DEATH in a SERENE CITY

At first he thought he was looking at a costume for *carnevale*. In the center of the pile was a full face mask that he assumed had been made to look old. There were red slippers and a torn, yellowed garment.

And then he saw the head—or rather the skull—covered with long black hair whose thickness and luster only made the sight more appalling.

A grin was frozen on its face as if to say, *Now you've really found something, you old fool!*

Other Books by
Edward Sklepowich
Coming Soon from Avon Books

FAREWELL TO THE FLESH

DEATH in a SERENE CITY

Edward Sklepowich

AVON BOOKS · NEW YORK

AVON BOOKS
A division of
The Hearst Corporation
1350 Avenue of the Americas
New York, New York 10019

Copyright © 1990 by Edward Sklepowich
Published by arrangement with William Morrow and Company, Inc.
Library of Congress Catalog Card Number: 90-35585
ISBN 0-380-71636-4

First Avon Books Printing: October 1992

AVON TRADEMARK REG. U.S. PAT. OFF. AND IN OTHER COUNTRIES, MARCA REGISTRADA, HECHO EN U.S.A.

Printed in the U.S.A.

RA   10 9 8 7 6 5 4 3 2 1

To my mother
Madeline Cacchillo Sklepowich

Mamma, solo per te la mia canzone

. . . the refuge of endless strange secrets,
broken fortunes, and wounded hearts.
—HENRY JAMES on Venice

O N one of those days when you feel you've seen just about all there is to see in Venice—have paid homage to every important canvas and stone, have taken in every recommended view from every recommended campanile and café, and have even allowed yourself the luxury of being lost, knowing salvation is only a few turnings ahead—you may consider the Church of San Gabriele in a remote corner of the Cannaregio quarter. There you may find a few others who have strayed from the nearby Ghetto in search of a boat stop or have mistaken San Gabriele for the Madonna dell'Orto and are wondering why they can't find the Tintoretto they've read so much about. A few of them, armed with thick, frayed guidebooks from secondhand shops, may even have purposely sought out this fifteenth-century church with its later lamentable additions to peer wearily at its disputed Tiepolo ceiling and the indifferent Cima on the left wall of the chancel.

You can be sure, however, that someone in the group you find yourself among is here to view a corpse—for the body of an obscure saint reigns supreme in the Church of San Gabriele. Put to the sword eleven centuries ago in her native Sicily, Santa Teodora is now enshrined in a crystal coffin in a chapel in the east transept, one more piece of booty seized by the Venetian Republic from the shores of the Mediterranean in the days when relics had a price beyond ducats. According to legend, however, this particular relic has a profane value as well because of prize jewels wound up with its cerements after the virgin saint was so rudely taken from Syracuse in 1309.

The dwindling faithful swear to the incorruptible state of the little saint even though not an inch of her supposedly inviolate body is now visible to the vulgar eye. The hands that clasp a flaking leather prayer book so demurely are gloved in faded crimson material, the body swathed in a tattered white gown from beneath which peep the tips of tiny scarlet slippers. Over her face is a silver mask fashioned in the nineteenth century by a craftsman from Florence after a competition among Venetians threatened to end in violence. All in all, from the top of this tarnished mask to the tips of her little slippers Santa Teodora measures barely five feet one inch as determined in 1932 by the last official Vatican examination by the Congregation for the Causes of Saints.

As you survey this holy plunder that survived the burning of the church originally built to honor it, you will notice small clusters of bouquets on the ledge of the catafalque, left in homage to the virgin saint by brides after their marriage ceremonies. You will be fortunate, however, to find any fresh bouquets among these offerings for the parishioners of San Gabriele are today, indeed, an elderly and dying lot.

Before you leave, gaze down at the silver mask again. Serenity, even for the dead, doesn't last forever.

Prologue

ACQUA
ALTA

1 HE was shaking and crying like a little boy although he was a man. The woman took him in her arms and looked into his tear-stained face. He broke away from her and ran across the uneven stones.

He went into the confessional at the front of the church and pulled the curtain across, closing out the dim light. He sat in darkness and silence, his head bowed. If there had been a priest, he would have confessed himself. He might even have cursed the woman and then done penance.

Outside the city was still in chaos.

2 LAPO Grossi, the gravedigger on San Michele, had seen many things during his fifty-odd years of service, but nothing like this. Entire parts of the cemetery island were under water. Sludge was almost a meter high in some places. Hundreds of tombstones had been leveled.

But worst of all was his special domain, the field of the common graves, where the disinterred bones of the poor and forgotten were dumped after a brief twelve years in their plots on other parts of the island. It was here that he saw his own fate, although the odds were against a flood like the one this November coming again during the twelve years of his own bones' rest.

In front of him all was a mad and pathetic jumble of skulls, ribs, thighbones, and indistinguishable shards that only an expert might identify. The scene looked like pictures he had seen after the war, pictures of those camps up in Poland. It reminded him of the Isle of Bones far out in the lagoon past Torcello.

The cemetery island was almost completely deserted. People were tending to the problems of the living today, trying to salvage what they could of their belongings, shoveling and sweeping and washing and picking through all the debris. Last night they had carried torches through the dark alleys of the city, trusting in God and their sense of direction to deliver them safely to their homes or to their parish churches where they could say their prayers of thanks for not having suffered even more.

Grossi was awakened from his reverie by a curt *buon giorno*. It was the priest from San Gabriele.

"What brings you here this morning, Don Marcantonio? No deaths, I hope."

"No, just this." The priest indicated the *campo* littered with its bones and mud. "Here you see the end of many of my parishioners." Bowing his head, he started to say a prayer but stopped and looked at the gravedigger.

The priest's gaze was so intense that Grossi lowered his eyes and after a few moments returned to his work. From across the lagoon the church bells of the city started to toll.

❧

3 THE glassblower shook his head.

"I know no one by that name. How many times must I tell you? I never heard of her."

The woman shivered.

"Can we go in by the furnace?"

"As you wish, but the answer will be the same there. I never heard of a woman with that name."

"*Una ragazza*," she said as they passed into the other room where an assistant was holding a long thin pipe in the mouth of the glowing furnace, "*una ragazza*, she was once a girl."

He shook his head and bent down to pick up a pair of shears lying on the floor.

"Girl, woman, *non c'è una bella differenza*." He put the shears on a table cluttered with other tools. "All women were once girls, isn't it so?"

The woman looked at him with dark eyes that reflected the glow of the furnace.

"*Sì*, but not all girls become women."

He was sure she must be thinking of her own dead daughter. More gently than before he said, "Perhaps that is your answer, Signora Galuppi. This girl you speak of, this Domenica, maybe she never became a woman."

Something like the beginning of a smile gathered at the corners of the woman's lips but never got any farther, certainly not to those dark eyes.

"Alive or dead, I must know."

She turned away, gathering her long black coat around her, and went out to the *fondamenta* where a chill wind was blowing. Bent over against it, she went along the canalside street past the Glass Museum until she reached the Church of San Donato.

Inside she knelt by the marble sarcophagus holding the bones of San Donato. If he hadn't slain a dragon, she would probably never have prayed to him. When she did, she sometimes confused him with that other, more famous slayer of dragons, San Giorgio. But this one, too, was one of God's chosen and although he could never hold the place in her heart that San Giorgio did—or, of course, Santa Teodora—she prayed to him from time to time.

As she knelt there in the gloom, however, she didn't pray to San Donato but to a saint she knew almost as little about: Santa Domenica. She had borrowed Don Marcantonio's book on the saints and read about the girl from the Campania named after the Sabbath who had been martyred in some faraway place she didn't remember.

On these visits to the island it seemed particularly appropriate to direct her special prayer to this saint who, according to the priest's book, was one of doubtful authenticity.

On this November afternoon her prayer was the same as always.

"Santa Domenica, *carissima Santa,* have pity on an ignorant woman who asks you to bring to light what is hidden, to reveal what has long been in darkness, to cleanse your own blessed name of a dark stain. Let her be known, this evil woman whose life is a dark shadow of yours, a woman who corrupts and destroys. Listen to a humble woman who asks for only the truth. Listen to her and grant her prayer. *Nel nome del Padre, del Figliuolo, e dello Spirito Santo.* Amen."

Before she left the church for the cemetery island, she went behind the high altar where the bones of the dragon slain by San Donato were hung. She spent several moments contemplating them. These bones always gave her hope when she remembered that the saint, they said, had killed the monster by spitting at it.

❦

4   TWO friars and several weary-looking women passed her an hour later as she went through the cloister to the cemetery. An old man stood staring at the notice of disinterment posted on the office window. No one paid any attention to her. She was just one more among hundreds of the bereaved who visited their dead and tended the graves. Today there were more than usual. The flood after the Day of All Souls had destroyed so much.

She went to a burial field in a far corner where graves weren't bought in perpetuity. She stood by a bulldozer listing in the soft soil and surveyed the litter around her—caskets, crosses, urns, bones. She bent down to touch the soil and raised her hand to her forehead, leaving a smudge. It looked like the ashes she was given each year at San Gabriele but Ash Wednesday was still more than three months away.

❦

5   ZIA Caterina couldn't sleep.
She went to the cabinet and took out the bottle of grappa she kept for such occasions. For a woman of seventy-three the occasions were getting more and more frequent. She poured some into a glass, being careful to be quiet although she knew her nephew and his wife would wake only if they heard the chink of coins or the rustle of *lira* notes.

Dio mio! Hadn't they almost slept through the storm and sirens the night of the flood?

She took her glass and went over to her chair by the window. After a life of traveling as far away as Siena to visit the home of her patron saint, it seemed that, as with so many of the old people she knew, her life had been reduced to the view from a window, day and night, night and day.

And what could she see, even during the busiest hours, even with the little mirror her nephew had attached to the outside wall? Not much. Only the *calle* and the small *campo* beyond it with its covered wellhead, only Cecilia's windows across the way and Antonia's above them. If she contorted herself slightly, she could also get a glimpse of one lone window of Lodovico's glass factory. Despite her arthritis she frequently made the effort, not so much for curiosity as for the sake of sentiment. There had been a time after the first war when she and Lodovico had come close to marrying.

Two in the morning might not be a good time for contortions but it was certainly a good hour for sentimental reflections. These she indulged in for half an hour, sipping her grappa. Although warmed and soothed, she knew she would still have trouble sleeping. She would have to give herself another half hour and probably another half glass.

She was about to get up for the bottle when there was a flickering in front of her eyes. The next second she wasn't sure she had seen it. Then it came again.

"Is this how it's to be?" she thought. "A flicker of light, then darkness, and they'll find me dressed like a fright in front of an open bottle of grappa!"

But the flicker came again and she could tell it was coming from outside. She bent closer to the window and then, this time not for sentiment but for a clear view that might settle the question once and for all, she twisted her head to look in the direction of Lodovico's glass factory.

There the flicker was brighter. Even with her poor sight she could see the flames. She got up from the chair and hurried as fast as she could to wake her nephew.

But the wail of the fireboats was piercing the air before she reached his room.

· *Twenty years later* ·

Part One

THE
SLIPPER
ON THE
GRAVE

1 URBINO Macintyre was sure about one thing. The poor woman had wanted to die.

He gazed up at the ceiling of the Church of San Gabriele. It was in almost as poor condition as the rest of the church, an old Gothic building dating to the early fifteenth century and flaking now from age, dampness, and the cancerous exhalations from the mainland industries. No thoughts of the ceiling's deterioration preoccupied him this morning, however. Nor was he scrutinizing its cherubs and blessed souls, its angels and clouds, its hovering Virgin and Child, for some indisputable evidence of Tiepolo's fresh hand.

Instead, all he could think of was the painful contrast between its airy, floating images and those last desperate moments of the poor woman's life.

Yes, she must have wanted to die.

Why else choose two in the morning in a quarter where almost everyone but insomniacs had been asleep for hours? In a city where a cry, echoing from stone and water, had more chance of sending help in the opposite direction than of leading it to the right place?

That is, he reminded himself, if a cry had even been uttered. No one seemed to have heard anything. And neither did anyone know if in her leap from the bedroom window at the Casa Silviano, she had hoped to die by drowning in the canal below or by cracking open her skull on the prow of the gondola, breaking off the *ferro*, just the way she had.

These thoughts about the recent death of the American writer Margaret Quinton were not motivated by personal curiosity. He had barely known the woman, having met her only once at an exhibit at the Glass Museum and a few times at the Contessa da Capo-Zendrini's.

What he had was a professional interest, however, the professional interest of someone who spent a great deal of time reconstructing the lives—and the deaths—of those who had gone before.

He pulled his gaze away from the ceiling—Tiepolo or otherwise—and rubbed the back of his neck. His eyes wandered around the dim interior for a few moments before they fixed on the glass casket of Santa Teodora. It was hard to avoid. The diminutive martyr, dressed in faded white like a bride of long ago and recumbent beneath crystal, dominated the church almost as much as the high altar with its Vivarini of the Archangel announcing the news to the Virgin Mary.

Now there you had a figure he wouldn't dare touch for his *Venetian Lives* series. It wasn't only because he was perhaps unsuited for hagiography—hadn't one reviewer detected what she called an "iconoclastic strain" in his lives of Goldoni and Canaletto?— but also because the saint was encrusted with so many legends that the truth could never be known.

Having put aside his thoughts of Margaret Quinton's last moments, he slipped from the pew and went up to the casket that sat on a small platform in a side chapel. When he bent down over the glass, for a few confusing seconds it was his own face—gaunt and sharp-featured—he saw instead of the silver-masked one of the saint. He peered down at the tarnished mask, yellowed gown, and crimson gloves and slippers. The card placed alongside the coffin above desiccated bridal wreaths told the story of the little saint in simple Italian, most of it probably fiction except for the description of how her body had been taken from Syracuse in the fourteenth century and brought to Venice. The card managed to glorify the raid by calling it a *"sacro furto"*—a sacred theft—a fine distinction that amused Urbino.

"*Buon giorno*, Signor Macintyre. If you will permit me."

Urbino turned around. It was Monsignor Marcantonio Bo, the pastor of San Gabriele, a thin, wizened man in his mid-seventies with a narrow fringe of white hair and thick round glasses behind which he blinked haplessly at the changed world around him. He was dressed in a black cassock and held a small bottle of green liquid and a white cloth.

"*Buon giorno*, Don Marcantonio."

Urbino moved aside to let the priest clean the glass coffin. He made it a special point to do it himself every day, a duty only slightly less important than wiping the paten and chalice at the end of every Mass. It wasn't that he didn't trust Carlo, the sexton, or one of the sisters from the Convent of the Charity of Santa Crispina to do a good job. It was that this attention made him feel that the relic was actually his and his alone. He had been doing it almost every day for more than fifty years.

Quite simply, the body of Santa Teodora was his most prized possession. Not even his well-thumbed copy of the flagellant Jacopone da Todi's *Laude*, which he had had since his first year in the novitiate and had shown so proudly to Urbino, could come close.

Urbino left Don Marcantonio to his work and sat down again. He looked at his watch. It was a few minutes after seven. He still had some time before he needed to be off.

Don Marcantonio rubbed hard with his cloth at a persistent smudge above the masked face. He frowned with what might have been concentration or disapproval. Did he resent all the fervent lips pressed against the glass or was he grateful for them for giving him the opportunity to display his own devotion to the saint? He rubbed away with the energy of someone at least twenty years younger.

Don Marcantonio believed the saint knew how well he cared for her and gave him what he needed to go on, day after day, year after year. He had once given Urbino one of his favorite examples of the saint's protection. Hadn't he been blessed with an upsurge of energy the day after his last battle with the Vatican official who had come to press for new measurements?

"But we must know if she is shrinking," the official had said. "After all, Venice is still sinking, *a poco a poco*," he had added, referring to one of the many legends of the saint—that she was shrinking in direct proportion to the sinking of her adoptive city.

But Don Marcantonio had given his usual reply:

"The Church of San Gabriele has nothing to do with centimeters!"

As the priest continued to rub the glass casket, Urbino imagined him saying over and over to himself as if it were a litany to the Virgin or the Most Precious Blood, "Nothing to do with centimeters, nothing to do with centimeters!"

Several years ago Angela Bellorini, who did charity work in the quarter—mainly bringing meals to the infirm and recently widowed—had suggested to Don Marcantonio that a better-known Santa Teodora was sure to mean more money in the collection boxes. Urbino could still remember the look on the priest's face when he had told the story—eyes wide, upper lip trembling.

"No centimeters!" the old priest had shouted. "Never! They can say she will be as popular as Sant'Antonio in Padua or San Gennaro and his blood down in Naples! Never!"

Urbino could easily imagine Don Marcantonio cursing against centimeters on his deathbed. And how far away could that be for a man his age? The Vatican and its officials would be forever, and Padre Marcantonio would not always be able to shelter his little saint from what he saw as impious violations. Urbino supposed it was even possible that some day Santa Teodora might be removed from the Church of San Gabriele for the malodorous corpse many had been saying she was since Vatican Two. Like Santa Filomena she might even end up struck from the roster of saints.

Don Marcantonio's labors were interrupted by the sound of one of the front doors opening and closing. He paused to turn around and watch Tommaso, the florist, come slowly down the nave with two urns of flowers, nodding to Urbino as he passed.

"Aren't you early?" Don Marcantonio scowled at the florist.

"Just a little, Don Marcantonio." Tommaso put down the urns, breathing heavily. He was an overweight man in his late forties. "I still have to deliver some flowers for Roberto's funeral on Murano. There's no one to help me."

The priest didn't seem to hear him. He was looking down at the urns.

"Roses in January! White roses! What will the Contessa think of next!" His voice had no admiration or approval but only irritation, which, along with piety, was one of his two dominant moods. "Santa Teodora makes no distinction between roses and—and weeds!"

"But if our Contessa ever saw weeds in her urns—*Dio mio!*—we would never hear the end of it, would we?"

"You certainly wouldn't—and she might find her way over to Liberato at the Madonna dell'Orto and there would go your big bundle every year!" He bent down and reached for one of the urns from yesterday filled with bright purple flowers. "And you can tell the Contessa that these purple ones would have been more fitting for Septuagesima. She's almost a month ahead of herself."

"Allow me, Don Marcantonio, they are much heavier than they look." Tommaso moved the urns away from the glass casket. "The Contessa doesn't choose all the flowers for the little saint herself, you know. These were *my* choice." He touched one of the purple blooms gently. Then, almost to himself: "Still so lovely. They could last several more days."

"And so they will if you can arrange it! But hurry. We don't have all the morning for this business."

"Sì, sì, Padre, but remember it's all for the little saint."

"All for the little saint! That's what the Contessa wants everyone to believe but some of us think differently."

Tommaso looked nervously at Urbino, then placed the urns of white roses in front of the casket. He walked a few paces away to look at his arrangement. He moved the urn on the right a fraction, then contemplated it all again.

"Bellissimo!"

"Sì, sì, bellissimo! Now just get these out of here so I can finish. Mass is in less than half an hour."

Tommaso picked up one urn, then the other, and bade good day to the priest. He nodded to Urbino again as he shuffled past beneath his burden. He seemed to want to get out as fast as he could but, perhaps knowing Don Marcantonio was watching, he put down the urns to bless himself at the stoup.

The priest shook his head, a gesture that seemed to say that the man, like his flowers, was all for effect, and returned to his work with renewed energy.

2   IN one of the chapels on the other side of the church the misshapen figure of a man had been watching the early morning activity. Carlo Galuppi preferred this chapel to the others not because of its *Madonna and Child* in the manner of Gentile Bellini but because of its deeper darkness. If Don Marcantonio saw him, he would be angry. He should be in the vestiary waiting for the boys and preparing everything for Mass. Sacristans had their many duties and a pastor like Don Marcantonio made sure that his performed each and every one.

Carlo was known as the Quasimodo of San Gabriele. Through one of those situations that could be taken as proof of either the startling symmetry of accident or the considered plan of Providence, Carlo was perfectly suited to Don Marcantonio's crumbling old church. His ugliness was surely far less excessive than that of the Parisian bellringer and his hump was at times almost unnoticeable, depending on the clothes he wore and the way he carried himself. But then wasn't this all as it should be since the Church of San Gabriele wasn't anywhere near as impressively Gothic as Notre Dame? The one lonely bell that Carlo rang several times a day had none of the thunder of those in the great cathedral's tower and the only chance of his becoming deaf from its sound was if he were to use his own huge head as a clapper—and there were some people in the parish who said he was stupid enough to do just that one of these days, and the sooner he did it the better.

Now, as Carlo watched from the chapel of the Madonna, the dark shadows there mercifully smoothed out and concealed his irregularities. You might not even have noticed his large nose, slightly protruding teeth, and the brown, hairy wen on his brow. You might have thought, seeing him indistinctly as you went by, that he was only a large-boned, unattractive man who knew how to keep as still as a cat watching a bird.

Surely, you might think, there was something more to be admired than feared in someone so large keeping so silent.

3 ALTHOUGH Urbino had noticed Carlo in the Chapel of the Madonna, he gave no indication. Why upset the man by showing him that his idleness had been observed? Carlo, almost as much as Don Marcantonio, was as sensitive about his duties at San Gabriele as he was dedicated to them. Only last

month he had had an anxiety attack at Jesurum's where he had asked the Contessa and Urbino to help him pick out a birthday gift for his mother. The large store with its vaulted ceilings had been crowded and it had taken them a long time even to get the attention of a clerk. Carlo had ended up rushing down the staircase into the late afternoon gloom and leaving them behind so that he could be back at San Gabriele to see if everything was in order for Sister Veronica and her tour group.

As Urbino walked up the aisle, these thoughts of Carlo Galuppi inevitably led back to his previous ones about Margaret Quinton, for the sexton had watched over her Pomeranian in the vestiary whenever she had come to Mass, being sure it made as little noise as possible. The poor man had become frantic only the week before the novelist's death when Dandolo had started barking—almost diabolically—during the Consecration. Margaret Quinton had hurried from her pew to comfort the animal but told the Contessa after Mass that the hunchback had required almost as much attention as had her Dandolo.

4 AS Urbino came out into the chill January air, Maria Galuppi, Carlo's mother, was walking up the steps of the church. Although close to eighty she had a vitality that, if you didn't look too closely at her heavily lined face and thinning white hair beneath which her scalp gleamed pinkly, might lead you to believe she was much younger.

Five years ago he had almost decided against having her do his laundry when the Contessa suggested it. How could he impose such a physical burden on a woman her age? Surely there were many younger women who could do the job.

"That's just the point," his friend had said. "There are *too* many younger ones who can, and all of them from the mainland. Maria is losing a lot of her clientele to them. What will become of her and Carlo? She would never accept charity."

And so Urbino had agreed although he still felt uncomfortable whenever she, instead of Carlo, picked up and delivered his laundry. Never in the past five years had the woman complained or accepted anything but the rather modest amount—modest at least from his point of view—that he gave her every month.

"Good morning, Maria."

"*Buondì*, Signor Urbino. You are up and about early this morning."

She squinted a smile up at him.

"I'm taking an early train to Padua."

"Two already left."

Obviously she had a completely different idea of earliness.

"I'm taking the *rapido*."

"The *rapido!*" She shook her head in disapproval but there was an unmistakable amusement in it. "How much faster? Five minutes? Ten? And for that you pay thousands of *lire* more!" She reached her hand out to touch his sleeve. "Listen to me, Signor Urbino, you must slow down, yes, you must slow down." Then she added something in the Venetian dialect that he didn't catch but was sure addressed in homely fashion the dangers of always being in a rush.

Her advice was at odds not only with his temperament but also with her own active life so that Urbino had a hard time suppressing a smile.

"I'll try, Maria. I should know after living here that Venice is no city to rush around in—or away from, for that matter."

She nodded her head.

"And remember, Signor Urbino, no matter how we rush it all comes to us in the end. Yes, with time it comes to us all."

With this sobering comment she went into the church as he held the door. He was about to strike out across the *campo* for the train station when the door opened. It was Maria again. She put her hand in the pocket of her old black coat and took out a ten-thousand *lira* note.

"Here, Signor Urbino."

He was so surprised that he took the money without any hesitation.

"When you go to the Basilica, you must do me a favor. Get a candle for my daughter Beatrice, put it with the others near the altar of Il Santo so the priests will light it."

How could he tell her he would be on a tight schedule in Padua and that he was going to be nowhere near the Basilica? His business in Padua was for his *Venetian Lives* series. There was a man near the Scrovegni Chapel who had known Ezra Pound during the poet's years in Venice.

"God bless you, Signor Urbino. You make an old woman very happy."

❧

5   THE Contessa da Capo-Zendrini leaned back against the maroon banquette in the Chinese salon at Florian's. Outside was what Napoleon had called the finest drawing room in Europe although on this afternoon its charm was compromised by a chill, damp wind and pools of water reflecting a dull, leaden sky.

"*La poverina,*" she said with a sigh.

She put a languid hand to her nape in a habitual gesture. As usual there were no derelict locks. She was an attractive woman in her mid-fifties who looked a decade younger, not so much because of the subtle art which only a close scrutiny would have detected but because of the generous stamp that nature had given to her cheekbones and upward-slanted gray eyes.

"To be so plain, poor thing, so gauche, and to come to such an end."

She sighed again and took a tea cake from the tray, looking at it from various angles before taking a bite. Everything about the woman—her aristocratic bearing, her stylish coiffure, her gleaming string of pearls, her subdued makeup, her tasteful suit and hat—made it clear that she was in no way the kind of person who could ever be either plain or gauche herself. She was displayed in one of her best settings here at Florian's with all its mirrors and paintings under glass, its velvet, walnut, and marble, its bronze lamps and intricately patterned ceilings—and she knew it.

"She also had a talent. Don't forget that, Barbara."

"A talent, you say? Was it such a very great one?"

Her intonation implied that only its greatness might compensate for the dead woman's appearance and manner. She took a last bite of the cake and picked up another. As he watched her, Urbino sensed something other than hunger was responsible for her uncharacteristic appetite this afternoon.

"Great enough, *cara*, to make me want to read some more of her books. I've read only one of her novels, *A Green Paris*."

"It was about Paris?" She seemed mildly surprised. "And to think she was writing another one about Venice when she died. You Americans are quite voracious, aren't you!" she said, unaware that the adjective might just as well apply to her this afternoon. "She might have gone on to all the cities in Baedeker, Michelin, or whatever your poor American equivalent is. I'm convinced it's partly because you Americans never had an empire. Look at the way you keep adding people to your *Venetian Lives!*"

"How do you know she was working on a novel about Venice?" As usual he ignored her reference to his biographies, which she alternately accused of being dilettantish and voyeuristic. Now she seemed to have found another basis for criticism. He took a sip of Bardolino, tea not being his idea of a suitable drink at five in the afternoon despite the chill outside.

"How do I know? You would have known yourself if you had spent more time with her. I know because I spent hours and hours with her, just the two of us. I also know because she borrowed books from my library."

"You never told me that."

"My dear Urbino, do you assume I tell you everything about my life?" She looked at him flirtatiously from beneath the long lashes that he still, after all these years, couldn't be sure were false or not. "We women must have some secrets from even the best of you."

"I'm pleased to fall into that category, Barbara."

"You do—despite your youth and rather lamentable American origins."

"Thirty-six isn't all that young, and I haven't been in the States for almost eight years now."

She waved a much-beringed hand in the air. He was surprised to see that it didn't hold another tea cake.

"It doesn't matter, *caro*. American you were born and American you'll stay. You can live in the Palazzo Uccello for the next forty years and not change that. It's indelible! In fact it's the reason you've become so Italian—or should I say a veritable *americano venezianizzato*? You did it much more quickly than I—and I married into it! As for thirty-six being old, I take that as a distinct insult."

As she turned to look out at the Piazza San Marco, her face went slack and Urbino could see, even in profile, the tiny lines of concern.

He followed her gaze. The sleet that had been coming down since he had returned from Padua an hour ago had stopped. The Piazza nonetheless still had a deserted look, even for early January. Only a few people were walking across the square or under the arcades, quite obviously native Venetians from their look and manner. On the opposite side of the Piazza an old waiter was cleaning the pavement in front of the café Quadri with a little broom and shovel while a group of expectant pigeons followed close behind. One of them perched on his shoulder and he seemed to be talking to it as he went about his work. A tall, thin young man muffled in several scarfs was pushing a cart of post-cards, flags, and guidebooks toward the Molo San Marco.

It was hard to imagine that in little more than a month *carnevale* would turn this whole placid scene into something more suited to the old days on San Clemente, the former island of the insane. All the more reason to appreciate the city now in its deepest serenity, a calm that might have been monastic except that even in fog and silence every stone spoke to the senses.

When he took his eyes away from the scene beyond the windows of Florian's, he saw that the Contessa was no longer looking at the Piazza. She was looking at him.

"You look a little tired today, *caro*. Why not change your mind and come tonight?"

"If I were tired—which I'm not, I assure you—shouldn't I stay in and rest? It would be the best thing for me, I would think."

She gave him an exasperated look and picked up another tea cake.

"Except that you wouldn't really rest, would you? You would probably spend half the night poking around in other people's lives or watching movies on that abominable machine of yours."

"They're old films, classics, as you well know. A dozen were just sent from Milan yesterday. If there were such 'abominable machines,' as you call them, a hundred years ago, you can be sure Des Esseintes would have had one."

"Des Esseintes, Des Esseintes!" she came close to shouting. The waiter, tending to a nearby table, looked in their direction. "Am I never going to hear the end of that—that disreputable Duke of yours! The way you refer to him you would think he was a living, breathing person instead of some outdated character in a novel."

The Contessa was referring to Huysmans's *Against Nature*, a French novel about a reclusive bachelor, after which, purged of its many decadent excesses, Urbino had patterned his own secluded life in Venice. When she had returned his gift copy during the first year of their friendship, she had said, "A better title would have been *Perversion*." She had refused to add it to her library or to keep it anywhere in the Ca' da Capo-Zendrini.

"Well, my friend," she was saying now, "don't you think it's about time you laid the poor man to rest?"

"Never! Since he's one of the main reasons, in a manner of speaking, that we two are here with each other at Florian's, it would be rather inconsiderate of me, don't you think?"

"No, I don't!" She took a big bite of another cake. "I think it would be good sense. You're too old for such things."

He laughed. "Ah, then you do admit my age. That's some improvement."

"I admit nothing except that there are things one might be too old or too young for, and your—your obsession with this disreputable character is definitely one of them."

"To each our obsessions. I know of a respectable British woman—an *inglese venezianizzata*, to use her own expression—who makes it a point to collect every book she can find on Venice."

Perhaps he could get the conversation back to Margaret Quinton and her Venice novel.

The Contessa stared at him blankly for a few moments and put down the tea cake. She didn't defend herself by pointing out that her book collection had been started a long time ago by the da Capo-Zendrini family and was one of the best in the city. Instead the lines of worry came again.

"Something seems to be bothering you today," he said.

She shrugged.

From his seven years of friendship with her he knew that she liked to be coaxed. Almost a game between them, it seemed to have less of sexual coyness in it than a reluctance to commit herself to something that might give her too much pleasure or someone else too much discomfort.

He reached for her hand.

"What's the matter, Barbara? You don't seem yourself today.

You're a bit on edge. Are you upset with me about anything? If you are—"

"Don't be silly, *caro*. It has nothing to do with you. It's my party tonight."

She was giving a party to celebrate the anniversary of her marriage, a date she kept religiously even though her husband had been dead for more than ten years. Not being a person who felt comfortable at large gatherings, Urbino had declined the invitation as he sometimes did.

"Are you sure it's not because of me?"

"Don't be so self-centered. It's because of Clifford Voyd. He's coming."

"But you've been singing his praises ever since you met him. I thought you liked him."

"I do—or at least I *did*. I still do, it's just that . . ."

"It's Margaret Quinton, isn't it?"

"Yes! He's responsible—and don't try to tell me any different."

"But she committed suicide."

"Suicide, *caro*, can be prevented—and it can be caused."

Two things about the Contessa that Urbino had never doubted were her intelligence and her morality. If her morality sometimes seemed inflexible, it wasn't reserved only for others. She conducted herself in accordance with the strictest principles. Urbino would have been shocked to learn otherwise. He never listened to any of the gossip that circulated within the insular, suspicious society of long-established Venetians who still considered her an interloper after thirty years.

"But surely you aren't implying that Clifford Voyd—the great Clifford Voyd—did anything that could have led that poor woman to throw herself from her window in the middle of the night? From what I understand they were great friends."

"My dear Urbino, how much longer will you have to live before you realize that it isn't the things we do that cause the real sorrows of our life but the many, many things we don't?"

Then, as if he might have missed her point, "Sins of omission, you know."

Yes, he knew. Bless me, Father, for I have sinned, I accuse myself of not . . . The list was by now too long to contemplate.

"What is it that the great Clifford Voyd didn't do?"

"He didn't see what he should have, that she was in love with him, that she felt encouraged, that she hoped."

"They were friends."

She took a sip of tea before she said with emphasis, the cup still in her hand, "In that kind of friendship it's always the woman who suffers. Such men should know themselves better. They should curb their charm."

It was as if she were talking about such men getting their hair cut or dressing down for certain social occasions.

"Voyd does have a great charm—and a great talent."

"Is it so great, his talent?" she asked, echoing what she had asked earlier about Margaret Quinton.

"You know it is, Barbara. You've read his books. He's one of the best. He's won all the prizes except the big one and his name is on the list every year."

"All that isn't good enough for me. It wasn't good enough for Margaret Quinton either."

Once again she stared out at the Piazza. It had started to rain and people were taking shelter under the arcades. Something seemed to catch her attention.

"Don't be upset, Urbino," she said, turning back to him, "but it's Stefano."

He had no idea why she thought he might be upset. He looked out the window to see Stefano Bellorini hurrying across the Piazza from the Mercerie, his head with its fringe of fading Venetian-red hair angled against the rain.

The Contessa must have realized he was puzzled by her comment.

"I mean about being interrupted," she clarified.

From the slight frown that worried her face, however, it seemed that she was the one upset by the entrance of the craftsman. She had just time to tell him that Bellorini wanted to show her the sketches for the frames he was making for some small family photographs of hers before the man hurried into the room and came up to their table.

"I'm so sorry, Barbara, but I can't find them," he said before even saying hello.

The fiftyish Bellorini looked crestfallen. He took out a handkerchief to dab at the top of his head. Droplets of water glistened in his full beard and moustache that had most likely been grown to compensate for the almost complete absence of hair above. Bellorini had the understandable vanity of a man whose youthful good looks had been cruelly treated by time. One of the few remnants was his deep blue eyes that hadn't faded with age. They were troubled now.

"I told you there wasn't any need to bring them here. They can wait until this evening. You'll find them."

"But to bring business to your celebration, Barbara!"

He took off his glasses and wiped them.

"I was just trying to convince Urbino to come this evening. Maybe this will give him an additional reason."

"You are not going? I would not believe it!" He had spoken this time in his precise and formal English, something he rarely did with his two native English-speaking friends, feeling self-conscious. "But you are not ill?"

The Contessa couldn't resist the opening.

"He does look a bit tired, doesn't he, Stefano? I was just telling him as much."

Urbino felt uncomfortable under their scrutiny.

"My party would be good for him, would lift that weariness right off his face, don't you think? But do sit down. Have some tea or a drink."

She looked around for their waiter.

"Thank you, Barbara, but I can't stay. The least I can do is be sure I have the sketches for tonight. I know I haven't lost them. I just have to find them—wherever they are! I hope you'll be there to see them yourself, Urbino. Until later."

As he was going into the foyer, he collided with an impeccably dressed young man whose annoyance was evident in his glaring look. He shot out sharp words at the departing Stefano whose pinkish face acquired more color than usual. With an exaggerated straightening of the collar of his camel-hair coat, the young man walked through the Chinese salon to the Oriental salon next to it and surveyed the occupants from the doorway next to Urbino and the Contessa. His blond, good-looking head held high, he turned and went back into the foyer.

"Poor Stefano," the Contessa said, "so talented but so absent-minded. Do they always have to go together like that?" But she didn't seem to want or expect an answer. She looked at Urbino with her earlier worried expression.

"You don't think Voyd should be enjoying himself in public, do you?" he asked, picking up the thread of their interrupted conversation.

"You put it so bluntly to make it seem silly of me but, yes, I'm old-fashioned enough to hold with such things. There should be greater respect, especially when there's been such responsibility."

"Cancel your party, then. Reschedule it."

"It's too late for that as you well know. I suppose I should have done it when I heard about Margaret's death. At any rate, to call off the party would be to let the man off the hook. If my party is any kind of temptation for him, it's not for me to remove it because of his weakness."

Not wanting to provoke an extended lecture on the ethics of the Garden of Eden, which she was quite capable of delivering, he asked how she knew Voyd would even be at the Ca' da Capo-

Zendrini tonight. Hadn't the invitations gone out a week before Quinton's death? He might have called in his regrets while they were here at Florian's.

"Be assured, my dear Urbino, the man will most definitely be there." She took another sip of tea, then set the cup and saucer down with a clatter. "That's why I wish you would come."

"What good would that do?"

"It would do *me* a great deal of good just to see you there. And who knows? You might be able to find out exactly how the great Clifford Voyd feels about her death."

"You mean that after all you've just said you think he might be racked with remorse?"

"Anything is possible. Believe me, I gave up the luxury of being surprised at the age of forty."

6 TWENTY minutes later, as Urbino made his way from Florian's, he left the arcade and strode briskly through the Piazza. He didn't mind that the rain was now coming down heavily or that the Contessa had insisted that he walk home instead of returning with her in the boat.

"Go for one of your walks," she had said. "Think it over."

She knew that he loved his walks and that he especially loved Venice in the rain. Perhaps she thought that she stood the best chance of seeing him later if she let him mull things over as he got himself good and wet.

It wasn't that he had a particular preference for rainy days in themselves. There had been enough of them in New Orleans to last him a lifetime, and here in Venice they could penetrate to your very core even if you never ventured out. It was just that the rain usually cleared the narrow streets and squares of even the

Venetians themselves and he could indulge in his harmless little fantasy that the city was a bit closer to being his alone.

Now, as he turned his umbrella to the rain that was being driven in by the wind from the lagoon, no one else was in sight except for a man rushing toward the shelter of the portico of the Mercerie, a copy of *Il Gazzettino* held over his head. A few seconds later another man emerged from the Mercerie, going toward the Molo San Marco at a leisurely pace, protected by boots, a mackintosh, and a shapeless hat. Despite his unhurried gait, he did not stop to look up at San Marco, as if to illustrate the truth of Ruskin's exaggeration that Venetians pass its splendors by regardlessly.

Urbino, however, despite what the Contessa might think about his having been "Venetianized," never ceased to see it. He stopped now before he got any closer to see it the better. The Basilica didn't loom above him as other great cathedrals did but seemed almost to prostrate itself in Oriental fashion before the high tower of the Campanile. And yet the ornate Basilica, with its onion domes, colored marble, mosaics, statues, arches, and porches, had all the splendors of a sultan reclining on his cushions, while the bell tower with its plain brick facade resembled a servant of the realm standing silently at attention. This was one of the many scenes to be found throughout Venice whose appeal was due to the improbable, the excessive, and the unexpected.

Raised planks had been set up in front of the Basilica so that people would be able to avoid the water that might well up through the paving stones of the Piazza or wash in from the lagoon if these rains continued. Although he knew full well not only the inconvenience of finding his route through the labyrinthine city detoured almost endlessly by flooded streets but also the serious damage done by floods, even small ones, Urbino nonetheless came close to wishing for an *acqua alta*, came close to saying, like one of Banquo's murderers, "Let it come down," as he looked at the even darker clouds now rolling in from the north.

Family and friends who came to visit often spent much of their time complaining about the odor of the canals in summer and the rains and flooded streets in winter. But Urbino himself was the kind of lover who transformed even the most brutish of faults into the most engaging of virtues—or willed himself blind. Love that did anything else didn't deserve the name. If his brief marriage right after college had been an exercise in just such blindness, it hadn't warned him off completely.

If it had, he might never have been captivated by Venice ten years ago following the death of his parents in a car accident. He had arrived during the madness of the tourist season, intending to finish his business and return home, where his biography of the chess player Paul Morphy had just been sold to the films. Instead, amid all the heat, the odors, the crowds, and the noise, he had decided to stay forever.

He had come to Venice to decide what to do with the Veneto-Byzantine palazzo in the Cannaregio near Santa Fosca that had been in his mother's family for generations. His mother, an only child like himself, had seldom traveled far from her native New Orleans, although she had often talked about the city where her grandfather had been born.

She had known little about the property except that it was called the Palazzo Uccello. She didn't even have a photograph. When Urbino saw it, he laughed out loud for it was little bigger than the houses in his neighborhood near Tulane. It was ironic that the relatively small, run-down building was called the Palazzo Uccello while a much more impressive building next door was simply the Casa Maddalena.

During his weeks in Venice the city worked its magic on him. Where others have loved Venice but felt alienated from it, as if they have wandered into a world that can never be theirs, Urbino had loved it almost immediately as the home he had been waiting for. He had seen it in innumerable photographs, paintings, and movies, read about it in stories and poems and travel accounts, yet when he had seen the real thing he hadn't been disappointed. The city exceeded his expectations.

It is questionable, however, whether Venice would have had such an impact on him if he hadn't, at a more impressionable age, read the book the Contessa had been chiding him about, the book that—he had never dared tell her—was said to have corrupted Dorian Gray. He had found an old, illustrated edition of the French novel in a dusty bookshop in the French Quarter. This story of a neurotic aristocrat who retires to his mansion outside Paris to lead a self-contained, eccentric life of the mind and senses had grabbed hold of Urbino. At the age of seventeen, when most other boys are thinking about a life of commitment, Urbino dreamed instead of one that would bring him seclusion on his own terms.

He had copied out several passages from the novel into a note-book and then illustrated them. One of his favorites was the description of Des Esseintes's fantasy of a special domicile for himself:

> Already he had begun dreaming of a refined Thebaid, a desert hermitage equipped with all the modern conveniences, a snugly heated ark on dry land in which he might take refuge from the incessant deluge of human stupidity.

Ten years later, when he had come to Venice to inherit the Palazzo Uccello, he realized that to live in a palazzo, however small, in this museum city would be to go Des Esseintes one better. In fact, like Urbino's own watercolor illustration for the passage—a gleaming boatlike building—the palazzi lined up on either side of the Grand Canal resembled ornate ships brought to permanent berth.

The decision to commit himself to the city had come suddenly. Walking through the damp and moldy *pianterreno* of the Palazzo Uccello the day before he was scheduled to leave, he had told the *agente immobiliare* with him that he didn't want to put the building up for sale after all. He would keep it. He would make it his home. The only way he could finance the needed repairs was to sell the house in New Orleans. For almost a year he lived in one room at a *pensione* near the train station while the work was being done.

When he eventually moved in, it was with considerable excitement and not a little nervousness. All the income from his books, supplemented by the inheritance from his parents, had to go into the upkeep. Although it was difficult, he had never regretted his decision.

The Palazzo Uccello was, he liked to think, a delightful ark within the greater ark that was Venice. Behind its walls he was far away from the crowds yet close enough to the flow of life to make him feel snug in his solitude.

On this late afternoon, however, despite the attractions of the Palazzo Uccello, he didn't turn down the Mercerie but went through the Piazzetta past the column with the winged lion to the Molo San Marco. He stood at the balustrade in front of the Royal Gardens, deserted now of painters and souvenir sellers. Only one other person was there, a thin old man beneath a battered umbrella standing next to the telescope and staring off toward the low line of the Lido.

With the broad expanse of the lagoon stretching from the Riva degli Schiavoni to the Giudecca, Urbino felt as if he were on the deck of a ship. The Church of San Giorgio Maggiore with its classical brick facade and tall bell tower floated in the near distance on its own island. To its right on the Giudecca rose the Redentore, chaste and dignified among the unimpressive scramble of buildings around it. At the mouth of the Grand Canal, beyond the Dogana di Mare and its golden ball on which Fortune perched, the baroque whiteness of the Salute gleamed with its oversized cupolas, little tower, and graceful flight of steps, its wide quay obscured by the landing stages along the Molo between Urbino and the church. Vaporetti, motorboats, yachts, and barges crossed the lagoon and slipped in and out of the Grand Canal and the Giudecca. Passing each other in the middle of the lagoon were a car ferry headed for the Lido and a dark tanker with the Greek flag plying toward Porto Marghera. The wakes from all this water traffic rocked the tarpaulin-covered gondolas and motorboats moored along the quay and slapped against the foundations of the balustrade and wooden walkway beneath him.

Between the balance and harmony of the two Palladian churches and the extravagance of the Salute, Urbino always felt at peace, as if the two sides of his nature were here externalized and shown to be compatible.

As he turned away from the lagoon, he was in a benevolent frame of mind that made him want to please. He would go to the Ca' da Capo-Zendrini tonight. Not only that but he would try to engage Clifford Voyd in a conversation that might set the Contessa's mind at ease.

There was no need to keep the Contessa wondering whether he would show up or not. He went back to the Piazza, to Florian's. The rain had driven many into its warm, comfortable rooms. Most of the tables and banquettes were taken by tourists drinking their mandatory Bellinis. A few Venetians had their teas and cognacs. Two elderly women in dark tweeds had taken the Contessa's place in the Chinese salon, a tray of sandwiches and pot of tea on the marble table next to a copy of *Casa Vogue*. They smiled at him hesitantly, as if they weren't sure if they knew him or not, but returned to their conversation when he went back into the foyer and on into the bar. He learned from their waiter that the Contessa had left shortly after he had.

As he was going out under the arcade, Angela Bellorini, Stefano's wife, came hurrying toward him from the Piazza. She was drenched and carrying a small black leather portfolio under her arm.

"He's still here then," she said.

"I'm afraid not, Angela. He was here for only a few minutes. Barbara's gone now too."

She frowned. It did nothing for her narrow face and close-set eyes.

"Did he go back to the Ca' da Capo-Zendrini?"

"I think he went back home to look for his sketches of the frames."

"For these." She held up the portfolio. "They were in here all along." She shook her head with amusement and affection.

"Barbara said he should bring them over tonight."

"Tonight?" There was a blank look on her face, then: "Of course, the party. I see I've rushed for nothing then."

As Angela darted out into the Piazza, clutching the portfolio to her breast, Urbino wondered whether her haste in coming had been inspired by consideration for the Contessa or the generous commission her husband was getting. Yet Angela had never seemed anything but selfless to him. For more than thirty years she had been doing charity work in and around the Cannaregio quarter, spending her own money on the meals she brought from restaurants to the widowed and housebound. And certainly the childless couple had little reason to be concerned with money, having inherited a great deal from the elder Bellorini.

Urbino felt guilty enough to quicken his steps toward the Mercerie. Hadn't he been priding himself just a few minutes ago on his benevolent frame of mind? If he hurried, he might catch up with Angela and they could walk back to the Cannaregio together.

❧

7   IN a little trattoria near the Church of the Madonna dell'Orto in the Cannaregio, Maria Galuppi stopped for a drink. She put down her basket of laundry and nodded to Bettino Tullio, the *padrone*.

Bettino brought her glass of anisette to her usual table next to the heater. There were five other people in the restaurant, all of them men and all sitting at the corner table playing cards silently and without much enthusiasm on this winter afternoon.

Bettino leaned against a chair back. He enjoyed chatting with Maria. There had been a time when he had thought her the most beautiful woman in the Cannaregio. Her daughter at the same age hadn't really held a candle to her. Now, of course, she was nothing like her former self. Over the years her poor eyesight had lent her face a perpetual squint that had hardened her features. Yet her dark eyes still had a warmth that could rekindle some of the feelings he used to have for her. He was glad she had always refused to dim their charm with glasses, however much they might have helped her vision.

"A little late today, aren't you?" He indicated the basket.

"With the rain everyone was using the machines." She took a sip of the anisette and closed her eyes.

"How's Carlo?"

"The same. The death of the American signorina gives him bad dreams. I think he is remembering his sister—although that wasn't the same at all." She opened her eyes and darted a look at him. "But what can I do? Last night I stayed up with him and spoke well of her. Ah," she sighed, *"la poverina!* We had some good talks, the two of us, a stupid old woman like me, can you imagine! I only hope she got as much from the little I could tell her as I got from what she had to tell me. But I doubt it." She smiled to herself, not looking at Bettino but down into the glass of anisette. "Yes, I doubt it. What I learned from that poor woman was as priceless as—as—" She groped for just the right expression. Then, the smile broadening into a grin: "As priceless as the body of Santa Teodora in her glass coffin!"

She drained the glass. Bettino picked it up to refill it but she stood up quickly.

"Only one, you know that well. It hasn't been any different all these years. Besides, it's time I was getting this back. I'll be helping out at the Contessa's party tonight."

"Since Carlo isn't with you today, why not have one of the boys playing in front of the Madonna dell'Orto help you?"

She shook her head.

"My last weakness will begin when I depend too much on the strength of someone else. It's just me and Carlo. We can take care of each other."

She rebuttoned her long black coat and picked up the basket, breathing heavily. Bettino wondered how much longer she would be able to push herself like this for her son's sake. The poor woman's needs were few but he knew that her son's uncertain future had started to trouble her deeply. Yes, it was all done for him now.

He watched her from the window as she walked slowly down the *calle* and up the steps of the bridge toward the Madonna dell'Orto. He hoped that her last weakness was a long, long way off.

8   AT eight-thirty that evening when Urbino reached the bridge that provided the only land access to the Ca' da Capo-Zendrini, he was beginning to feel as if he shouldn't have come after all.

He stopped on the bridge, delaying the moment when he would enter his friend's *salone*.

The *calle* that began on the other side of the bridge was empty. The intricately patterned globes flanking the iron door of the Ca' da Capo-Zendrini and the lighted windows of the *piano nobile* only made the alley seem all the more cold and forbidding. It was strange that no one was coming and going through the large iron door. Were most of the guests using the water entrance on the Grand Canal?

He heard a scratching sound behind him and then a little splash. Most likely a water rat, one of the city's nastier realities that he tried to ignore.

He stood looking up at the front of the Ca' da Capo-Zendrini—or rather its humble back, for most of the decorations on the eighteenth-century building were concentrated on the Grand Canal side where it presented a classical facade in Istrian stone with an elaborate attic frieze of lions. Like the Palazzo Labia farther up the Grand Canal, the Ca' da Capo-Zendrini had been designed by Cominelli, but unlike the much more sumptuous building it couldn't boast frescoes by Tiepolo or trompe l'oeil decor and certainly not that notorious palazzo's reputation for lavish entertainments. Instead there were some passable frescoes by Zugno and Cignaroli and the Contessa's subdued gatherings as the one this evening was sure to be.

Although the building was now known as the Ca' da Capo-Zendrini, the Contessa's husband's family had owned it for only the past seventy years, after having sold their smaller palazzo in the San Polo quarter near San Cassiano. By the time the Contessa—then simply Barbara Spencer of Cadogan Place—had married Alvise da Capo-Zendrini thirty years ago, the building had been denuded of many of its decorations and severely damaged by the recent war and industrial pollution from the mainland.

The Contessa had made it her mission—at least her first one—to restore the palazzo to its former glory. She had been so successful that she had received both the praise and the envy of many established Venetian families who had neither the money nor the imagination to do what should be done with their own buildings.

Before he had met the Contessa, Urbino had heard gossip about her hard line with the architects and restorers, her scrounging throughout Italy and Europe for the perfect pieces to fill in the gaps in the Ca' da Capo-Zendrini's furnishings, her physical and emotional exhaustion afterward and extended stay in a Swiss sanatorium. Although the gossipers had thought they were painting a picture of someone that the young American would never want to meet, their talk had had the opposite effect. His interest in the woman had only increased for he perceived in her passion for her adopted city something very similar to his own. And when they had met at a reception during the Biennale seven years ago they had discovered an instant rapport. Ever since they had been close friends and confidants. With much amusement the Contessa had told him that they were referred to as "that Anglo-American alliance."

His thoughts about the Contessa having sharpened his sense of responsibility, he went down the steps of the bridge and along the *calle* to the iron door and rang the bell. The door was buzzed open and he walked through one of the palazzo's two gardens, this one small and formal. The inner door was opening as he approached it, giving its view of the impressive staircase sweeping up to the *piano nobile*. Mauro, the Contessa's majordomo, bade him good evening and closed the door behind him.

9 IT was proving much easier to talk to Clifford Voyd than he had thought it would be. The stout fellow was downright garrulous.

For half an hour they had been standing at the far end of the *salone* near the closed doors of the loggia that overlooked the Grand Canal. In front of them in the brightly illuminated room the Contessa and some of the most prominent men and women of the city formed small groups among whom the maid Lucia, Maria Galuppi, and two young men walked with trays of drinks and hors d'oeuvres. Maria looked uncharacteristically stern and severe, a result not only of her crisp black dress and white apron but of the set expression on her face that seemed close to disapproval.

The large room was dominated by several sixteenth-century tapestries of biblical and mythological scenes and an entire corner was devoted to icons and a portable altar of the Virgin, St. Ambrose, and St. Gregory. Urbino surveyed the scene as he talked with Voyd. The Contessa, although engaged in close conversation with Stefano Bellorini and the curator of the Glass Museum, kept sending anxious glances in their direction.

She might have spared herself, however, for things were moving along swimmingly.

"I hear you have a veritable passion for that old decadent Huysmans," Voyd had said for openers after striding across the room as if he had been waiting for Urbino to arrive. He was a heavyset, good-looking man about the Contessa's age. "Your reputation has preceded you in more ways than one."

"As has yours, Mr. Voyd."

Somehow the man managed to look both sheepish and vain at the same time.

"Tell me," he said, "if you love that book so much, do you go for all its ideas? Are your rooms in colors that look best by artificial light? Do you favor orange and a lot of episcopal violet and cardinal purple? Indigo moldings as well? And absolutely thousands and thousands of richly bound books and exotic flowers, preferably artificial ones that look real and real ones that look unmistakably artificial? And—and all the rest?"

"Not quite, Mr. Voyd. I have no gold-plated tortoise encrusted with jewels either and I certainly don't compel my maid Natalia to wear a costume of Flemish grogram with a medieval coif. But I take what suits my sensibility and character and leave all the rest."

"But I'm still as much up in the air as before."

"Let me put it this way, Mr. Voyd. If you were to come to the Palazzo Uccello you wouldn't find anything very strange."

"Because there's nothing strange there or you keep it all well hidden? Pardon me if I josh you in this way, but I find your enthusiasm for Huysmans rather unusual. In my youth—my *first* youth, that is," he added, smoothing down his bald spot with a wry smile, "I found him deliciously wicked but still could never understand how poor Dorian Gray could have been corrupted by him."

After a few moments of silence Urbino thought that the man was finished teasing him, but then the writer said, "I've also heard that you're one of those men most to be feared." He paused for a few beats for Urbino to suffer whatever response had been sought. Fear? Confusion? Amusement? It was difficult to tell. He smiled broadly. "I mean, of course, that you write biographies. Tell me, do you really believe we gain anything by seeing the naked man—or the naked woman, as the case might be?"

"Such biographies have their place. What you call nakedness is sometimes nothing more than the person stripped of myths and distortions, frequently of his own creation. My own books, I like to think, make a small contribution to a more balanced perspective."

"Be assured I was speaking only generically," Voyd said with the air of soothing a tender ego. "I regret to say I haven't read any of your little lives." He shrugged apologetically—not, it seemed, for the slight of the *"little lives"* but for the neglect of an unfortunately busy man. "I do seem to remember a review of one or two of them, though."

He smiled broadly again.

"But don't take what I say personally. I know many intelligent people who wouldn't be caught dead with fiction in their hands, no matter who the author. It's just that I have a mortal dread of the biographer. I do all I can to thwart him. I feel as if I am always making moves against an opponent perhaps not even born yet, someone who will want to reveal what should be kept in the dark and who will make up all the rest." He gave Urbino an exaggeratedly judicious look. "Who knows, Mr. Macintyre? It might even be you."

"I doubt it. I'm committed to my *Venetian Lives*. If I do anyone who isn't Venetian, he must have some close relationship to the city, like Browning or Wagner."

"I like your choice of words. 'Do'! We Americans living abroad sometimes end up using the most unusual expressions. But you may be tempted yet to 'do' me one of these days. I've always wanted to have a *pied-à-terre* here in Venice the way you do."

"It's much more than that. It's my only home."

"So much the better for you."

At this point Voyd launched into a monologue on Venice that had Urbino wondering why he even wanted to visit a city he seemed to have so much disdain for. He had little good to say, pointing out that it had been a long time since there had been any real life in the city and lamenting that today it wasn't much more than a tomb and a vast museum, a cross between an Oriental bazaar and a sideshow.

"The Philistines are everywhere. A vulgarizing mob has taken hold of this once great city—and they're not all foreigners either but Venetians themselves. One of these fine days I won't be surprised at all to have to buy a ticket before I'll even be able to step out of Santa Lucia."

Urbino didn't feel like rising to Voyd's bait and defending the city. Instead he changed the topic to Rome. From Rome they soon passed on to Paris and London and eventually to their mutual expatriate existence.

"It isn't at all what it used to be," Voyd said several times.

Whether he was referring to his own long experience as an expatriate or to the twenties and earlier, Urbino couldn't decide and didn't get an immediate opportunity to ask, so expansive and fast-talking was the man.

Then, just when Urbino had begun to despair of introducing Margaret Quinton into the conversation, Voyd brought the dead woman up himself.

"My friend Quinton told me last year that she felt in many

ways the Bedouin during her years abroad, taking up and pulling down the same old tent in different places. Only the thought of a room back in Schenectady gave her the strength to stay. Schenectady! Can you imagine! She doubted if she'd ever see that room again. She described it down to the wallpaper pattern and windowpanes. I could almost see it myself. She said she was going to make one last try here in Venice this winter, not the most auspicious of places for such things. Well," he sighed, raising his glass of wine to his thin lips, "we all see how that worked out, don't we?" He drained the last of the wine and stared at the empty glass.

"Poor, poor Quinton," he went on after a moment. "I liked to think she had no idea what she was doing, that she must have been in a daze. She had the influenza, there was all that medication, fever, who knows what came over her? The last time I saw her, the day before she—she died, she looked older by a decade than her fifty years. She was sitting up in bed in the same room she threw herself from the next night, and you'll never guess what she was doing. She had one of my early books propped up on her knees and was copying the whole damn thing out in longhand! She was up to the fifth chapter, *Passing into the Picture* it was. She said that she was beginning to understand how I had managed to bring it off. She was certainly an unusual woman." He lifted his empty glass in tribute to her memory, then added, "She was deaf, you know."

Urbino had been so taken aback by Voyd's unsolicited flow about the dead woman that it was a few seconds before he realized that the last comment, unlike the others, expected an answer. Voyd was waiting and seemed amused, as if he had caught Urbino out in being either too much or too little interested in what he had to say about Margaret Quinton.

"No, I didn't know."

This seemed enough for Voyd who, after exchanging his empty glass for a full one from Maria's tray, went on to explain. "Not completely deaf, you understand, but with seriously impaired hearing. Well, with whatever problems she had or thought she had, big or small, she's gone from us now, and there's much that needs to be done because of it."

While Voyd had been talking, a man in his mid-twenties came up to them in time to hear the last words. He was dressed in a dark-brown velvet suit and had a shock of unruly blond hair over his smooth forehead. It was the man Bellorini had collided with earlier at Florian's.

"As usual you exaggerate, Clifford," he said with a slight accent that sounded vaguely Germanic. "There's not that much to do, is there? You're almost finished, in fact. You work fast." He looked at Urbino. "Excuse me, my name is Kobke, Christian Kobke." He extended his hand.

"Urbino Macintyre."

The good-looking young man turned again to Voyd, who was looking at him with a mixture of amusement and irritation.

"You do go on, Clifford. You give the impression that you are absolutely inundated with things. But the truth of the matter is, Mr. Macintyre, that everything has been done that needs to be done. My friend here is most efficient when it comes to these things. He brought everything out this afternoon in several large boxes. I was staggering under their weight."

"Now who is exaggerating?"

"Nonetheless—"

"Yes, nonetheless, my dear boy," Voyd interrupted, "it's a disturbing duty I must perform. I'm Quinton's literary executor, Mr. Macintyre. And in addition to all her writing, her niece has asked me to help go through her other things and kindly said I might take what I want."

"Which was about twenty or thirty letters he'd written her—or were there even more?"

"They fall within the domain of my literary executorship, Christian, as you well know. This is a duty I would most gladly relinquish, believe me. As for poor Quinton's *objets*, I've limited myself to a painting, a few books, and a trinket here and there, none of them worth much. The painting's a Riva degli Schiavoni in the manner of Sargent, a bit heavy-handed but the two of us found it on one of our many forays together."

"It has what you might call sentimental value," Kobke said with a little smile.

"Sentimental value can often make up for a lot of mediocre art," Urbino said, thinking of some of his own favorite pieces at the Palazzo Uccello.

Kobke looked at him sharply.

"You aren't an art critic, are you, Mr. Macintyre?"

"Not at all."

"I'll leave the explaining to Clifford. Meanwhile, I'm off in search of that glowering old woman with the tray, the one who looks like the witch in 'Hansel and Gretel.' I wonder if she'd let me do a sketch of her."

"You'll have to excuse Christian," Voyd said when the young man had left. "He's rather out of sorts at the moment. He just learned about a poor review back in Copenhagen. He's an illustrator. Believe me, his work is absolutely of a charm. Perhaps if you come by some time he'll be in a better mood and show you what he has with him. We'd be delighted to see you."

"Where are you staying?"

"The Europa e Regina. We can almost see right through the doors of the Salute from our balcony when we're brave enough to venture out in this weather. You'll have to visit us. Perhaps we can continue our conversation about my friend Quinton if you'll allow an old man to indulge himself. You seem a sympathetic listener, so rare to find in any man. And I would be interested in your own impressions of her. Give me a ring but don't wait too long. We leave before carnival."

"I thought that might have been why you came."

"You amuse me, Mr. Macintyre, you really do. We have a great

deal to learn about each other. Carnival! Never! But excuse me,"
he said as he looked at his watch, "I must find our dear hostess and
say good night. I won't be able to stay for dinner. Eating late has
never agreed with me, recently less than ever. And it seems my
best writing here is done between midnight and three—although
tonight this might make a great deal of difference." He held up his
empty wineglass. "Good-bye, my new young friend. Don't forget
to stop by. The Europa e Regina."

No, Urbino said to himself as he watched Voyd join the Contessa, he wouldn't forget. Hadn't Voyd implied that he would like
to tell him more about Margaret Quinton? It was as if the writer
needed someone to talk to about the unfortunate woman, someone more receptive than the ironic Kobke. Or was it that Voyd
had sensed Urbino's eagerness for information about her and was
tempting him with the prospect of future revelations?

Whatever it was, Urbino was sure of one thing. The great
Clifford Voyd felt more than a little guilty about the death of his
friend. He wondered how the Contessa was going to take the
news.

10 "BUT just a few opals, Barbara, *ti prego*," Stefano Bellorini was saying when Urbino joined him and the
Contessa in one of the side alcoves with windows looking out
over the water. Urbino had waited until Voyd had made his
farewell to the Contessa. The writer, however, had not yet slipped
away but, with an impatient Kobke, was talking with a professor
from Ca' Foscari and his wife who was handing him a book and
a pen. "Not for all of them, you understand," Stefano continued
after greeting Urbino. "No, not at all, but for your lovely *nonna*."
He was referring to the photograph of the Contessa's grand-

mother. "And it might even be less expensive. *Per esempio*, we could—"

The Contessa shook her head impatiently.

"I am not concerned with saving money on this little project, Stefano dear, as you well know, and neither should you be. You will never be able to convince me by arguing expense when it's a matter of opals. They're bad luck, aren't they, Urbino?"

"Some people think so but—"

"That's quite good enough for me. And it will have to be the same for you, Stefano, even if you aren't superstitious. Not that I am myself but—but I believe my grandmother was," she finished somewhat lamely.

"You are more difficult to deal with than my father was," Stefano said, making one of his well-known jokes, "except that he *was* always trying to save money!" His father, dead for thirty years, was still remembered in the Cannaregio for his miserly ways and domination of his wife and only child with a fortune made in the shipping trade. "I will say this for you, Barbara, you know what you like." He took several sheets of paper from a small table and handed them to Urbino. "Here they are."

They were the sketches he had misplaced earlier in the day. It was difficult to tell exactly what the finished frames would look like but Urbino was impressed as he knew he would be. The designs, each ornate and decorative in its own distinct way, were striking.

"Lovely," he said, handing the sheets back to Stefano. "They remind me of Art Nouveau, with a touch of the Pala d'Oro, but yet they're very much your own."

The artist beamed behind his thick round glasses.

"Art Nouveau! Exactly! That's why I wanted opals. But don't worry, Barbara. We artists have almost always listened to our Popes and other patrons! But you must excuse me. Cavatorta is monopolizing Angela disgracefully and even after all these years I'm still a bit of an Othello. One good thing my father did was see to it that I didn't lose Angela to someone else."

He frowned in the direction of his wife and Cavatorta, an ex-priest and now a mask maker in the Cannaregio. The Bellorinis had a strained relationship with Cavatorta that was said to go back to the time of their marriage, when there had been a disagreement of some kind over a gift given by Cavatorta's father. Those who disliked Angela spread the story that she had acted in a haughty manner that went with the Candiani blood and the Bellorini money. Equally vociferous were those who couldn't abide Cavatorta. Surely a man who had never been known even in his youth to pass by an opportunity to make others look worse than himself had enjoyed taking malicious advantage of a mild misunderstanding and fanning the flames over the years.

Urbino had always found all this rather amusing than otherwise. Venice, a small, inbred place, was rife with such gossip, petty jealousies, and rivalries.

If Angela had a condescending side—something that he didn't necessarily discount despite, perhaps even because of, all her charity work—she had never shown it to him or to the Contessa whose good friend she was. Through the Contessa, Angela and Stefano had become, if not his friends, then his close acquaintances and had been particularly helpful during the second stage of his renovation of the Palazzo Uccello. Often they had known better than the restorers where to find matching marble for the fireplace and the best terracotta bricks and tiles for the *andron*.

As for Cavatorta, he had an irritating snideness. Urbino suspected that his behavior was an understandable, if mean-spirited reaction against the ill will many people had for him since he had left the Church. It must not be easy for him, living in the same quarter in which he had been a priest.

After Stefano had bustled off to rescue his plain-faced wife from what seemed the rather bored attentions of the mask maker, the Contessa put her hand on Urbino's arm.

"So how does our writer feel about his poor dead friend? Is he racked with remorse as you so colorfully expressed it earlier?"

Urbino started to go over his conversation with Voyd and his friend Kobke. He was just warming to the topic, trying to remember as best he could everything that had been said, when the Contessa interrupted him.

"No more details, Urbino, if you don't mind."

"But the details are particularly interesting."

"But they might make me try to find excuses and the man doesn't deserve any. He feels guilty because he *is* guilty and knows it. It's a simple question of morality and the workings of the conscience. There you have it, my dear."

Urbino didn't go on but he disagreed with her. For him details were almost everything. Wasn't it one of the main things he loved about the city, its mad jumble of details that somehow all came together so beautifully? And all those lists of flowers, of perfumes, of painters in Huysmans? The Contessa had once accused him of losing a sense of "the one true bright thing," as she had phrased it, because of this love for details. "But I'd be lost, adrift without them" had been his answer. "I'd be lost forever if I indulged in them" had been her own quick response.

The Contessa was smiling at him now, her head tilted slightly to one side.

"I know what you're thinking, *caro*. You're saying to yourself, 'For a bright old woman Barbara has her peculiarities.' You're saying, 'Barbara and her blasted morality!'"

"Not quite but you're close. Tell me, though, does all this mean that Clifford Voyd has seen the last of his invitations here?"

She gave him a look from which everything was absent except the reproach.

"My God, Urbino, what's your opinion of me! Of course not. He'll be back, I'm sure, if he cares to come, and his handsome young friend is welcome too. It should be interesting to see what costumes they wear for *carnevale*, don't you think?"

"We'll never find out, I'm afraid. They leave before then. Voyd doesn't care for *carnevale*."

"Now that's a surprise. I would have thought otherwise. We'll just have to get along without him then. Do you think we can manage?"

"Considering that neither of us is particularly fond of *carnevale* either, don't you think that the question is more one of how we'll be able to survive it under any circumstances? But it's not for a whole month yet. For now all I'm concerned about is managing the walk back home."

She looked up at him with a playful smile.

"What is it going to be tonight? *Casablanca? Brief Encounter?*"

"*Camille.*"

She gave a self-satisfied nod and patted his hand.

"She got what she deserved, that woman!"

With this she went off to say good night to the curator of the Glass Museum, who was about to leave and was looking for her. Urbino, now ready to leave himself, saw that he would be obliged to stop and say something to the Bellorinis and Cavatorta who were at the other end of the *salone* by the staircase. Voyd and Kobke, a little closer to making their exit, joined them a few moments before Urbino did but Kobke and Stefano gave no indication that they had met earlier at Florian's.

Cavatorta, a thin man in his mid-fifties who somehow always managed to look unkempt no matter how he was dressed, was describing the history and design of Venetian masks. The Bellorinis, who most likely knew a great deal about masks themselves, had bored expressions.

"For example, color," Cavatorta stressed, looking at Voyd as if he were the only one who could understand or appreciate what he had to say. "Color, now, is of extreme importance. It is essential, in fact." He took a sip of his whiskey. From his thick, slurred speech it was evident that he had already had too much to drink. He had something of a reputation in the Cannaregio, if not for outright drunkenness, then for a chronic state of mild intoxication that often led him to say or do something that gave offense. "The *moretta* is always black, always, and should be made of velvet although these days I usually use plain cloth. Now the *domini* should be made of silk but they can come in many different colors, red and gold and purple and yellow and green." As he said this he took in Angela's bright green dress and added, "Yes, color is of the essence. Color gives personality, it reflects it. For example, brown suits you, Signor—Signor—"

"Kobke," the Dane said less than enthusiastically.

"It complements you. And look at our famous author—austere and priestly in his black, but our friend Signor Macintyre here knows that black doesn't quite suit his coloring so he wears midnight blue." Briefly, his eyes flicked in Angela's direction again. "And as we say, 'He—or she, as the case might be—who wears green must be very sure of himself.'"

It seemed an invitation to look at Angela that none of them was able to resist. The bright green of her dress made her complexion even more sallow and emphasized the dark circles beneath her eyes. A woman of a certain age who was not attractive to begin with, she obviously had gone to a great deal of trouble with her hair and her dress for the party. Stefano glowered at Cavatorta and seemed on the point of saying something, but to say anything would have drawn more attention to his wife. Beneath his evident anger there seemed to be something else—uneasiness, almost a touch of fear, perhaps for how his wife was taking the comment. His concern for her was, the Contessa often said, what she admired even more than his talent. He gave his wife a strained smile. Then, taking her arm and saying an abrupt good evening, he brought her over to join Rebecca Mondador, a young architect talking with a reporter from *Il Gazzettino*.

"That Cavatorta," the Contessa said a few minutes later when Urbino had described the incident to her, "he manages to rub everyone the wrong way. I don't know why I invite him here."

But Urbino knew why. Although she readily admitted being prejudiced against the mask maker because of his abandonment of the priesthood, his father had been one of her husband's most faithful friends. If the sins of the father were often visited upon the sons, perhaps the virtues of the father could in some way make up for the wrongs of the son—at least up to a certain point.

Perhaps she was thinking of the same thing for she said, "Now his father was a good man, the best. He sold a building over on Murano just to start Luigi up in business after he left the priesthood. Sold it at a loss, too, to one of the glassmakers who needed space for a showroom. If he had held on to it, it would be worth a fortune today. All that old Cavatorta got out of it was the satisfaction of pleasing his son and the dubious comfort of a discount on whatever he wanted to buy at the glassmaker's. I wish I could remember his name—what was it now? Oh, there's Sister Veronica. I didn't think she would be able to come. She might know."

Sister Veronica, dressed in a simple dark gray suit and black shoes instead of the modified habit she wore when she was about her official duties at the Convent of the Charity of Santa Crispina, came up to them. Urbino knew he was old-fashioned to think so, but although he liked and admired her, he couldn't get used to the considerable freedom she enjoyed, a freedom that had her going to parties like these and often joining the Contessa or Angela or some other woman from the parish on shopping trips or outings as far away as Milan and Florence. And it wasn't as if she were one of the younger sisters who had grown up in a more liberal church. She was only a few years younger than the Contessa.

As it turned out, the Contessa didn't ask Sister Veronica the name of the glassblower. Instead they started to talk about Margaret Quinton. After a few minutes Urbino, feeling that the two women wanted to be alone to discuss the ill-fated writer, said good night. He was amused to see that Voyd was still there, a fresh wine in his hand. Kobke was nowhere to be seen.

11

ALTHOUGH *Camille* was one of his favorite movies, Urbino's attention continued to wander from the divine face of Garbo.

He was thinking about Margaret Quinton. Although he had met her only a few times, she was vivid in his mind. She had been a large woman who wore cumbersome shoes and dresses with little shape. Barbara had assured him, however, that the dresses were custom-made in Milan and Paris. What Voyd had told him tonight about her being slightly deaf helped him understand the intense look she had had whenever she was listening to him. He now wondered, despite all her nods and smiles, how much of what he had said to her she had even heard. He could still see the slightly pained look on her long, thin face when he had gone into considerable detail about his dislike for the *centro tavola* in the form of a garden with fountain on display at the Glass Museum. At the time he had taken it for disagreement but now he realized she had probably been straining to hear.

He wished he had been more attentive to her, had invited her to the Palazzo Uccello, had drawn her out more about the history of glassmaking that Barbara said she knew so much about. It might have helped just a little to dispel her vague, forlorn air.

He promised himself that he would take Voyd up on his invitation. He wouldn't mind learning a few more things about the woman. She was much more interesting to him now in her death than she had been in life.

The realization so startled him that he decided to banish any more thoughts of her for the rest of the night and to start the movie over again. Before he did, however, he went across the hall to the library and took down one of Quinton's books, *A Knot of Clowns*. He would read it as soon as he finished the George Sand novel about Venice that he had just begun.

After making a note to order flowers from Tommaso Soli for the funeral the day after tomorrow, he settled himself in front of *Camille* again with an almost easy conscience.

❧

12 AS Urbino sat next to the Contessa and the Bellorinis in the English Church of St. George, so unlike the nearby Salute and the other baroque, Gothic, and Byzantine churches throughout the city, he was struck with how suited the simple building was to the impression he had of the woman. He wondered, however, if Voyd, dressed in the same impeccable black of the Contessa's party and looking appropriately somber, might not have preferred more grandiose surroundings for his eulogy. His manner seemed to cry out for something more Latinate.

The Contessa was muffled in dark furs and a matching hat that concealed her face except when she lifted it to look up at Voyd. Her expression was almost completely blank, which probably meant there was a great deal of emotion behind it.

Several pews in front of them was Margaret Quinton's niece, Adele Carstairs, her bowed head covered with a black lace shawl. Beside her was the nurse who had come up with Margaret Quinton two months ago from Rome. The American consul and his wife, looking alternately bored and impatient, were across the aisle from the two women. Next to them was Sister Veronica, who kept glancing at her watch. This was the time that she usually began her tours with guests from the Santa Crispina hospice.

The dead woman had kept to herself and had made few close friends despite the entree given her by the Contessa. Other than the chaplain and the organist there was only one other person in the Church of St. George: Maria Galuppi. Whether it was shyness or unease at being in a church not of her own faith for perhaps the first time in her long life, she kept to the shadows to one side of the entrance where she stood in her long woolen coat, her gloved hands clasped loosely in front of her. When Urbino turned around at one point, she was staring at their pew with a grim expression. Perhaps she couldn't bring herself to look up at Voyd in the pulpit as he spoke about mortality.

Voyd's sonorous tones washed over the small group along with the steady sound of the rain outside.

"To die in Venice," he was saying, "is to be in good company. Wagner, Browning, Diaghilev, Pound, and so many noble others, the unknown as well as the famous, those of modest talents as well as those of great genius. Our Margaret loved this city dearly and she was giving honor and praise to it in the way that meant the most to her and would certainly have meant a great deal to us. With all of her fine discrimination she was making it the setting for one of her incomparable fictions. But that, alas, is among the things that shall never be. There is much sad obscurity surrounding her last moments at the Casa Silviano—of this let us speak freely and openly as she always tried to do in her work—but we must not let their darkness hide for us the light and gentleness and talent that were Margaret Quinton. She was a woman we were all privileged to know but a woman who never once would have considered it such.

"I will leave you not with my own feeble words but with the shining ones of Quinton herself, something I marvelously chanced upon last night as I was glancing through some of her writings which it is now my dolorous duty to oversee. It is written in that fine spidery hand that seems to come from another age and that any of us who has ever seen it will never soon forget."

He slowly took out his glasses from his vest pocket, unfolded a sheet of paper, and after clearing his throat, read even more sonorously than before:

" 'Venice, like love, is much described and little understood.

Venice, like life, is both a reality and a dream passing away. Venice, like the only beauty to be truly valued, was born to die and in that dying and death to become, if possible, even more beautiful. I look from my windows at a romantic little canal, the kind that Sargent loved to paint, and sounding in my ears like some inner echo I hear that lovely aria from *I Due Foscari: "Ecco la mia Venezia, ecco il suo mare."* Someday may she rest in peace beneath the waves of time and tide like all past dreams and forgotten or abandoned loves. Someday— but let it be a long, long day from this one—let her rest in peace, this serene dream upon the water.'"

Voyd paused after finishing, bowing his head for what seemed much longer than necessary. Then, slowly putting away his glasses and the paper, he looked out over the heads of the small gathering to the back of the church where Maria was standing and said in a stage whisper, "And let us all say, let her rest in peace, this woman who brought us all such light and joy, this woman who had the soul to perceive beauty and the talent to create it herself. Amen."

Urbino had the impression that Voyd, as he stepped gravely down from the pulpit, considered the rest of the service nothing but anticlimax.

He wondered what the Contessa felt about the writer's performance. A quick glance at her face showed that it was—if possible— even more expressionless than it had been before.

13   FOR most tourists the cemetery island is only a stop on the way from Venice proper to Murano but for Urbino it was someplace special, its tombs and graves more curious and interesting than anything on the glass island could ever be.

"Would you think me strange, Barbara, if I told you that I find this part of San Michele among the loveliest places in all of Venice?"

He knew he was being perverse, for the Protestant graveyard was overgrown with unkempt grass beaten down by the rain that had only recently let up. The older grave markers, most crowded beneath massive trees that themselves looked half dead at this time of year, were eaten away by time and weather, their surfaces sometimes as smooth as the wall that set the area off from the lagoon and the rest of the cemetery. Where letters and dates could be traced, they frequently spelled out the melancholy story of those foreigners who had probably been surprised to meet their deaths in Venice so far from home.

"Since I thought you strange, *caro*, from the first time I laid eyes on you admiring that abominable painting at the Biennale, I've grown accustomed to such things."

She looked around them. The graveyard was empty of everyone else except two attendants filling in the grave. Even fewer people had come to the burial than to the church service. The American consul and his wife had hurried from the church to their waiting boat and Maria and Sister Veronica had gone about their duties. The Contessa's boat had dropped Stefano and Angela off in the Cannaregio before continuing across the lagoon to San Michele.

There had been one graveside mourner, however, who hadn't been at St. George's. This was Kobke, Voyd's young friend. Urbino had noticed him idling on the other side of the Campo San Vio when they came out of the church. Kobke had joined Voyd, Adele Carstairs, and the nurse in the same funeral boat to San Michele.

"You know," the Contessa said as they walked down one of the leaf-strewn paths to the gate that led into the rest of the cemetery, "I've never been able to decide if this is a good city to die in since we must all die somewhere in the end or if it might not be a bit—oh, I don't know—redundant. But obviously Clifford Voyd thinks it a marvelous place for dying, considering the lineage he gave."

"Such melancholy thoughts, Barbara. You surprise me—you with your love for Venice."

"It's Venice I love, not dying." She shot him a vulnerable, troubled look that went straight to his heart. "I can't say that I care for all its associations with death. It's impossible to escape them."

"But didn't one of your countrywomen—I don't remember who it was—say a long time ago that there was no other city better for the retreat of old age?"

"That's hardly more consoling."

They walked in silence for a few moments. Urbino assumed they were on their way to the boat landing until the Contessa said, "Indulge me for a few moments. I'd like to visit the Orthodox section."

He didn't have to ask why. It was to visit Diaghilev's grave. Her mother had been a close friend of Diaghilev's and had always regretted not having been at his funeral, not because she had missed Diaghilev's friend jumping into the grave but because she had been unable to pay her last respects to a man she had loved and admired. As they made their way into the Orthodox compound and down to the wall to Diaghilev's simple stone, Urbino even knew what his friend would say.

"There's another one." She pointed to the ballet slipper on the top of the tombstone. It had lost its shape and color. It was filled with decayed leaves, and a spider had spun a web across its opening. "I wonder who leaves them. In all the times I've been here I've never seen anyone even looking at the grave."

"It's one of Venice's romantic mysteries. After all, Venice is a city of love as well as death—and they're not too far apart. Remember that Wagner not only died here, as Voyd reminded us, but he also wrote the "Liebestod" of *Tristan und Isolde* in his palazzo on the Grand Canal. Love-death, death-in-love, love-in-death, love's death," he reeled off with an inappropriate grin.

Then, right there in the corner of the Orthodox section against the wall by Diaghilev's grave, he startled the Contessa—and in fact himself—by breaking out into his weak, uneven tenor:

> *"Nun banne das Bangen,*
> *holder Tod,*
> *sehnend verlangter*
> *Liebestod!"*

And then, fearing his friend might have missed his point, he started over in English:

> *"Let fear now be banished,*
> *gracious death,*
> *yearningly longed-for*
> *love-in-death!"*

"That's more than enough, thank you! Come, I think we'd better go. You have the most peculiar sensibility for an intelligent man!"

Once again arm in arm, they left Diaghilev's grave with its lone, mysterious slipper and walked slowly back to the boat landing.

Part Two

BLESSED REMAINS

❧

1 EVERYTHING had gone well at the Glass Museum despite Sister Veronica's preoccupation with Margaret Quinton's death last week and her less than keen interest in glass. Although the daughter of a glassblower, she had little appreciation for the art. What she now knew about it had been learned long after her adolescent rejection of her father's profession and because of her tours of Murano for the guests at the hospice. Even now she still had large, almost willful gaps in her knowledge, something that couldn't be said of her knowledge of Tintoretto, her grand, if chaste passion.

At one point this afternoon Sister Veronica had thought there might be a problem when the chubby little boy from Perugia started to slide himself across the floor in the room of the Wedding Cup. His momentum had almost carried him into the showcase with reliquaries but fortunately his mother had stopped him at the critical moment. She had just shrugged at Sister Veronica as if to say, Well, what can we do? He's a boy!

Now, two hours later as they stood in the Church of San Gabriele, the boy was being so quiet that Sister Veronica was getting nervous. She knew, from her own nephews down in Naples, enough about the silence of children to realize that it usually boded no good.

And the boy wasn't just quiet. He was as still as one of the sculpted figures of death looming behind him on the mausoleum of a prominent Cannaregio family.

The reason soon became evident as she followed the direction of his wide-eyed stare. It was the body of Santa Teodora in her glass coffin.

Wouldn't it be best to mention the precious relic before he said anything irreverent that would reverberate through the church with its eerie acoustics?

"And that," she said with almost indecorous haste, not having yet mentioned the disputed Tiepolo ceiling and the Cima painting, "is the body of Santa Teodora."

The boy went up to the coffin, knelt on the catafalque among the wilted bouquets, and pressed his face against the glass.

"But I thought it was Biancaneve!"

His mother and the three other guests started to laugh at his confusion of the saint's body with Snow White but quickly restrained themselves. Laughter didn't seem appropriate in these Gothic surroundings. But Sister Veronica saw no need for restraint. Her own laughter rang out clearly.

"Very good, *piccolino*. She does look like Snow White in a way. When I saw Santa Teodora when I was a little girl, I thought the same thing."

The boy took his hands away from the case, leaving behind smudges that Don Marcantonio would be sure to notice later. He turned to Sister Veronica.

"Does she have a handsome prince to wake her up?"

This time they all laughed heartily. The sound of their laughter echoed from the vault and came back strangely distorted. Sister Veronica thought she heard a mutter of disapproval from somewhere in the back of the church.

She turned to the boy, put her hands together, and looked over his head at the glass coffin.

"Many years ago," she began in the same tone of voice she used when telling fairy tales to her nephews, "there lived a little girl named Teodora of Syracuse. She had many brothers and sisters and was a good girl, a *very, very* good girl," she emphasized with a glance down at the boy. "She made a promise to God that she would never marry but instead would give all her time and devotion to Him and only to Him. But there was a young prince from far away"—at this the boy's face lit up—"a young prince who wasn't at all good, not one bit. He loved Teodora. Everyone loved Teodora, of course, but the prince loved her in a different way. He asked her to marry him and to go away with him to his kingdom. Teodora thanked him very sweetly but said she couldn't marry him or anyone else because of her promise to the good Lord. So what did the prince do but go to the governor and tell him that Teodora refused to marry him because she was a servant of the Christian God and not of anyone else. You see, this was during the time when good Christian souls were severely punished for their faith. The powerful governor couldn't accept such behavior and so his soldiers killed Teodora." Sister Veronica paused and then added, "With a *very big* sword. She became a saint and now she's with us here in Venice."

The boy didn't say anything for several moments. He seemed to be thinking.

"But Syracuse is in Sicily and Sicily is a long way from here," he eventually said. "How did she get all the way up here? We had to take a bus and a train and we came only from Perugia."

"She was brought here by two Venetian merchants who thought she would be happier in Venice."

There was a puzzled frown on the boy's face as he went over to the glass coffin again and looked in.

"You mean they just took her? And why would she be happier here? I don't think anybody ever knew if she was happy or not because she was dead. And besides, she was wearing a mask. Did she always wear one?"

There were so many things she might explain that she wasn't

sure which to take up first. Obviously this afternoon she wasn't going to deliver the neat lecture she had perfected over the years on the legend of the blessed Santa Teodora. It was probably just as well. The boy's questions were the ones most people wanted to ask but were too embarrassed to.

"But you see, *piccolino*, they didn't just take her. The Doge, the ruler of Venice in those days, was interested in Santa Teodora, very interested. He thought that his city—with all its money and beauty and power—was a better place for such a wonderful saint. And there was another thing: one of the first saints of the city was San Teodoro—you can see a statue of him with his crocodile on a column near the Doge's Palace—and the Doge thought it would be nice if Venice could bring Santa Teodora here too and he had this special case built for her on Murano where we just came from."

When she looked at the adults, she saw that they were more absorbed in her story than her listeners usually were. Perhaps inadvertently, with the help of the boy from Perugia, she had discovered a better way to tell the story of Santa Teodora.

The boy, however, wasn't satisfied.

"The mask," her reminded her.

"Ah yes, the mask. The mask came later, much, much later. It was made in Florence in 1839 so that her head wouldn't fall off."

The boy edged slowly away from the glass coffin. He turned around and looked up at the arches of the church, at the stained-glass window of the Virgin and the Archangel Gabriel, at the Cima. He seemed to be looking for something to focus his attention on instead of the body of Santa Teodora.

He found it. He pointed to the other side of the church.

"That old woman there looks scary. I think she's a *strega*. Yes, she's a wicked witch, the Mala Regina, and I want to know why she's here!"

Sister Veronica, though patient before, was now upset. Without waiting for the mother to calm or reprimand him, she knelt down and said, "Be quiet, you mustn't say such things! She's a very good woman. Her name is Maria, like the mother of Jesus. She loves Santa Teodora."

"I don't care who she loves," he cried. "I think she's ugly and a witch! I want to go home!"

He ran to his mother and buried his face in her coat.

※

2 HALF an hour later a young British couple were examining the masks in Cavatorta's shop in the Calle dell'Arcanzolo a few steps from the Campo San Gabriele.

"That one is Arlecchino, Harlequin," the mask maker said, "the buffoon." He started to explain the character when the wife, an attractive blonde, interrupted him.

"You speak English very well but your accent isn't by any chance . . . ?"

"Yes, Australian. My teacher was from Perth." He scratched his beard. "And I have cousins in Australia who visit from time to time."

"How interesting. And this?" She took another leather mask from the wall and put it in front of her pale face.

"That's Pantalone."

"Pantalone?" said the husband. "I'm afraid I'm not familiar with these characters."

"Pantalone, now," Cavatorta began with enthusiasm, lighting a cigarette, "is most interesting. He's an old Venetian merchant, the husband who—how do you say in English?—who wears the horns. What is the word?"

Neither of his customers helped him but from the expression on their faces he could see they understood. The wife put back the mask and took down another. This could go on forever. It was already long past five and he was in a hurry to close early. He had pegged these two from the moment they walked in as browsers.

If they bought anything, it would be only one of the pamphlets on mask making stacked next to the cash register.

"Now this one," the wife said. "Let me guess." She held up the black papier-mâché mask with its prominent cone-shaped nose to one of the lamps placed throughout the shop to illuminate the display. She turned it in profile. "Yes, I know! Pinocchio!"

Cavatorta smiled.

"A logical guess but also a logical mistake. It's the *medico*."

"*Medico*? It means 'doctor,'" she said for the benefit of her husband, who seemed bored. Cavatorta wondered if he would get even the price of a pamphlet from these two. The wife gave him a puzzled look. "But I don't understand. Why is this one the doctor? Is he another one of those characters from the Italian theater—what is it called?"

"The commedia dell'arte." He shook his head and took the mask from her, pointing to the nose. "It's not really a nose. It's a device to protect the doctor from the plague in the old days. Some chemical or other was put here"—he turned the mask over and indicated the deep hollow—"and the doctor breathed safely, or so it was thought."

"I see." Then to his irritation she took down yet another mask, one that he didn't feel inclined to talk about. "And this one? It's lovely." She cupped the delicate silver papier-mâché mask in both her hands as if it were a face.

He crushed out his cigarette.

"That's a replica of the mask covering the face of Santa Teodora over in San Gabriele." That should be enough but then he risked adding, "I'm the only mask maker in Venice to have the honor of making copies." He probably shouldn't have said it but maybe he would make a sale and they would leave him alone. "Do you like it? It can be shipped anywhere you want. It isn't as fragile as it looks."

The husband frowned. He took the mask from his wife and put it back on the wall.

"We must be going, Jill. We've been out all day."

Looking embarrassed, the wife thanked Cavatorta and started to follow her husband into the Calle dell'Arcanzolo. Noticing the pamphlets, she picked one up.

"How delightful." She riffled through the pages, then looked at Cavatorta with a bright smile. "I'll take one." She gave him a ten-thousand *lira* note. "Make that two. I have an actress friend. She should find it interesting."

Then, with the air of someone doing her bit for local art and culture and a starving not-so-young artist, she told him to keep the change.

As soon as they left, Cavatorta went outside to pull down the metal shutters, holding himself back from banging them down the way he wanted to.

3 THE couple went down the Calle dell'Arcanzolo to the Campo San Gabriele where the wife stopped to look through her guidebook for a few minutes, frowning at a page and then up at the facade of the church. With a quick glance over her shoulder at her husband, she went across the *campo* and up the steps of the church. The door was locked.

"This way," she said, as she went down the steps and along the *riva* that bordered the canal. "Let's slip in here."

She pointed to a partly open door.

"But the church is closed, Jill."

"Don't be afraid, darling. She's been dead for a long time."

She gave a nervous laugh. It echoed from the other side of the canal and came back to them dead and hollow. She shivered, looking down at the dark, murky waters beside the footpath. Her laugh had sounded like a stranger's. Yet one more weird transformation of the city. It must have something to do with all the water and all the stones—there was hardly anything else in the city. Nothing was what it seemed here. Some of the time you couldn't even be sure if you were looking at the real thing or its reflection.

Her husband was still hesitating.

"Come on, Andrew. You know how I love these churches. Indulge me and then I promise we'll go straight on to Harry's."

"I swear they would have hanged you for a Papist in the six-teenth century. To think your dear old pater is a respectable Oxford atheist. Come on then. Let's get this over with."

He pushed the door open a bit but when he saw how dark and empty the hall ahead was, he hesitated once again. Thirty-one years of queuing up and never ignoring a sign or sensible advice held him back now.

"We'll barely see anything, it's almost completely dark. Why don't we come back first thing in the morning?"

"Because we're off to Murano then. And tomorrow's not today."

"Don't delude yourself, sweetheart, your father will know of these tendencies. I'm not sure how he'll react. They're shocking enough for me to discover in my new bride."

But before he had finished speaking she had pushed past him and was already halfway down the narrow hall. He sighed. Here it was their honeymoon and it seemed she was almost always bustling ahead of him. Either that or waiting for him with a touch of impatience. But the dear girl always seemed to know exactly what she wanted to see and exactly where it was, perhaps not so remarkable in Rome or Florence but in Venice it was a downright miracle.

All day she had been talking about this relic. "What do you think it's going to look like? Do you think there'll be a postcard? Do you think they'll let us take a snap?" She had an old school chum named Theodora and thought it would be a scream to send her a card or a snap.

He imagined it would be. You go to your front door to pick up the usual bills and circulars only to find the face of some bloody RC mummy staring at you. And to make it worse it's got your very own name!

"Andrew dear, are you coming or not?"

Did he have a choice? He caught up with her. She was standing in front of a large dark portrait in a heavy frame.

"And who do you think *he* is?"

He looked up at a dour-faced man in red robes.

"A cardinal." He pointed to the man's head. "See the red hat?" He paused. "But there's only one problem. I don't see any portraits of his so-called nephews, do you?"

"You're impossible! Come on, let's finish this before the whole building falls down on your heathen head."

Once again she led the way, this time down the hall to a door. It opened smoothly, with barely a sound, showing them the dimly lit interior of the church. They entered a side aisle near the baptismal font. To Andrew it looked like just about every other church they had visited in the city, though shabbier and—from the smell of it—quite a bit farther down the watery decline. Perhaps to Jill it looked different. She certainly seemed spellbound.

Without saying anything she squeezed through a row of pews. She had told him that the glass coffin was in a chapel on the other side and he thought he could see a corner of it in a dim recess beyond. He followed, picking up a leaflet from a pew.

Jill screamed. He dropped the leaflet and ran over to her, tripping over a kneeling board.

When he reached the chapel, Jill had stopped screaming and had her hand over her mouth. At her feet sprawled a dark-clothed figure facedown. It was a woman, apparently an old woman with thinning gray hair. His first thought was that he was looking at the saint herself, for the casket was empty, the glass broken. Pieces of glass crunched under his feet.

A rivulet of blood was seeping from the woman's head. It was staining a large white cloth and collecting around the edges of some dried flowers.

Although he knew the RCs had numerous bleeding saints in their crowded pantheon, he couldn't believe that this indeed was one of them. He bent down to put his fingers to the woman's throat. She was still warm but there was no pulse.

❧

4   MARIA was late returning Urbino's laundry. During the week since his trip to Padua he had noticed that she was struggling a bit more than usual under the basket's burden. For this last pickup he had taken out some of the heavier items.

This was the first time she had been late. If she couldn't be on time, she sent Carlo.

Urbino put down the George Sand novel and went to get another glass of wine, pausing at the study window to look down at the garden. It was a mere postage stamp but incredibly precious in a city with barely forty acres of earth. Although he loved this time of year, he was anxious for spring with all its flowers, especially the bougainvillaea that cascaded over the garden walls.

On his way back to his chair and the amiable company of Sand's Consuelo the bell rang. Before he was even halfway down the stairs there was another long ring.

When he opened the door, it was Carlo. He started talking rapidly in dialect. Even in the best of circumstances it was somewhat difficult to understand him. All Urbino could make out was that he was asking for help.

Perhaps realizing that Urbino was confused, Carlo stopped speaking. He held up his hand. In it was one of Urbino's monogrammed pillow slips. It was stained with red.

5 THE honeymoon couple had been gone only ten minutes when Commissario Francesco Gemelli of the Venice Questura learned that Urbino Macintyre was on the line. Gemelli sighed. What did Macintyre want this time? He seemed to have an endless stream of complaints and suggestions for a better and safer Venice. The last time he had called was about some supposedly unauthorized renovation in the Cannaregio.

"Tell him I'm busy, Flora."

"I'm sorry, Commissario, but he insists it's urgent and wants to speak only with you."

Gemelli cursed under his breath. This was what came of socializing, he supposed. Ever since he had met Macintyre at one of the Contessa da Capo-Zendrini's parties, the American seemed to think he was entitled to special treatment.

"Put him on then."

Gemelli thought he was prepared for just about anything Macintyre might say but realized how wrong he was when the American said,

"Commissario, you must send someone over here right away. There seems to have been an accident. I have a pillow slip covered with blood."

"What?"

"Carlo Galuppi, the son of the woman who does my laundry, just came here with a bloody pillow slip, one of *my* pillow slips."

"Are you sure it's yours?"

"It's monogrammed."

"Listen, Signor Macintyre, do whatever you can to keep Galuppi there."

"I'm afraid he's already gone."

"He just came and went, leaving you with a bloody pillow slip?"

"Not quite. I had him come in and sit down. He was very upset, almost incoherent. He was asking for help from what I could understand. I went for some brandy but when I got back he was gone. I'm afraid he's been hurt."

"Not him, his mother. Maria Galuppi had her skull bashed in at San Gabriele and that saint's body was taken. If Galuppi returns before my men arrive, try to keep him there this time. Talk to him, give him that drink, serve him dinner if you have to. Do everything you can—everything, that is, except physically restrain him. We don't want you to put your own life in danger. Just keep reminding yourself that you're probably entertaining a murderer."

6 THE rest of the Corvo was doing nothing to dull the pain Urbino felt about Maria's murder or to reconcile him to the possibility of Carlo's hand in it. Gemelli's men had come and searched the Palazzo Uccello, then taken away the pillow slip and posted a guard for the night.

Maria murdered? And possibly by her own son? Such things happened in someone else's world, certainly not his, nor that of people like the gentle, hardworking Galuppis. And yet Maria was lying at this moment in the city morgue and her son was somewhere out there on this January night afraid, confused, and—if the Commissario was right—someone to be feared. Anyone could be the victim of violence, Maria or anyone equally gentle and harmless—of this he had no doubt—but he wasn't cynical enough to believe that anyone, given the proper set of circumstances, might be the perpetrator of violence. And certainly not Carlo, not the Carlo he knew.

He was going over once again his encounter with Carlo and his conversation with Gemelli when the phone rang. As soon as he heard the Contessa's voice he realized he had made a mistake in not calling her.

"I can't believe what I just heard, *caro*," she began, the ache in her voice cutting into him, "I just can't. Sister Veronica rang me a few minutes ago with the most terrible news, you won't believe it either, *caro*. It's Maria—Maria Galuppi—"

Her voice broke, her fabled control deserting her. There was no way he could let her go on.

"I know, Barbara," he said quietly. "She was murdered."

There was a short silence, then:

"How long have you known?"

"An hour."

"An hour!" It was as if he had said "days." "My God, Urbino, whatever is the matter with you! What were you thinking of? Why didn't you ring me?"

"Try to understand, Barbara." And then he told her how he had come to know about Maria's murder, giving her all the details of Carlo's visit, his conversation with Gemelli, and the search of the Palazzo Uccello. "There's even a guard posted outside."

She didn't say anything for several moments but when she did she said it quietly yet with a clear edge of urgency: "We must do something, Urbino, we must."

"Do something?"

"Well, Carlo asked you to help, didn't he?"

"Barbara, nothing can be done now. I'll go to the Questura tomorrow to make a statement."

"I'm not talking about doing something at this moment, Urbino, and I'm certainly not talking about making a statement at the Questura. I think it would be disloyal to make a statement anyway."

"Disloyal? To whom?"

"Can't you see? To Carlo. And not only to Carlo but to Maria, too. She loved her son, no one will convince me any different— and he loved her." She paused. "And there's someone else to take into consideration, in case it hasn't occurred to you."

"Who?"

"Me! I'll never forgive you if you do anything to prevent the return of Santa Teodora."

How his friend had reached this point in her logic was far beyond him, but he had come to expect such things of her.

"Aren't you being a bit extreme, Barbara? I'm only going to make a statement at the Questura. That can only help everyone concerned. At any rate, I don't have any choice, do I? I'm sure it's required by law."

"Oh, the law!" she said angrily. It was a few moments before he realized she had hung up.

❧

7   EARLY the next morning he went to the Questura to make his statement. On his walk to the plain building in the quarter beyond the Bridge of Sighs he put from his mind any thoughts of disloyalty. He was a man going to do his duty, something he would have done with just as clear a conscience back in New Orleans.

He gave his statement to Gemelli and a stenographer as gulls screeched outside the windows. The sound startled him, making him realize he was more on edge than he had thought. When he finished describing what had happened the night before, the stenographer left to have his statement typed for signing.

Alone with Gemelli, a dark, good-looking man in his early forties, with a military bearing, Urbino decided to take a direct approach.

"For what my opinion is worth, Commissario, I don't believe Carlo Galuppi is the culprit here."

Gemelli raised his eyebrows.

" 'Culprit,' Signor Macintyre? Come, come, you know our language very well. I prefer 'murderer.'"

"But he wasn't acting like a criminal at all. He was afraid, yes, but in a pathetic kind of way. His speech impediment was more pronounced than usual. No, Commissario, I don't believe it. In all these years I've known him I—"

He broke off as Gemelli shook his head.

"Murderers are seldom strangers to others, Signor Macintyre. In fact, they usually know their victims very well. And believe me, they have family and friends like everyone else. They can even give to charities and love children and animals."

"What I meant, Commissario, is that Carlo Galuppi is not the kind of person who would do something like this."

"I am well aware of what you meant, but let me say again that I disagree. Galuppi is our primary suspect precisely because he *could* have done something like this, as you express it. Once again your euphemism is amusing. 'Something like this' happens to be the brutal murder of an old woman and the theft of the body of a so-called saint. I call it theft, but perhaps I could just as easily call it body snatching or grave robbing or the kidnapping of a prominent figure; we've seen enough of that in this country lately."

"But what motive could he possibly have had?"

"Forget about motive for a minute. Galuppi had opportunity. He's one of the few people who can come and go freely in that church at any time. Despite his deformity many parishioners have probably stopped seeing him. He's just part of the scene. As for motive, he hated his mother, for one thing."

"Hated her? If my observation of human nature means anything, Carlo Galuppi—"

Gemelli waved his hand in the air.

"All right, maybe hate is too strong. Call it resentment, deep resentment. I've already had two phone calls from people who, understandably, want to remain anonymous. But both said the same thing: Galuppi had good reason to hate his mother."

"What exactly did they say?"

For the first time since Urbino had come into his office Gemelli looked uncomfortable. "Excuse me, Signor Macintyre, but I shouldn't have mentioned the calls at all. I only did it to impress on you that Galuppi might have had reason to kill his mother. I don't want to frighten you but it's not at all inconceivable that you might be in danger yourself. Perhaps you don't know as much about our Italy as you should. How could you? But we understand crimes like this. A wife poisons her husband, a father shoots his daughter, a sister stabs her brother."

"But a son killing his mother?"

"Ah yes, this is perhaps a little more difficult to understand in our country of *la mamma*, but such a son, such a mother?"

Urbino rose from his chair.

"Excuse me, Commissario, but I don't think you should be so quick to form judgments about these people or the crime itself. It's not the best procedure for someone in your position, I would think. Isn't it just as logical to assume that Maria was there in the church when someone came in to steal the relic? Why would Carlo want to take the body of Santa Teodora? And why would he take it after he had already struck out at his mother? No, I'm not Italian but it's possible I know more about these people than you do. Maria Galuppi was a simple woman who loved her son and Carlo, despite his appearance, is a gentle soul, more to be pitied than feared. You speak of crimes of passion, Commissario, but Venice isn't Sicily."

Gemelli had risen too. A flush was creeping over his face. As Urbino knew from the Contessa, Gemelli was originally from Sicily.

"I'd appreciate if it you wouldn't imply that I don't know my job, Signor Macintyre. What you are giving is your opinion. We will take it into consideration along with all the others but so far yours is in the minority. Our two callers both said that Maria Galuppi mistreated her son, at least verbally, and even Don Marcantonio has told us that Carlo seemed afraid of her at times. In fact, he's heard them arguing in the sacristy on one or two occasions; he thinks he even heard them mention Santa Teodora. And don't forget that Carlo did show up at your door last night with a pillow slip stained with blood, the same blood type as Maria's and, I might add, blood that came from a female, not a male. I've just received the laboratory report."

Gemelli shook his head. The flush was gone now. In its place was a slightly irritated, weary expression.

"Listen, Signor Macintyre, we appreciate your concern. Not everyone would be so quick to defend an old washerwoman and her son who's something of a frightful joke in the Cannaregio. But Galuppi is all we have to go on at the moment. He's our primary suspect and until we get more evidence—something the scene-of-crime unit comes up with or perhaps a ransom note or information about someone suspicious in and around San Gabriele— well, until then my report must reflect the information we have up to this point. We know that Galuppi was in San Gabriele shortly before his mother's body was found. We also know that he appeared a short time later at the Palazzo Uccello with the bloodied pillow slip. He's nowhere to be found. He's fled, he's hiding somewhere. You mentioned that I shouldn't be too quick to form judgments but here in Italy we move differently than you do in America." A smile came over his face as he said, "I have a cousin, an *avvocato* in New Jersey. He visits us maybe once every two, three years, and we always end up arguing about the differences between the handling of crime and punishment in our two countries. We never reach a conclusion; we never convince each other. What more can I say, Signor Macintyre? Galuppi is all we have at the moment. This doesn't make him guilty, but neither does it make him innocent. If we are lucky—and luck plays a larger role in these cases than you might imagine, luck and informers, that is—yes, if we are lucky then this affair will be cleared up by *carnevale.*"

"Or else it might be bad for business, mightn't it?"

"The Questura isn't concerned about business. We leave that to you Americans, along with some decidedly naïve notions about guilt and innocence."

Assuming that this was his dismissal, Urbino started to put on his coat.

"Excuse me, Signor Macintyre, but you aren't finished yet. We need your identification."

"My identification? But surely someone else has already—"

"Not the body, Signor Macintyre, your laundry." There was a hint of a smile on Gemelli's handsome face. "Come with me."

Urbino followed Gemelli to a small, dark room at the end of the hall. It was filled with file cabinets, bookcases, and wooden and cardboard boxes. Gemelli pointed to a carton on top of a file cabinet.

"If you wouldn't mind going through it, we would appreciate it." As Urbino approached the carton, Gemelli added, "The blood-stained pieces are still at the laboratory. There were several. You'll get everything back eventually."

Urbino examined a few pieces, then turned to Gemelli.

"They're mine."

"But is it all there? Not counting the bloodstained pillow slip, a white monogrammed towel, and two pieces of underwear—unmonogrammed."

"Commissario, there is no way for me to be sure everything is here. I wasn't in the habit of making out a laundry list. Perhaps I'll notice something missing later when I need it."

"Like another pillow slip? People usually have at least two."

Urbino went through the laundry piece by piece.

"There were two."

"We have only the one. May I ask why you have such large pillow slips, Signor Macintyre? Three, four times the usual size?"

"Because I have such large pillows, Commissario. Both the pillows and the pillow slips are custom-made in Milan. But I don't see what importance their size has."

"In addition to indicating a man who likes his peculiar comforts, it gave the murderer a convenient way to carry away the body of Santa Teodora."

"But surely her body could never have fit!"

"From what can be determined there probably isn't much substance left to the body. Even a body five years old would have been in poor condition in Venice's damp atmosphere, but one from the tenth century—even given a miracle if you believe in such things—would probably be only dust by now, dust and some bones. Who really knows what condition that body was in? Don Marcantonio has resisted any attempt to have it examined since he's been at San Gabriele. Even throwing in the garments, the shoes, the mask, and—who knows?—those legendary jewels, it's not hard to imagine everything fitting into one of your pillow slips."

After helping put the laundry back into the carton, Gemelli detained Urbino in the hallway for a few more minutes.

"Try to understand our position here at the Questura, Signor Macintyre. We have a delicate situation. It's not just the murder of a defenseless old woman. That would be bad enough. We don't have many violent crimes here in Venice—thefts, yes, frauds, purse-snatchings, graft, the city is rife with these. We handle them as a matter of course, and sometimes we feel we're going crazy, especially during the tourist season. Murder is an ugly thing. I'll never become accustomed to it and I never want to. If I had my way—which, contrary to what you Americans might think, the police in this country definitely do not have—but if I did, I would go after whoever killed Maria Galuppi with every one of my men here.

"But there's another factor, the relic. The Vatican has already contacted us twice and they're sending an official from something called the Congregation for the Causes of Saints. And, believe me, the Vatican won't be satisfied until that relic is returned and although they won't go on record, you can be sure, they seem much more concerned about finding the relic than the murderer."

"Is that so much of a conflict, Commissario? Whoever took the relic also murdered Maria Galuppi. Find the relic and you'll find the murderer." It all seemed so clear to him.

Gemelli shook his head and smiled.

"I'm not so sure of that. You see, Signor Macintyre, I'm not as quick to form judgments as you think. If you need to speak with me, my secretary will put you through right away. Good day."

8 ON the way to the Piazza Urbino bought a copy of *Il Gazzettino*. There were several front-page articles about Maria's murder but he only glanced at the headlines before putting the paper in his coat pocket. He would read it at Florian's over a much-needed cup of coffee.

As he passed the café-bars with their stacks of sweet rolls and small crustless sandwiches or *tramezzini*, the boutiques, souvenir stands, and pastry shops, he barely glanced in their direction, and returned the occasional greetings absently. He thought only about his conversation with Gemelli.

When a young couple asked him to take their picture with the Bridge of Sighs in the background, he just stared at them for a few blank moments until they repeated the request. Then he took the camera and pointed it vaguely in their direction, handing it back without a word.

Almost everything Gemelli had said was disturbing, and not only what he had said but also the way he had said it. Although Urbino understood that under the circumstances Carlo couldn't be anything but the prime suspect, he also realized that for Gemelli to be so self-satisfied about it was far from professional behavior in a high-ranking officer of the Questura.

But maybe Gemelli hadn't been completely straightforward. Last year in the same office with the gulls screaming outside he had made a point of telling Urbino just how little he understood the laws protecting the buildings in the city, although Urbino had known that it was Gemelli himself who was either misinformed or hoping his version would be believed. There had been a strain between them from the time they had first met and today's encounter hadn't helped any. He wouldn't be surprised if the man had some ulterior motive for making it seem he believed Carlo was the murderer, for misleading him. Perhaps he even—

"Well, if it isn't Mr. Macintyre!"

Urbino, who only a few moments before had entered the Piazza, was startled to see Clifford Voyd standing almost directly in front of him between the Basilica steps and the elevated wooden planks for the *acqua alta*. The writer had a big smile on his face. Had Voyd been watching him from the time he had entered the square oblivious to everything but his own somewhat unsettling thoughts?

"And what dark, shameful deeds of your current victim are you mulling over, my friend? You will allow me to call them your victims, won't you?"

Urbino just stared at him.

"Your mischievous little lives, what else!" He used the same diminutive about Urbino's biographies that he had the evening of the Contessa's party. Before Urbino could say anything, the writer added, "But I suppose I'm not in any position to be criticizing you, my friend, even if it is so mildly and playfully." He held up a copy of *Il Gazzettino* in a gloved hand. "This unfortunate business at San Gabriele has started me thinking about a little story, the mother of two ill-fated children, daily trips to the shrine, a sizable amount of her hard-earned *lire* spent on candles, only to be— But no! It's too melodramatic, much too unbelievable! It would have to have a different ending."

He looked over Urbino's head toward the clock tower as if it might provide the ending he needed.

"A comforting convenience of fiction, wouldn't you say, Mr. Voyd?"

He had tried to keep his tone light but he knew that an edge of sarcasm and irritation had crept into it.

"So I suppose it is, my friend, and where would any of us be without that particular little convenience? And it's not only in fiction either. I've read quite a few biographies that play fast and loose with the facts themselves. But don't take it personally. As I said at the Contessa's last week, I have yet to read one of your own little lives. I see some are honored with shelf space in the library." He nodded toward the Biblioteca Marciana on the other side of the Campanile. "I might get to one of them before I finish here, who knows?"

And with that he said good day and walked off in the direction of the library, the newspaper carefully folded and tucked up under his arm.

When Urbino was settled at a window table at Florian's, he took out his own copy of *Il Gazzettino*.

One article was a brief history of Santa Teodora, describing her martyrdom in Sicily and subsequent removal to Venice by what the article called "two reverent sailors from the Lido." Being familiar with the story, he only skimmed it, smiling at its description of the sailors who, from his own understanding, had been the Doge's hirelings whose only reverence was for *scudi* and the safety of their own necks.

Another article was about the Church of San Gabriele and Don Marcantonio. A photograph at least twenty years old showed a smiling Don Marcantonio in the Campo San Gabriele in front of the church. The caption beneath said: "Monsignor Marcantonio Bo, pastor of the Church of San Gabriele for almost fifty years, in happier days." The article praised his devotion to the relic of Santa Teodora and described his efforts to protect it over the years from "the encroachment of the modern world and its skepticism and profit-motive." Mention was made of his "ecclesiastical battle behind closed doors" with his former assistant, Luigi Cavatorta, who had wanted to install a modern system of lighting and coin-operated recorded lectures. Cavatorta's failure in this attempt was underlined by the last line of the article: "Luigi Cavatorta has since left San Gabriele and the priesthood."

Across the top of the first page were two large photographs. Both were of the body of Santa Teodora, one of her in her mask, the other showing the body in the same reclining position but without the mask. It was the first time Urbino had seen the face of the saint. Although the photograph was a poor one taken before Don Marcantonio had come to San Gabriele, Urbino could make out all the features in profile. What would the old priest think of this exposure of his beloved saint?

The face, with its prominent nose and receding chin covered with mummified flesh, bore a strong resemblance to La Befana, the witch of the Epiphany, a holiday they had just celebrated on the sixth of January. On her head was a high tiara from which trailed backward a long piece of pale material that might have been some fashionable accoutrement in a previous age. The material fell from the head onto the ornate pillow and then off the edge of the catafalque. Except for the pillow these were all details he was seeing for the first time. He wondered where the tiara and veil were now.

He read the article beneath the photographs.

MURDER IN CANNAREGIO
Theft of the Remains of Santa Teodora

"All that might remain is a big sack filled with dust."
This is the fear of the police who have initiated a search

for the person or persons who committed a murder before stealing away with the remains of Santa Teodora from the Church of San Gabriele in the Cannaregio.

The belief that the relic was heavily damaged in the theft is supported by the fact that the body's extreme fragility made necessary in the last century a face mask to hold together the cranium of the saint.

The reconstruction of the crime presents many puzzling aspects. A British husband and wife on their honeymoon entered the Church of San Gabriele by a side entrance at approximately 5:30 yesterday afternoon. The church had been closed for the night and the six o'clock Mass had been canceled because of the indisposition of Monsignor Marcantonio Bo, pastor of San Gabriele. No one is believed to have been in the church when the couple arrived.

The honeymoon couple found Signora Maria Galuppi of the Cannaregio lying on the floor in the chapel devoted to the saint. She was pronounced dead a short time later by Professor Alberto Lago, the medical examiner. Signora Galuppi was a frequent visitor to the shrine.

The police could find no traces of the person or persons involved. Neither could they find anyone in the area who saw anyone fleeing or acting in a suspicious manner.

The double panes of glass of the coffin holding the body of the saint were most likely broken by a candelabra, also believed to be the murder weapon, found on the floor of the chapel. It is believed that the remains were stuffed into a pillow slip that was among the laundry the dead woman was returning to her client, Signor Urbino Macintyre of the Palazzo Uccello, Cannaregio.

It is speculated that the unfortunate woman was murdered in the course of the theft of the remains of Santa Teodora, the motive for which is unknown. Several possibilities are being considered.

It might have been perpetrated by a political or religious group or individual intending to ask for ransom.

It might be the crazed deed of drug takers of which our city has seen a considerable increase. It might even be the result of a centuries-old rivalry between Syracuse and Venice for possession of the saint.

However, sources close to the Questura claim that the authorities have not ruled out the possibility that Maria Galuppi was the main focus of the crime and that the theft of the body of the saint was either an afterthought or a final insult to the dead woman.

Police are searching for Carlo Galuppi, son of the murdered woman and sexton for twenty-five years at San Gabriele, in the hope that he will shed light on this tragedy.

On the inside page of obituary notices was a brief piece about Maria Galuppi:

LAUNDRYWOMAN MURDERED

Maria Galuppi, the widow of Ignazio Galuppi of this city, was murdered yesterday afternoon at the Church of San Gabriele. She was 78 years old.

Signora Galuppi, who lived all her life in the Cannaregio where she was a familiar figure, was a laundrywoman and occasional domestic until the time of her death.

She is survived by her son, Carlo, also of the Cannaregio. A daughter, Beatrice Galuppi, predeceased her.

After reading the articles, his coffee forgotten, Urbino felt that same peculiar pull and tug of curiosity he always did when he was about to commit himself to a new *Venetian Life*. It always began with a question but never one as disturbing as the one he formulated now to himself.

Who had killed good, gentle Maria Galuppi?

The lives he dealt with usually involved people about whom the unanswered questions were subtle and complex rather than disquieting. And he was never in any way emotionally involved with his subjects, having understood from the first the dangers of too close an identification or too strong an antipathy.

He could see that the untroubled, serene life he preferred would be almost impossible as long as there was no satisfying answer to the question of who had killed Maria.

And there was something else. Despite the disdain for contemporary society that in large part was behind his decision to live in Venice, he found himself fascinated by this example of just how repulsive that society could be. He had thought himself beyond any real interest in such brutish things, had believed he could willingly remain aloof, isolated, yet here he was at Florian's, surrounded by its emblems of a sane and civilized life, finding what could only be called a perverse pleasure in contemplating that very brutishness.

It was an unsettling position to be in, and he wondered where it all might lead.

❧

9   "A penny for your thoughts? Isn't that what you Americans say?"

Urbino looked up into the smirking face of Christian Kobke. Noticing the newspaper on the table, the young man added, "But the answer is self-evident, I suppose. *L'affaire San Gabriele.* It doesn't surprise me, though. In fact, it's the kind of thing we northerners have come to expect of this country. Old washerwomen giving all their pennies—or rather *centesimi*—to the Church and being murdered when some fanatics steal a moldy old corpse. By the way, you wouldn't mind if I sat down for a few minutes, would you?"

Without waiting for an answer he put his briefcase on the floor and sat across from Urbino. When the waiter came over, he ordered an espresso and Urbino asked for a fresh cup of coffee.

"This will have to be fast. I have to be at the Marciana Library in"—he consulted his watch, an expensive Swiss model—"ten minutes. If I'm not, Clifford will absolutely have my head. Some business about Quinton. I'm bringing some papers of hers that Adele gave me this morning. I think the girl has them stored away and is doling them out piece by piece, for what possible reason I have no idea."

Urbino still hadn't said anything and it looked as if he might not have to for several more minutes. He wondered what conversations between Voyd and Kobke were like since they both seemed to prefer monologues.

"I almost didn't come down from London with Clifford, you know. Who wants to be in Venice this time of year, I thought. So beastly dull, and I knew Clifford would never stay for carnival. We were at Nice last year and he hated it. But now there's this bit of excitement to keep us going for a while, murder and body snatching and only the Pope knows what else. Not dull at all but fascinating in a macabre sort of way."

While Kobke was going on in this way that made Urbino slightly uncomfortable since it was a bit too close to what he had been thinking himself, Stefano Bellorini came into the room and approached their table.

"I don't think you should be joking about such a thing, Signor—?"

His usually cheery face with its fringe of red beard shot through with gray was grim and tense.

"Kobke." Far from being disconcerted the Dane seemed amused. "I believe we've met several times before. At the Contessa da Capo-Zendrini's and"—his eyes moved quickly to the foyer—

"right here earlier the same day although you might not re-
member. You're Bellorini. You're making those frames for the
Contessa's dead relatives. Surely someone of your interests can
appreciate what I mean. All that pulling and tugging at the body
of some *soi-disant* saint dead for hundreds and hundreds of years!
What a magnificent subject for a painting, a Bosch version of that
Tintoretto at the Accademia—what is it called?—*The Theft of the
Body of St. Mark*."

Bellorini made no response. Instead he asked Urbino if the
Contessa was there yet.

"I wasn't aware she was coming this morning."

"We had an appointment. She was going to do something at
the Marciana first."

"She probably can't pull herself away from Clifford."

When the waiter brought over the coffees, he said to Bellorini,
"The Contessa da Capo-Zendrini called a few minutes ago. She
regrets she will be unable to see you this morning."

Kobke downed his espresso in one swallow like a native Italian,
grabbed his briefcase, and stood up.

"I must be off. Good day, gentlemen. The next coffee is on me,
Mr. Macintyre."

He was barely out of the room when Stefano said, "I may not
understand English well enough to say this but just about everything that young man has to say is irritating. Doesn't he have any
regard for other people's sensibilities? The less I see of him the
happier I'll be."

"I agree with you. The two of them won't be around much
longer. You would think he'd have the sense to be less flip about
it even if he didn't know Maria."

"Even if I hadn't known her myself I'd find the man offensive.
I'm glad Angela wasn't here to hear what he had to say."

"Would you like some coffee?"

It would help to discuss Maria's murder and Carlo's possible
role in it with someone who might be depended on to have more

than a little sympathy. And it might be a good opportunity to ask about the incident with Kobke last week at Florian's that the Dane had just referred to.

But Stefano declined.

"I should take advantage of the rest of the morning although I'm afraid I won't be able to do much concentrated work under the circumstances. If you see Barbara before I do, would you tell her I came all prepared with a convincing argument in favor of the opals?"

After he left, Urbino ordered another coffee and read through the articles again. As he was paying his check twenty minutes later, Kobke walked slowly past the window, seeming abstracted. He didn't look in. Urbino extended his conversation with the waiter so there would be little chance of meeting the Dane out in the Piazza.

❧

10 THE murder of an old woman in a back quarter of Venice is local news even in a city that, as Gemelli had pointed out, sees relatively few homicides. But the theft of a religious relic that happens to be a centuries-old corpse is national and even international news.

In the days following the murder and the theft, hundreds of thousands of words, official and unofficial, written and spoken, reverent and irreverent, were generated about the case that the media were calling the "Relic Murder." As for the people of the Cannaregio and the other quarters, they didn't have to give it a specific name. All they had to do was start talking about it in even the most indirect way and everyone knew exactly what they were referring to.

Il Gazzettino continued to run articles during the week after the murder even though there was nothing new to report, the editors knew when they had a good story. They hoped it would carry them into *carnevale*. There was hardly an issue without a photograph of either the relic, the Church of San Gabriele, Don Marcantonio, or Maria Galuppi. There were interviews with the police, friends of the murdered woman, Don Marcantonio, and the church officials, including the Monsignor from the Congregation for the Causes of Saints. Many letters were written speculating about the case, the large majority of which agreed that the murder was the unpremeditated act of religious fanatics who wanted the remains returned to Sicily.

Don Marcantonio, who might have been expected to agree with a religious motive, however twisted, believed firmly in an economic one. "The body of our dear virgin martyr has surely been stolen for ransom by those who see only what most of the modern world sees: dollar signs. We all pray for the safe return of the blessed remains of Santa Teodora," went his statement in *Il Gazzettino*, "and of course for the repose of the soul of Maria Galuppi who defended the saint so spiritedly."

As one day followed another with neither a ransom note nor statements from any religious or political group, Commissario Gemelli maintained, albeit unofficially, that the murder and theft were the acts of one man, Carlo Galuppi. Why else had he fled? Why else hadn't he turned himself in? In fact, it was rumored that the Substitute Prosecutor, a relatively young man recently transferred from Bari, was already preparing the case against him.

Depending on whom you talked with, Maria Galuppi was either praised or criticized. Some—these mainly the elderly of which the quarter had many—called her a martyr herself who had died in defense of her beloved saint. Others said that she had merely gotten in the way of something bigger than the life of an old laundrywoman and that it was only fitting that if one relic had been stolen, another should have been left in its place.

11 THE funeral of Maria Galuppi was a simple affair as befitted the woman herself. At the urging of the authorities the service was being held not at San Gabriele but at the Church of San Michele on the cemetery island, where it would be easier to detain Carlo Galuppi if he made an appearance.

The illogicality of this amused Urbino. What sense did it make to assume that Carlo, after hiding away as he seemed to be doing, would risk his neck by paying these last respects to a mother he had supposedly murdered? And if they really believed he might, wouldn't it have made more sense to have had the funeral at San Gabriele in accordance with the common belief that the criminal revisited the scene of the crime?

Urbino sat with the Contessa, Sister Veronica, and the Bellorinis near the chapel of the Zorzi family of Doges. Perhaps the change to San Michele was the reason or perhaps it was the weather—the rainy end of a *bora*—but very few people from the Cannaregio were there. Only Bettino and Netta Tullio from the restaurant near the Madonna dell'Orto, Cavatorta, two elderly sisters from the Convent of the Charity of Santa Crispina, and five old women in what looked like identical black coats and scarfs. The strategically placed police outnumbered the mourners at least two to one.

Urbino was surprised that Don Marcantonio, who had been permitted to say the Mass on the cemetery island, didn't deliver a eulogy. He seemed to try to make up for it, however, by infusing the requiem service with more emotion than was usual with him, especially the long sequence before the Gospel that had an uncanny appropriateness:

> *What horror must invade the mind*
> *When the approaching Judge shall find*

And sift the deeds of all mankind!
For now before the Judge severe
All hidden things must plain appear;
No crime can pass unpunished here.

There were even references to Maria and a thief, and although they were the Blessed Virgin and one of the crucified thieves, Urbino was moved by the coincidence.

After the Mass Urbino and the Contessa followed the plain wooden coffin from the church to the boat landing for its short trip to the other side of the island. Sister Veronica and the Bellorinis joined the Tullios. When Urbino started to guide his friend toward their boat to follow the coffin, the Contessa shook her head.

"I want to walk. The rain has let up."

He told Don Marcantonio they would go to the grave on foot. He took the Contessa's arm and they walked slowly across the cloister and through the gates into the cemetery. They walked in silence down the graveled paths with the crosses, tombstones, and markers stretching out all around them. Many of their inscriptions were familiar to Urbino from his wanderings but this morning they held no interest for him other than as memento mori, the circumstances of Maria's death having taken away their romantic aspects.

"We would have to be passing one of these fields," the Contessa said with a stiff nod in the direction of the *campo* on their left. It was in the process of being disinterred and was littered with piles of broken pottery, slivers of wood, crosses, votives, memorial photographs of the dead, and withered flowers. This was the field of the poor where the dead's rest was now ended and room had to be made for the ones who were to come—who, in their own turn, would have to relinquish their narrow space to others yet alive.

They continued on in silence to Maria's open grave, which was surrounded by the coffin, Don Marcantonio, and the small group of mourners.

Once again, the usually phlegmatic Don Marcantonio gave the words of the service special emphasis: "Give us grace to make ready for that last hour by a devout and holy life, and protect us against a sudden and unprovided death. Teach us how to watch and pray that when our summons comes, we may go forth to meet the Bridegroom and enter . . ."

Urbino's mind wandered. It was the reference to Christ, the Bridegroom, that did it, for he was reminded of how the body of Santa Teodora had often been likened to Snow White awaiting the kiss of Prince Charming and of how Maria used to call the saint her *"bianchissima."*

By the time he brought his mind back, Don Marcantonio was asking for the perpetual light to shine upon Maria Galuppi.

As the coffin was lowered into the grave, Urbino wondered what the point was in asking for perpetual light when Maria Galuppi's body, like those of most of the Venetian poor, was being commended to a mere twelve years' rest in the marshy soil. Wouldn't it be better to cast it at once on the pile of crosses, votives, and dead flowers from which the Contessa and he had averted their eyes?

Despite his love for his adoptive city there were some of its customs he would never understand.

❦

12 TWO days after Maria Galuppi's funeral, the Patriarch of the city, an old man with gaunt ascetic features and an abundance of unruly white hair, visited the Church of San Gabriele to pledge his solidarity to the faithful and to say Mass. It was shortly after eight in the morning.

The notoriety of the recent events and this participation by the usually reclusive Patriarch had attracted a large crowd at this early hour. As he sat with the Contessa, Urbino realized that this was the third service associated with death and violence they had attended in the past week. Last night over dinner the Contessa had said that she was finding it all very distressing. She did in fact look strained. The lines around her eyes and nose were more prominent and there even seemed to be a new, or deeper, one between her eyebrows.

Many of the sisters from the Convent of the Charity of Santa Crispina were there, among them Sister Veronica with a small group of hospice guests. There were many more dark-clothed old men and women than usual and even quite a few young ones.

No one's presence, however, not even that of the twenty or so curiosity seekers craning their necks for a good view or the noisy journalists and photographers in the back, surprised Urbino as much as that of Clifford Voyd and Kobke. The Contessa had drawn his attention to their late arrival by a regal inclination of her black-hatted head.

The two men were taking their seats when the Patriarch started to address the congregation in a melodious voice that many years ago had earned him the title of the modern Chrysostom, the golden-mouthed.

"This most monstrous and senseless act has struck deeply into the heart of our entire community here"—he made a gesture that included the gathered group—"as well as far, far beyond into the hearts of all those who, regardless of their faith, cherish life and the good examples of the Lord's servants. The body is a sacred temple. This we learn when we are but children still filled with the first wonder of life and the world. To pass beyond this world into the blessed next we must, we know, be again as children. And now, faced with these two most senseless acts that violated the sacred temples of a good, simple woman and the saint she loved so well, we must be as children in the expression of both our horror and our fervent hope. Maria Galuppi is among those who have passed beyond this world in which such trying events are a common occurrence. Yet she is also with us this January morning. Surely she joins us not only in our deep hope that the person or persons responsible are soon apprehended but also in our prayers that Santa Teodora may be found unharmed and be restored to her proper place here in the Church of San Gabriele. Let us pray."

The Patriarch bowed his white head.

Behind him two fidgeting altar boys and Don Marcantonio, looking ashen in his green robes, sat on a long bench. The old priest kept glancing at the empty chapel now barred by a thick scarlet cord. Propped on the catafalque was a small sign written in a shaky hand that asked the faithful to "pray for the safe restitution of the blessed body."

13 AS Urbino and the Contessa walked up the aisle after the service, a flurry of movement and slightly raised voices came from around the holy-water stoup. It was Clifford Voyd in the midst of several photographers who pursued him into the vestibule between the two sets of doors. When they went into the vestibule themselves, Voyd was standing in front of the glass-enclosed notice board with its various death announcements and parish information. Over his left shoulder was a black-and-white obituary photograph of Maria. The photographers were taking his picture. Kobke, leaning against the wall, his hands thrust into the pockets of his camel-hair coat, looked on impassively.

"Good morning," Voyd said when the photographers had finished. "Yet another tragedy brings us together. Let's hope this is the last."

Urbino, remembering their meeting in the Piazza and Voyd's

somewhat callous comments about Maria's murder, allowed the
Contessa to commiserate with him. He hadn't mentioned Voyd's
comments to her.

"I was indisposed for the poor woman's funeral—my back—but
I felt I absolutely had to be here today for her sake."

"And for Quinton's," Kobke said in an insinuating tone.

"I was just about to mention her, my boy. Youth is so impatient." He gave Kobke a quick glance that made him straighten up
and assume a less insolent pose.

"Margaret Quinton?"

"Yes, Contessa, my dear friend Margaret Quinton—and, it
would seem, the dear friend of Maria Galuppi as well."

"Something he learned only yesterday or else he might have
made the effort despite his back," Kobke said with a slight quaver
in his voice. It was difficult to tell whether this was meant as a
helpful clarification or some kind of thrust at Voyd. The writer
ignored him this time.

"I knew Quinton had an interest in this poor dead woman. She
mentioned it in several of her letters. I was looking through them
a few days ago. Perhaps I read them rather hurriedly the first time
through, but there it was as plain as milk in mud. Quinton used
only her first name, you understand, but there's no question it was
this Maria Galuppi who has come to such an unfortunate end. I
suspect Quinton was on the lookout for material as usual—as all
of us always are. Stories can come from the most unlikely
places"—this with a significant glance at Urbino—"and although
she wasn't of your religious persuasion, Contessa, she was fascinated by your Santa Teodora. In fact she didn't seem to be able
to get enough of that sort of thing here in Italy. She had leanings,
as we say. Surely you must have known that yourself, Contessa,
you knew her well enough for that. So I came here this morning,
you see, for poor Quinton's sake as well as the old woman's. I
believe Maria Galuppi was at Quinton's service and, as I said, I
was indisposed for her own."

"In any case, Mr. Voyd, we are certainly pleased to have you here today, a man of your concerns and responsibilities."

There was no irony detectable in the Contessa's tone. Considering her feeling about the man, Urbino found this remarkable and perhaps one more proof of her talent at dissimulation. She went on to ask Voyd if he had yet had a chance to read what Margaret Quinton had written while in Venice.

"Merely a few scraps here and there but there's a fat notebook I haven't yet got to. It promises to be most interesting."

"And not a little sad, I'm sure," the Contessa added.

"Ah yes, that too."

"Clifford, don't forget your appointment with Adele. It's already past nine."

"What would I do without your fine Danish precision, my boy? Once I cross the Alps I'm inclined to forget time and tide altogether."

The Contessa was amused at this.

"But we dare never forget the tide here in Venice, Mr. Voyd, south of the Alps though we are. As for time, well, that's something we're all too eager to forget, and Venice is a better place than most, isn't that so, Urbino?" she added, trying to draw him into the conversation. He only nodded.

They soon parted company on the steps of the church. Voyd and Kobke struck out into the *campo*, crowded now with shoppers, children, and deliverymen. Before they were halfway across, the writer turned around and called back, "Now don't forget, Mr. Macintyre, I'm still expecting you—and you as well, Contessa. The Europa e Regina."

Urbino watched the two men until they turned down into the Calle dell'Arcanzolo and then gave his arm to the Contessa. As they walked across the *campo* she said, "He's perhaps not such a bad sort after all, is he? But I'm not so sure about his friend Kobke. He's a handsome enough young man but there's more there than meets the eye."

Urbino smiled to himself. In her own unpredictable way he supposed she was being consistent. Her disapproval was still there but she had neatly switched it from the writer to his young Danish companion.

"And now, *caro*," she said as she gave his arm an affectionate tug, "I would like you to come with me to Signora Castaldi's for my dress fitting. Don't frown like that! You know very well she has Mutinelli's book on Venetian costume to keep you occupied. After that I have to stop by the Fortuny, but then I absolutely promise we'll go to Florian's."

❦

14 "WELL, Urbino, what do you think?"
It was several hours later and they were finally ensconced at their usual table by the window in the Chinese room at Florian's. Coffee, tea, and a tray of small sandwiches were on the table.

"That leaves a great deal open, Barbara. What do I think of what?"

"Don't be coy with me, Urbino. It doesn't suit you and it makes me suspect you have something to hide. You're the person least able to conceal anything from me. I'm quite obviously referring to what we've been avoiding talking about ever since we left San Gabriele—this whole miserable affair of Maria and Santa Teodora. What have you been doing—that is, other than paying visits to the Questura?"

"I only went the once. There's no need for me to go again. I'm finished with them."

"But are they finished with you? I know this system. I might not have been born in a gondola either but I've spent a much longer time in this city and country than you have. Your naïveté only reminds me of my own age, and there's no need to draw more attention to that than is necessary."

She smiled and poured out some tea for herself. Today more than usual she seemed to be paying a dear price for having been born with a mobile face, expanding so often over the years into astonishment and anger and diminishing into sorrow, puzzlement, and suspicion. Just about every line and indentation, so useful in her first and second youths, stood out now at Florian's.

"So what conclusions have you come to? Everyone from street sweepers to cardinals has an opinion."

"There isn't much to base an opinion on, is there?"

"That's why there are so many of them. Everyone's imagination is working double time. A lot of people seem to believe whoever it was was after the jewels that were supposed to be somewhere in the casket. The police and more people than I want to think about are convinced it was Carlo, and Don Marcantonio is waiting for a ransom note he probably thinks the Vatican Bank will take care of or—who knows?—maybe even the English Contessa he hasn't shown much fondness for before."

"Would you?"

"*And* there are some who think—believe it or not—that you might be involved yourself."

"Me!"

"Oh, not in a direct way of course but talk might eventually make it seem so. After all, your pillow slip is still missing and Carlo did come to the Palazzo Uccello right after his mother's body was discovered."

"But that's just coincidence about the pillow slip. And Carlo's coming to see me—who knows why he did that?"

"That's all true enough but it doesn't mean that people will stop talking. Listen, Urbino, surely it's no secret to you that they're not particularly quick to accept *forestieri* in this city, even *forestieri* from other parts of Italy! At times like this these feelings surface."

"I really can't concern myself with it. What I *am* concerned with is Carlo and the way the Questura seems to have placed him right at the top of their list."

The Contessa reached for a sandwich. "Yes, but we both know that's ridiculous." As she was about to take a bite, she looked at him and added, "Don't we?"

"No matter how many times I've been proven wrong I still trust my impressions. Carlo just doesn't seem the criminal type even if appearances are so much against him—and I'm not talking only about his—his ugliness," he added reluctantly.

"There you have it. It doesn't help that he's one of the few people with easy access to San Gabriele, especially on that particular afternoon. The murder and theft had to take place between five and five-thirty. Sister Veronica and her group were there until almost five. She locked up. She has a key, as you know, for her tours, since the church is usually closed at that hour. It would have been reopened before the six o'clock Mass as usual if Don Marcantonio hadn't been ill."

"Does Don Marcantonio open and close the church every day?"

"Usually it's Carlo. That's one of his jobs as sexton. He was a little upset when Don Marcantonio gave Sister Veronica a key last year."

"So Sister Veronica locked the front doors but the side door was open."

"She has nothing to do with the side door."

"I wasn't suggesting that she had but the fact that it was open must mean either that it was never locked to begin with or that someone opened it after it had been."

"But that side door is usually kept locked even when the front doors are open."

"An oversight on Carlo's part?"

"I doubt it. You know as well as I do that he's not the kind of person to take his duties lightly. It's just about everything the poor man has had for the past thirty years. He's dedicated to San

Gabriele. He feels more at home there than in those rooms on the Rio della Sensa. He even—"

She broke off abruptly and put a hand to her throat, staring out the window. He followed her wide-eyed gaze and saw a man under the arcade reading *Il Gazzettino*. He was absorbed in the back page but it was the front page with its photograph of Santa Teodora, the one without the mask that showed her receding chin, that arrested his attention as it obviously had the Contessa's. Above the photograph was the headline RANSOM LETTER FOR SANTA TEODORA.

Urbino hurried out to get a copy of the paper from one of the kiosks by the post office behind the Piazza. When he brought it back to the table, the Contessa had her reading glasses on and her hand out.

"Let me, please."

He handed her the paper. She glanced quickly over the page and then, in her clearly enunciated Italian, slowed now for emphasis, she read:

> "A ransom note was received early this morning in the country's most unusual kidnapping. The ransom request involves no money, and the victim has already been dead for some time—more than a thousand years in fact.
>
> "The anonymous letter received in the Bologna office of ANSA begins: 'The conditions for the return of Santa Teodora's body, which Santa Teodora herself would have agreed with, are the following: In every junior high and high school in the entire Veneto region one page of Antonio Gramsci's book, *Letters from Prison*, should be read at choice.'"

The Contessa stopped, a puzzled expression on her face, and asked if he knew the book. He nodded but told her to go on.

> "The letter, typewritten on a piece of ordinary white paper, was postmarked January 17 from Bologna.

"It was entitled 'For Publication,' and it goes on to say, 'We are neither glory-seekers, nor fanatics, nor terrorists. The only ones who can be called glory-seekers or fanatics are those who try to get some money in exchange for a little pile of bones.'"

"A little pile of bones!" the Contessa repeated. "Can you believe that!"

"Is that all?"

Skimming ahead, she said, "There's a section on that Gramsci person." She took a sip of tea and continued:

"The book in question, published posthumously in 1947, was written by Antonio Gramsci, who founded the Italian Communist Party in 1921. The author, born in Sardinia in 1891, wrote numerous notes while mortally ill in Fascist prisons. These notes were later collected together and published as *Letters from Prison*. Gramsci believed that the disorganization and lack of individualism in Italy were the consequence of the capitalistic system and that only Communism could effect a cure. He died in Rome in 1937."

When she lowered the paper, Urbino thought she had finished but then she raised it again and read the last lines:

"One ANSA reporter observed, 'It is difficult to establish a connection between the book and the theft of Santa Teodora's relics, except for one coincidence. Gramsci—like Carlo Galuppi, son of the murdered woman of San Gabriele and one of the major suspects in the case—was a hunchback.'"

The Contessa put the paper down, almost upsetting her teacup. Then, for the second time within an hour but now with a rasp of impatience to her voice, she asked, "Well, what do you think?"

"It's obvious, Barbara."

She shook her head. "Tell me. Make me feel like a *cretina* if you want."

"Some crackpot group or person is taking advantage of the murder and the theft to make a point."

Her face brightened.

"Mightn't it help Carlo?"

"It could do the opposite. All that business about a hunchback will only draw more attention to him. It's an unfortunate coincidence."

"Maybe it's not a coincidence."

"Gramsci was a hunchback, Barbara."

She shook her head impatiently.

"What I meant was that it seems just a little *too* convenient that both this Gramsci and Carlo are hunchbacks. Someone may be trying to point a finger at him."

"That's hardly necessary."

He was beginning to wish he had ordered something with alcohol instead of coffee. He looked around for the waiter.

"I don't know why you're being so obstinate! I thought you believed Carlo is innocent!"

He covered her hand with his.

"Of course I believe he's innocent but I don't believe it because of nonsense like this." He nodded toward the paper.

"It may not be nonsense at all. Sometimes I think anything is possible in this country! Alvise and I used to have the worst arguments about it, almost right up to the end. I love it but I despair of ever really understanding it."

"Didn't you say just a little while ago that you knew more about it than I did?"

"Yes, I did, but that was only to point out how abominable your own ignorance is!"

"Vincible, however."

"What?"

"Vincible ignorance, to use a good old theological term. Just give me time."

"Ah, time! You have such a knack for bringing up the most disagreeable topics!"

❦

15   AT about eleven that night Urbino was once again trying to get into Sand's *Consuelo.*

He was nearing the end of a chapter when he heard a noise in the hallway outside the study. It sounded like a footstep. He had let Natalia go right after dinner, and although she had a key, he couldn't believe she would come back from Mestre at this hour.

He put the book down and went to the door. Before he quite reached it, however, it started to open slowly to reveal the misshapen form of Carlo Galuppi. Urbino had one quick rush of fear that he was almost as quickly ashamed of. The hunchback looked as if he were about to collapse.

"Carlo! However did you get in?" He helped him to a chair next to the door. "Let me get you some brandy."

It all seemed so much a repetition of what had happened before that he expected Carlo to be gone when he returned a few minutes later with a glass and the brandy decanter but there he was, still sitting, his large head in his hands. Urbino poured some of the brandy and handed it to Carlo. He gulped it down.

When he finished, he started speaking rapidly. It all sounded such a mad jumble of elisions, dropped consonants, strange words, and an extravagance of *z*'s that Urbino cursed his unfamiliarity with the Venetian dialect and wished the Contessa were there. Even she, however, might not have been able to make much sense of the man's gibberish, a result not only of dialect but also of his speech impediment and the quite palpable fear that reached out to grip Urbino himself. But the man had sense enough to slow down and repeat what he had been saying so that gradually Urbino came to understand that once again Carlo was asking for help, this time with considerably more desperation.

"Please, Signor Macintyre, you must help me, I beg you—I could see and hear nothing, nothing!—the confessional—always I did what she told me—our saint was our protection, she said, we needed no other—she watched over all we did and all we had—soon everything would be different for us—but the blood—I was afraid—I—"

He looked up at Urbino, his face streaming with sweat, and held out the empty glass. Urbino refilled it.

After waiting for Carlo to gulp this one down, too, he put his hand on his shoulder. His earlier, momentary fear was forgotten. It seemed ridiculous in the presence of this so obviously shattered man whose ugliness only made his vulnerability more touching.

"Carlo, listen to me, you must go to the Questura," he said with exaggerated slowness, foolishly assuming the man might be as confused by his proper Italian as he had been by Carlo's dialect. The words sounded hollow to his own ears but what choice was there? Then, to convince himself as much as Carlo, he added, "You have no choice. They'll help you. I'll see that they help you."

Carlo stood up abruptly, dropping the glass. Just missing the rug, it shattered on the marble floor.

"No!" It was a clear negation shot through with fear. "I can't!"

He went into the hall and hurried toward the staircase. Urbino followed for a few feet, then stopped. What could he do? Carlo had stopped, too, and turned around. They looked at each other in silence. Urbino forced himself not to stare at the man's left eyelid that drooped so disturbingly, almost completely obscuring the eye.

"A favor, Signor Macintyre, not the Questura."

So mesmerized was Urbino by the power of the emotion behind Carlo's words that he said nothing. Carlo seemed to take his silence for assent.

"Call the Questura tomorrow if you have to."

He gave a grim semblance of a smile and went down the stairs. Urbino went to the staircase and looked down to see Carlo going not through the front door but through the one leading to the unused water entrance. So that was how he had got in. Had he come in a boat of some kind, an old *sandolo* he had cut loose from its moorings on a back canal? Getting around Venice that way would be a little less risky than using the alleys and bridges. Urbino silently wished him luck but exactly what this might mean for a man in Carlo's situation he didn't know. All he knew was that Carlo had come to him for help and that he had failed him.

16 AGAINST his better judgment Urbino didn't call the police that night. If someone had asked him exactly why, he might not have been able to give a definite answer. It had something to do, he knew, with Gemelli's attitude, his cocksureness about Carlo.

But beyond this was the feeling that he should be true to the assumption Carlo had left with. The man had seemed so desperate, had looked at him with such appeal, that to call the Questura would have been tantamount to betrayal, and Urbino was a man who believed betrayal was close behind murder as the most unpardonable of sins.

Carlo had come to him for help and this might be the most help he could give him.

The next day being Sunday, Urbino delayed longer than he had intended the night before. Surely not even the most diligent of Italian police officers would be at the Questura early on a Sunday morning, and he didn't want to talk with anyone but Gemelli.

It therefore wasn't until eleven that he phoned the Questura.

The woman put him through immediately as Gemelli had said she would.

"Commissario Gemelli? Urbino Macintyre speaking."

"Yes, Signor Macintyre, good morning."

He sounded weary.

"I'm a little surprised to find you in."

"Then why did you call?"

Urbino could imagine the little smile on Gemelli's face.

"You said to let you know if I saw Carlo Galuppi. I have."

"You have?" There was a strange note in Gemelli's voice that he couldn't identify. "When was that?"

Urbino braced himself. Perhaps he had broken some Italian law about cooperation with the police.

"Last night about midnight."

He gave the details.

Instead of berating him for having waited almost twelve hours, Gemelli said in a quiet, even voice, "Fortunately for you, Signor Macintyre, we've had a later sighting of Galuppi than that. I've just seen him myself." Urbino felt relieved until Gemelli added, "In the morgue. A workman on San Michele found him early this morning. He must have been desperate to kill himself. Slit his throat and then threw himself into a partly dug grave with about six inches of water in it. Kind of a joke in a city with so much of the damn stuff but there was enough to drown him, I suppose. The medical examiner is still trying to figure out if he died from drowning or loss of blood. A mere technicality as far as I'm concerned. There's no indication it was anything but suicide."

Gemelli gave him the opportunity to say something. When he didn't Gemelli went on: "In other circumstances your failure to call us as soon as Galuppi came there could have had unpleasant consequences but all we'll bother you about is another statement so that we can proceed with the closing of the case."

"But what about the ransom note?"

Although Urbino hadn't changed his opinion about it, he

brought it up to give Gemelli's self-satisfaction some check. Also, still shocked over the news of Carlo's death on San Michele, he didn't know what else to say.

"Surely you don't take that note seriously? Quite honestly we're more than a little surprised that there weren't any other letters, just as ridiculous, from every religious and political *pazzo* who can write and has the price of a stamp. We've seen all this before," he said, trying to give the impression that this case was in no way unique.

"But why are you so sure that Carlo Galuppi killed himself?"

Gemelli laughed in a rather unpleasant way.

"There's no doubt about that, believe me. We found a razor near the grave; the only prints on it were his. Really, Signor Macintyre, don't be too hard on yourself. Who knows? Maybe Galuppi would still have managed to kill himself even if you had called us right away. Until tomorrow morning, then."

❧

17 EARLY Monday morning along the Fondamenta Nuove across from the cemetery island, Matteo picked up the dustbin near the Bridge of the Mendicanti and put it in his trolley. After he had rolled it over to the garbage barge moored along the quay, he stopped and took out a flask of anisette from his coat pocket. It was cold and he needed another swig. After he put the flask back, he removed the lid of the dustbin and looked inside.

On the top was a sack made of what looked like good, though soiled cloth. Partly filled as it was with something whose contours were obscured by the rich folds of the material, it fired his expectations.

It was amazing what people threw out. His apartment on the Giudecca was furnished with some of the things he had found over the past ten years, even down to prints on the walls and dishes on the table. The clothes on his back as well as the shoes on his feet had once been the proud possessions of rich old eccentrics. Matteo never entertained the possibility that the things he had found over the years could have once belonged to people who had as little or even less than he had. Instead he considered all these things as so much ballast cast off by the rich to keep their palazzi from sinking.

He picked up the sack, disappointed not to find it heavier. He looked around nervously, not because it was against the law to take what no one else wanted but because his pride was almost as strong as his inability to resist temptation. To avoid any prying eyes from the buildings along the quay, he brought the sack into a deserted *calle* and emptied it on to the damp stones.

At first he thought he was looking at a costume for *carnevale.* In the center of the pile was a full face mask that he assumed had been made to look old. There were red slippers and a torn, yellowed garment.

And then he saw the head—or rather the skull—covered with long black hair whose thickness and luster only made the sight more appalling.

A grin was frozen on its face as if to say, Now you've really found something, you old fool!

❀

18 BECAUSE the body of Santa Teodora had been found across from San Michele shortly after Carlo Galuppi's suicide there and since no ransom request other than the Gramsci one had surfaced, the hunchback's culpability was clinched for the Questura and most of the public. What more proof was needed?

The press treated the murder as the bizarre act of an unstable son whose resentment against his mother had smoldered over the years. *Il Gazzettino* even found an old man now living up in Trento near the Austrian border who claimed to have seen Maria Galuppi slap her son on several occasions many years before when he was a resident of the Cannaregio. He had said nothing earlier because he had feared for his own life.

Now that Carlo was dead many people from the Cannaregio had stories to tell about harsh words between the mother and son or unusual forms of punishment, such as forcing him to sit quietly in a pew or to kneel in front of the coffin of Santa Teodora for two or three hours at a time. But none of these people could say for sure that such things had actually happened or, if they had, that they had occurred recently enough to have been a reasonable motive for matricide.

As to why he had also taken the body of Santa Teodora, most thought it was one final blow against his mother. A few others with a facile knowledge of psychology said that he was striking out at yet another symbol of female authority and that it was surprising he hadn't also mutilated the statue of the Blessed Virgin and the painting of the Madonna and Child.

Because no jewels were retrieved with the body, the legend about them was debated in the paper and in bars and cafés. Eventually almost everyone came to the conclusion that there had never been any jewels, valuable or otherwise. Even Don Marcantonio was quoted in *Il Gazzettino* as saying, "Santa Teodora always was and always will remain the only prize a true believer needs. It is almost sacrilegious to consider the need or existence of any other."

The case of the Relic Murder was closed. No one was more relieved than the Questura and the city officials and merchants who pointed out that *carnevale* was only a short three weeks away.

The city, especially the Cannaregio, rested more easily although there was some regret at the loss of an interesting topic.

The Patriarch and the Monsignor from the Congregation for the Causes of Saints made plans for the reconsecration of the body of Santa Teodora.

19

A week after Carlo's suicide, Urbino decided to try to get at some answers.

It was about two in the morning and he went to the library for something to read. He had gone to bed at eleven and slept soundly for two hours only to awaken refreshed and unable to get back to sleep.

Although he wasn't deeply superstitious, he put the George Sand novel back on the shelf, thinking it had already proved to be a peculiar kind of bad luck. No sense in testing the adage that things come in threes.

He settled down in a corner of the bedroom with a book that never disappointed him. He couldn't imagine better company during these dead hours than that of a man who wrote about Venice in sentences that resembled nothing so much as "those fast-gaining waves that beat, like passing bells, against the Stones of Venice," to use Ruskin's own words.

He soon put aside the book, however, as thoughts of Maria's murder intruded.

The day after her murder he had realized at Florian's that he wouldn't be able to rest until he had a satisfying answer to the woman's death—and by a satisfying answer he hadn't meant one that named Carlo as the murderer. It went against everything he felt about the man and about the man's relationship with his mother. Carlo's own death and the closing of the case only intensified this feeling.

Commissario Gemelli might pride himself on being a student

of human nature but in his own small way so did Urbino. Work on *Venetian Lives* had developed his ability to detect the truth—or the truths—behind appearances. This didn't mean that he always dismissed appearances as lies. He had too much respect for the truth to do that.

He opened *The Stones of Venice* again, sitting beside Ruskin as their gondola approached the city and walking with him through the Basilica as his guide convinced him, once again, that all the incrustation of the brick with precious materials only *seemed* insincere, that there was no intention to deceive, to be treacherous. Then, troubled thoughts of Maria receding into the background, he read what Ruskin had to say about San Zanipolo, the church of the Doges not far from where Santa Teodora's body had been found. When he finished, he put the book in his lap and mused on the image of Ruskin climbing a ladder in San Zanipolo to discover what he strongly suspected—that the profile of the sculpted Doge placed for all to see was faceless on the other side.

But what had been the point? Who cared? Why go to the trouble of climbing his ladder and risk breaking his neck?

And then the answer came not in a flash but, quite appropriately, like a gentle wave: To know, to know, as if knowledge, happy or sad, uplifting or disillusioning, was and should be reason and consolation enough for just about anything.

Ruskin hadn't hesitated to climb his ladder for the sake of the truth, even though it might not have turned out to be the truth that he expected and wanted.

The relevance of this to what he was going through himself struck him forcefully. And so, with the help and example of dear old Ruskin on this early morning in mid-January almost two weeks after Maria's murder, Urbino reached a point he wouldn't turn back from, no matter what.

Part Three

REMEMBERING HER DEAD

1 MARIA and Carlo Galuppi had lived in a narrow, dilapidated, four-story building that brooded along the Rio della Sensa not far from the house of Tintoretto.

In that same building four women now huddled in a room on the third floor to conserve heat and pass the dull afternoon hours. They might have been figures in a medieval or Renaissance painting about the ravages of age. The old woman talking reminded Urbino of the toothless hag in Giorgione's painting at the Accademia, except that Nina wasn't pointing to a scroll with the message COL TEMPO. Instead she warned what would happen to us all with only her face and body, but they were enough.

In some kind of ironic compensation, however, her voice was that of a young woman. She had just finished telling him, interrupted periodically by the other women, what he already knew about Maria: that she had been a hard worker, a devout woman, and a true daughter of the Cannaregio, having been born, married, and widowed there. "And murdered too," one of the women farthest from the stove cackled. She had snow-white hair but the blackest and bushiest eyebrows Urbino had ever seen. Nina shot her a glance and the woman looked away. It was evident that Nina, perhaps because it was her apartment, exerted an influence over the others.

They had deferred to her earlier when Urbino had asked about Maria.

"Don't be disrespectful, Eleonora. Death will come to us all, even you, my dear."

"We all have to die but we won't all be murdered," another of them said. She had a black lace cap pulled down over her head and a rather pronounced moustache.

"It's bad luck to say such things," a refined-looking woman replied. She had an abstracted air, as if she wondered what she was doing in the midst of these vulgar old women. She was sitting closest to the fire and took an occasional sip from what looked like a small medicine bottle she kept in the pocket of her robe. She didn't do it furtively, but rather with hauteur, and when she did, the faint odor of anisette wafted to Urbino.

"I don't think you ladies need fear any bad luck of that kind. The Questura is satisfied that Carlo killed his mother."

He threw it out to get their reaction. They hadn't said anything yet about Carlo except that he had lived with his mother on the top floor in the back.

"The Questura is satisfied with very little," Nina said with a sniff. "We knew Carlo since he was a little boy. He could never have done such a terrible thing, never."

"He was ugly is all, *un gobbo* like that statue on the other side of the Ponte di Rialto—if it's still there. I haven't left this house in years." Eleonora shook her head regretfully.

"He loved his mother," the woman with the medicine bottle said in a dreamy voice as if she were thinking of loves from her own past.

"And she loved him, don't forget that, Marietta," the woman in the lace cap said.

"Yes, Dorotea, she loved him," Nina agreed, "but she loved her daughter more."

"You can't compare love, it can't even be measured," Marietta said in her dreamy voice, looking off into a far corner of the room.

"It's not someone's fault if they love you more, or less, or if they can't love you at all. In my time there were three men all courting me, as different as could be, one of them was from Verona, the home of Romeo—"

"I don't think the *signore americano* is interested in the story of your life, Marietta," Nina interrupted. "He came here about Maria. We don't want him to leave with the impression that old women wander from one topic to another."

"Her daughter's name, I believe, was Beatrice," Urbino prompted.

"Beatrice, like Dante's love," said Marietta.

"Yes, her name was Beatrice," Nina said matter-of-factly. "I doubt, however, if her name had anything to do with Dante. I think it was Maria's mother's name."

"Perhaps her mother was named after Dante's heroine," suggested Dorotea with a little smile at Marietta. Marietta ignored her and took a sip from her medicine bottle.

"Whoever she was named after," Eleonora of the eyebrows said, "she was her mother's shining light. Maria would have followed her anywhere." Urbino wondered if Eleonora's image was merely fortuitous or if she actually knew who Dante's Beatrice was. She left the question no longer in doubt when she added, "Unfortunately *her* Beatrice led her down to an inferno, not up to Paradise."

"You exaggerate as usual," Nina said. "Beatrice loved her mother."

"But she loved someone else much more, I think," said Marietta, who by now held the bottle openly on her knee.

Nina looked at Urbino steadily and said in her little girl voice, "Marietta is right. Beatrice was most certainly in love. Oh, she was a beautiful young girl, fair, fair skin and bright blue eyes. Her hair was a marvelous black, like ebony. She was as different from her brother as you could imagine two children could be, not just in her beauty and slimness but in her quickness of mind. She was bright, very bright. She could have married well. That's what Maria hoped, that's what all mothers hope."

"What happened?" All he knew about the daughter was the little the Contessa had told him when he had hired Maria: that she had died very young, that she had been in love, nothing much more than that. Maria had never told her anything more, it seemed, nor had anyone else.

"What happened?" Marietta echoed him. "She fell in love."

"Love frequently leads to marriage. Did she marry the man?"

"Love sometimes leads to marriage," Marietta corrected with the air of someone who should know, taking a sip of her anisette.

"In the case of Beatrice, this love could never have led to marriage, I'm sure." It was Dorotea. She pulled her lace cap down more snugly and looked at Nina. "Am I not right, Nina?" She seemed to want to pacify the woman.

Nina nodded with a frown, then turned to Urbino and sighed. "My dear Signor Macintyre, please don't think ill of a group of old women. Maybe it's wrong to talk as we've been doing but it's one of our few pastimes and we mean no harm. It's only the truth we're telling. Haven't you noticed how the old usually tell the truth, no matter what? Yes, we tell the truth as we understand it. That's what we're trying to do, all of us, even Dorotea here."

"But what did she mean, Signora? Was the man married?"

She shrugged.

"We spoke of love, Signor Macintyre, but did we speak of love for a man who could or would marry her?"

"Who was he?"

She shrugged again.

"We never knew. Seventeen-year-old girls can keep a secret. I don't think her own mother knew. Beatrice took the man's name to her grave."

"Did Maria confide in you?"

"She never said a word about it, either before or after her daughter died, but we knew."

"I was the first to know," Marietta said. "I told the others."

"We would have heard too if we had been home at the time," Nina said. "Come here, Signor Macintyre." She got up and led him across to the window. It was covered with transparent plastic taped messily to the frame. "Do you see that?"

He looked out the window. All he saw was a small courtyard and the backs of three other buildings. Before he could answer Nina continued, "When all the windows are open we can hear almost everything because of the way the buildings come together, even if there's no shouting. But that afternoon more than thirty years ago there was a great deal of shouting."

"Yes," Marietta said, "and I heard it. You always talk as if you were the one to be home that afternoon."

"What did she hear?" The quickest way to get information would be to treat Nina as the source of it all. The woman beamed.

"An argument between Maria and her daughter. Maria wanted to know where she'd been. Beatrice laughed. 'Wouldn't you like to know!' she answered as sassy as you please. Then there was a slap."

"A loud one," Marietta added. "My cheek smarts to think of it."

"A sad situation," Nina continued. "That girl gave Maria sorrow but like most mothers she forgave her. Once Beatrice was gone she spoke only well of her."

"How did she die?"

Nina didn't seem as eager to answer this question as the other ones. Eleonora and Dorotea acted as if they hadn't heard it. Even Marietta, who might have been expected to take advantage of Nina's silence, said nothing. Then, with obvious reluctance, Nina said, "Three months later Maria found her dead upstairs." She nodded toward the floor above. "In the toilet."

"What happened?"

Again a silence until Marietta said, the bottle poised at her lips, "Just like Carlo except that she took poison. They say it runs in families." Then, after a sip: "But Beatrice did it for love."

✼

2   AS Urbino was making his way down the dark stairway a few minutes later, there were footsteps behind him on the landing above, then a voice called down:

"Excuse me, Signor Macintyre, could you help me to my apartment?"

It was Marietta.

"Of course, Signora." He went up to her. "Where is it?"

"Down on the next floor. I know it makes little sense," she said as she put her thin arm through his, "but it's more difficult going down. I pull myself up little by little but when I go down I get dizzy."

He guided her down to her door which was slightly ajar. She pushed it open, revealing a sparsely furnished vestibule and room.

"Thank you very much, you are most kind." The odor of anisette was strong as she leaned closer to him. "You deserve something for your kindness but unfortunately I have nothing to give you." She inclined her head toward her apartment and rubbed the pocket of her robe. From the way she had tipped the bottle the last time he knew it must be almost empty. "Virtue they say should be its own reward but I've never believed it. Just one of those things they tell you when you're a child to get you to do what you otherwise wouldn't." She smiled up at him, her face breaking into a thousand lines and wrinkles. "Are you shocked?"

"Do you want me to be?"

She laughed.

"I think you know the answer to that or you wouldn't ask. Old age would be no fun if we couldn't shock people from time to time."

"Then Signora, I'm exceedingly shocked. I've never heard such cynicism from anyone, old or young."

"Then let me tell you something else. I'm afraid it's nothing shocking but it might help repay you for your kindness. I said nothing upstairs because it's better that Nina thinks she knows everything. Otherwise she'll know my little smile is often at her expense—and then where would I be? Her rooms are the warmest in the building!"

"What is it that you want to tell me, Signora?"

"Just this: Maria always went to Murano the first week of every November. I don't think she missed a November in more than twenty-five years. Don't you find it strange?"

"Not so strange, Signora, if you'll pardon me," he said, realizing he might hurt her feelings. "Murano isn't far and it's a popular place."

"Maria had no interest in popular places! She hadn't been to the Piazza for years, she was proud of it! No, Signor Macintyre, it's very, very strange, especially since her daughter died in November."

She turned to go into her apartment but stopped.

"And another thing," she said, leaning against the door frame. "Maybe you'll find it of as little interest as what I've just told you. It's about a *cocorita*, a lovebird, a parakeet, whatever you want to call it. I heard Beatrice tell her mother as they went down these stairs here that her little *cocorita* had disappeared, couldn't be found anywhere. About two months after their argument it was, several weeks before she—she died. Maria said real sharp, 'Maybe she'll give you another one, your friend.' I said nothing of this to either that one"—she lifted her chin in a vigorous gesture to the floor above—"or anyone else. I'm not a eavesdropper and that's what Nina would have called me, she would have said I'm always listening outside doors and windows as if I don't have better things to do with my time!"

"Did Beatrice keep a lovebird?"

Birds were popular pets in Venice where space was so scarce. Perhaps the Venetians got pleasure out of seeing creatures more confined than they were themselves but ones which they could pamper. In a few months, with the coming of the good weather, cages would festoon the sides and sills of buildings throughout the city.

"Oh, no, I would have known, we all would have."

"Are you sure Maria mentioned a woman?"

"A woman, a girl, that I don't know, but a female, yes. Domenica was what Maria called her. But excuse me, it's almost time for my nap."

Before she closed her door, Urbino reached into his pocket. He took out a ten-thousand *lira* note and tucked it into the pocket of her robe.

"For some anisette, Signora."

She didn't thank him but lifted her head a little higher as she closed the door. There was a faint smile on her lips, however, probably the same kind of smile Nina saw so often and wondered about.

❦

3   TEN minutes later Urbino was at the rectory of San Gabriele. Sister Giuseppina showed him into the small parlor and went to summon Don Marcantonio and get some tea.

The room reflected Don Marcantonio's well-known austerity. There was a worn sofa, two chairs with high backs, a threadbare carpet, several lithographs of martyrdoms, and a small dark-wood table and matching sideboard with an old candelabra and two stuffed, mounted ducks.

A few minutes after Sister Giuseppina brought in the tea, Don Marcantonio, looking frailer than usual, came shambling down the hall from his private quarters. Urbino stood up.

"Please sit down, Signor Macintyre. Forgive me if I see you for only a short time but I'm not feeling well. All this sadness and confusion." He sighed. "It takes me twice as long and three times the energy to do everything. My new assistant was supposed to be here before Christmas but he has to look after his father in Rimini until some other arrangement can be made." He went to the sideboard and came back with a bottle of brandy and two glasses. "We'll have some of this. It'll do us both good on a cold afternoon, better than that stuff there." He sat down in the other chair and poured out two generous portions of the brandy. After taking a sip, he said, "Now what can I do for you?"

"I have some questions about Maria Galuppi."

"What kind of questions? I've already told the police what they wanted to know."

"It's just that I'd like to have certain things settled in my own mind. Perhaps some questions the police didn't ask you."

"They were very thorough, believe me. They had a long list of questions and people they wanted me to tell them about: Carlo, of course, Luigi Cavatorta, the Contessa da Capo-Zendrini herself, even some of the sisters at the convent." He took another sip of his brandy and held the glass up to the faint light coming through the window. "And they even asked me about you but fortunately—or unfortunately—there wasn't much I could tell them."

"Did they ask about Beatrice Galuppi?"

"Beatrice Galuppi? Why should they have asked me about her?"

"Anything that concerned Maria might be of importance, and surely her daughter—"

"She loved that girl," the old priest interrupted. "If anyone told you any different, they were lying." A softer cast came over his face. "Beatrice was blessed with beauty and although she was only a Galuppi she had the manner of a daughter of the Doges. I had great expectations for her. We all did here in the Cannaregio, most of all her poor mother."

"What happened?"

"I'm sure you already know, Signor Macintyre. If you've talked with anyone about Beatrice Galuppi, the first thing they surely told you was how beautiful she was and the second was about what happened to her. She died under a dark cloud—but don't think we didn't give her all the honors of a good servant of God when we laid her to rest. What man can say that there's not a shining heart in the darkest of clouds?"

Urbino wanted hard answers, not euphemisms. Best to take a more direct approach.

"What do you know about the person she was involved with?"

The priest's hand shook slightly as he raised his glass.

"What person?"

"Her gentleman friend."

The priest relaxed and took his sip, looking in the direction of the stuffed ducks as he swallowed.

"I'm sure you know as much as I do, Signor Macintyre. You impress me as being just as thorough in your own way as the police."

"Do you know who he was?" Urbino persisted. "Did Maria know?"

"Signor Macintyre, there are questions even a priest isn't required to answer—or should I say especially a priest."

"Let me ask you this, then: Was Beatrice Galuppi a devout girl?"

"It's not for me to judge and never was. I wasn't her confessor. In fact she seldom came to San Gabriele. She preferred the Madonna dell'Orto."

Even after all these years he seemed offended.

"But the Madonna dell'Orto isn't much closer to where the Galuppis lived."

"Actually it's a bit farther but distance had nothing to do with it. Beatrice had an interest in Tintoretto like our own Sister Veronica. As you know the Madonna dell'Orto was Tintoretto's parish church. Beatrice painted. She might even have had a talent but such judgments are beyond me. I never saw anything she did anyway. Sister Veronica has, Cavatorta too. He thought it good enough if you can trust his opinion."

"Could Beatrice's preference for the Madonna dell'Orto have had anything to do with her mother's devotion to Santa Teodora? When a girl reaches a certain age, it's not unusual for her to want to do whatever she can to distinguish herself from her mother."

"Beatrice had other ways of doing that."

"The gentleman friend?" The priest avoided his eyes. "Or was there something else," Urbino went on, "someone else, a woman friend perhaps, a bad influence, someone her own age, someone named Domenica?"

Don Marcantonio glared at Urbino.

"Who have you been talking to? I thought you were interested in a man. I don't know anyone named Domenica—except for an obscure saint from the Campania. It's not a common name here in the north."

He put down his glass and stood up. Urbino did too.

"I can't clutter up my mind with speculation, least of all gossip. Many here in the Cannaregio will accommodate you, I'm sure. As for me, I knew very little about Beatrice Galuppi's personal life, who she knew and who she didn't."

"Do you know if she had a lovebird?"

"What are you talking about? I really must say good day, Signor Macintyre. I need to rest before the six o'clock Mass."

Something Don Marcantonio had said was on Urbino's mind on his walk back from San Gabriele. When he got back to the Palazzo Uccello, he went into the kitchen where Natalia was chopping garlic. He had a question for her. Originally from Messina, she had ended up in the Venice area after hotel work in Zurich, where she had met her husband, an itinerant laborer from Mestre.

"Natalia, do you know anyone named Domenica?"

She looked at him with wide eyes as if it were the strangest question he had ever asked her.

"Not here in Venice, Signor Macintyre, but down in Messina, yes, I knew two or three girls with that name. There was Domenica delle Palme—Palm Sunday—although she preferred

Palma, a lovely name, don't you think? And can you believe she had a sister named Pasqualina!—Easter!" Then, her eyes filmed over with nostalgia, she added, "And there was Mimma Giuliana and her cousin Miccuccia."

"But I thought you said they were all called Domenica?"

"So they were, but those are pet names for Domenica and since both girls were named after their grandmother, one was Mimma and the other—she was fatter and older—was Miccuccia."

Having imparted this information, she waited for Urbino to tell her why he had asked. When he didn't, she gave an almost imperceptible shrug and returned to her chopping with a disappointed look.

4   THE Contessa's *salotto* was cluttered, not because it was small—which it wasn't—but because she had insisted on furnishing it with many of her favorite things. There was a story behind just about every painting, print, bibelot, and piece of furniture—from the Veronese over the fireplace to the collection of eighteenth-century ceramic animals on one of the smaller tables—and Urbino had heard all of them. Strangely enough—perhaps more a testament to the Contessa's talents as a raconteuse than to his as a patient and attentive listener—he had never been bored.

Tonight, as he was telling her what he had learned from the women at Maria's apartment building, Don Marcantonio, and Natalia, her eyes kept moving from object to object as if she were assessing them or trying to get comfort from their familiarity. She didn't say anything until he finished.

"I'm offended, Urbino."

She seemed so serious that he made a little joke: "At my success?"

"It's not such a grand success. Don't get more conceited than you already are. No, it's not that." She took a handkerchief from her pocket and wiped her nose in a thoughtful way. She had sneezed several times since he had arrived and she looked drawn. "It's about Maria's daughter. Of course I knew she had a daughter who had died a year or two before Alvise and I were married. I even saw her photo—a lovely girl standing in front of the Madonna dell'Orto—but I certainly never knew about a suicide or some mysterious friend named Domenica or about much else in fact." A strange expression came over her face and the next moment she sneezed. She took out another handkerchief from her other pocket and tended to her nose. "And perhaps it's silly of me when there's so much else of greater importance, but to think that Maria never even breathed a word about her daughter's painting or her interest in Tintoretto."

"Doesn't that indicate a mother who cherishes her daughter's memory and wants to keep it to herself?"

"No! It indicates a mother secretive about her daughter. Besides, you said that Don Marcantonio, Sister Veronica, and Cavatorta all knew about it." She ended the sentence on a whine and wiped her nose vigorously, making it even redder than it had been.

"Could it be, my dear, that you're a bit peeved? It's as if you were upset about not being included in a game everyone else has been playing. After all, you did know her daughter was dead and had died under strange circumstances. And you knew a man was involved."

"Oh, everyone knew that!" she said with disdain for what was common knowledge. Surely she was entitled to something more! "But I'm not completely out of the game, to use your expression, as you'll soon see," she added with an air of mystery. She got up from her chair and went to the table with the ceramic animals. Opening the drawer in the side she took out a piece of paper and brought it over to Urbino.

"What's this?" he asked as he took it.

"Something to show you I have my own little games to play. Well, don't just look at it! Read it!"

On the sheet was a long paragraph in the Contessa's elaborate handwriting. It was a detailed description of Maria Galuppi's last day, from the time she was seen leaving her building on the Rio della Sensa until Sister Veronica and her tour group saw her in the Church of San Gabriele about five.

Taking a sip of his cognac, Urbino read the sheet over again.

"Don't act as if you're wondering what it's for. Isn't that what's usually done? A reconstruction of the victim's last day?"

"But Maria's schedule has relevance only if we assume she knew her murderer or was murdered because she was Maria Galuppi. I suppose someone might have seen her talking to a stranger or noticed someone suspicious around San Gabriele, but no one has come forward, has he? Maria might have been in the wrong place at the wrong time, in which case your reconstruction here—"

"I don't accept any of that, Urbino, and I don't think you do either or else you wouldn't be showing such interest in Beatrice Galuppi, who's been dead for more than thirty years. That Maria might have been murdered during a theft just because she happened to be in the church at the time shakes my faith to its very foundations. It gives too much credence to accident, to chance. No, I can't accept it!"

"But accidents do happen, Barbara. I could be walking down a *calle* and have a brick fall on my head. The Palazzo Uccello could catch fire because of faulty wiring. You could—"

"Don't say anything more about what could happen. I'm talking about the murder of Maria, a woman who had a devotion to Santa Teodora, yes, I'm not denying that she had. And she died right there in front of the coffin, but that doesn't mean she died *because* of Santa Teodora, does it? There's a big difference. No, she wasn't killed by Carlo—this, I hope, we agree on—but she wasn't killed by chance or accident either, by being in the wrong place at the wrong time. I don't care what you think of my work there"—she nodded at the sheet still in his hands—"but let me ask you one question: If Maria was murdered in the course of a theft, then why hasn't anyone made his identity known if it was, let's say, a political act? Or why hasn't ransom been asked for, something other than that Gramsci hoax? No, Urbino, if the relic were at the center of this, we would have heard something long before now."

"What about the jewels?"

"I doubt if anyone has believed that story for years. People just like to talk about it, the way they do about St. Mark's body being buried somewhere beneath the Basilica."

"But maybe someone did believe it. They went after the relic, killed Maria, and took away the body of Santa Teodora. They searched for the jewels, found none, and are now some very disappointed and fearful thieves with no reason to contact anyone."

"I disagree. Let's assume they did believe there were jewels. Well, if they didn't find any and had Santa Teodora's body, why didn't they then try to get something for all their trouble and ransom it? If they did believe there were jewels, why didn't they search the garments then and there at San Gabriele? Why risk taking the body away like that? No, there are too many things that don't make sense. Even Commissario Gemelli said as much although he's not even entertaining the possibility of reopening the case. He made that clear enough to me this morning."

"Commissario Gemelli?"

"Yes! How do you think I got all that information? I'm not without my contacts and influence, *caro*, and I don't think I've ever abused them, certainly not in this instance. The main problem wasn't getting the information because of any technicality but convincing them that the information could possibly be of interest since the case has already been closed. Maybe they thought I was doing some research for you for one of your *Venetian Lives.*"

They sipped their cognacs in silence for several minutes. One of the things he liked about his relationship with the Contessa was the way they could fall in and out of silences like these without any self-consciousness. He read through the list again.

When he put it down on the table, he saw that his friend was smiling at him.

"So who will be next?"

"Next?"

"You know very well what I mean! I can tell when you're hooked. You're not going to stop with the old women on the Rio della Sensa, are you? Don't forget I know you better than anyone else does. I know that the very reason other people might assume you'd never trouble yourself is exactly the reason why you are doing so—and will continue to."

"And why is that?" he asked with a little smile of his own for her.

She held his eyes for a moment before answering.

"Because of your love for peace and quiet and order. You don't have them now, do you?"

"I don't know what you're talking about, Barbara. The Palazzo Uccello is as quiet as ever and despite all these recent troubles at San Gabriele, Venice is serene enough—and will be until *carnevale*."

But he knew what she meant.

"I mean in *here*." And she gently tapped the side of her head.

5   URBINO was about to leave when the outside bell rang. "That's Stefano, or at least I assume it is."

Urbino looked at his watch.

"So late? It's past ten."

"My, my, aren't you spoiled! Why can't I entertain other gentlemen at whatever hour I please? But don't sulk, it's the frames, simply business. He wants to look at the photographs again. Why, I'm not sure."

She got up as footsteps approached in the hall. It was Bellorini.

"I hope I'm not intruding, Barbara. I know it's later than I said it would be. Good evening, Urbino. I suppose I could have waited until tomorrow but . . ." He shrugged.

"We understand: the impatience of the artist. But you're not interrupting us. As a matter of fact you've come at an opportune time. Would you like something to drink? Help yourself." She indicated the table in the corner set up with decanters, glasses, and a pitcher of water.

As Bellorini went over and poured himself a whiskey, he asked, "Why do you say opportune?"

"Because we both need a break from too much thinking. Let me get the photographs." She went to the same drawer she had gotten the sheet of paper from and took out a marbleized envelope. She brought it back to her chair and produced three photographs of different sizes in black-and-white—of her husband, her mother, and her maternal grandmother. Urbino had seen them many times before but he looked at them attentively again before passing them on to Bellorini.

Bellorini handled them with almost as much reverence as the Contessa. After looking at each individually, he laid them in a neat row in front of him on a small table.

"Call it superstition or eccentricity, but they almost seem to have an influence over me when I go back to work on the frames. I wouldn't have to make these trips here in the middle of the night, though, if you had let them be reproduced." He picked one up again—the Contessa's grandmother—and looked at it closely, turning it to the lamplight. "But probably it wouldn't be the same at all. No, I don't think it would."

The Contessa was pleased. A flush crept into her cheeks as if he had flirted with her and had paid her a compliment that had gone straight to her heart.

"I'll leave you two to discuss matters artistic," Urbino said, getting up.

To his surprise the Contessa didn't urge him to stay.

6 AFTER leaving the Ca' da Capo-Zendrini Urbino went for a walk that took him across both the Rialto Bridge and the Accademia Bridge before he stopped at Harry's. The bar was crowded and smoke-filled and he left after only one drink, striking out in the direction of the Riva degli Schiavoni.

He paused as he usually did to take in the view of the Salute and San Giorgio Maggiore but his thoughts weren't his usual ones. Instead they were of Maria Galuppi and her love for her daughter. They said that a parent never really recovered from the death of a child, and to have had a child die by her own hand must surely have added to the pain in ways he couldn't even imagine. Maria had been a woman of simple faith. How much consolation had it given her? What kind of prayers had she offered up to Santa Teodora? And to think she had met her death in the presence of the little saint, perhaps even in its defense. The scenario wasn't difficult to imagine: an old woman of few pleasures enjoying some quiet moments in church at the end of her day, filled with thoughts and prayers for a dead daughter and a living son, and then being intruded upon and killed.

But why?

And where had Carlo been? When he had come to the Palazzo Uccello the second time, he had mentioned a confessional. Could he have been in the confessional when everything happened? Had he covertly watched his mother praying and wondered if she was thinking of Beatrice? The old women on the Rio della Sensa had said that although Maria had loved her son, she had loved her daughter more. Had he been aware of it? Had he resented his sister and her memory? Had he in fact had a motive for matricide?

Such suspicions started making Urbino uncomfortable, and he pulled himself back. As he made his way along the Riva degli Schiavoni, the lagoon stretching out on his right to the Lido, he turned his mind instead to his conversation with the Contessa. She was so sure that Maria hadn't been killed because of the relic, but what other than her refusal to believe in a disorderly universe of chance and accident was behind her conviction? He knew that there was no sense in pointing out that chance seemed so only from the limited human point of view, that from the larger perspective—the one she so fervently believed in—all was a fine and intricate pattern, all a providential design.

Within this context his friend's schedule of Maria's last day, folded now in his vest pocket, took its place as a somewhat feeble but earnest attempt to find a pattern in it all, not to rest content with what time and eternity would unfold. Urbino was sure that the medieval theologians so admired by Des Esseintes had had much to say about this kind of behavior. They might even have considered it some kind of grievous sin, like doubt or hubris.

Well, he wouldn't trouble himself with that. Let them both be careful, however, not to impose a pattern where one didn't exist, for that would be much, much different from discovering one.

As he let himself in to the Palazzo Uccello, the phone started to ring. It continued as he hurried up the stairs.

"Where have you been?" the Contessa asked querulously when he finally picked up the phone in the library. "You left more than an hour ago. I was beginning to worry. I know, you were walking. You're lucky you live in Venice. Most other cities would have you regretting your habit at this hour."

Urbino waited. He knew his friend didn't respond well to being rushed and he wasn't in the mood to coax her tonight. He didn't have to wait long.

"You know, Urbino, I've been thinking about our conversation ever since Stefano left and I can't seem to get one thing out of my mind. It's about Beatrice." It sounded as if she took a deep breath before going on: "About her mysterious female friend. I hope you won't think I have a strange mind or that I would like to believe in such things but something occurred to me and I wanted to mention it to you right away so you could tell me I'm wrong. But I warn you, do it in a nice way."

"Barbara, would you please just tell me what it is?"

"Well, that old woman on the Rio della Sensa said there were some sharp words between Maria and her daughter about this woman, something about a *cocorita*, a lovebird."

"That's right."

"I find that a little unusual, don't you? I could understand if her *other* friend had given her a lovebird"—the way she said it made it seem as if the poor dead girl had had only the two friends—"but why would some girl or some woman do it? I've been going over and over it, Urbino. The gift of a lovebird from one woman to another sounds rather—rather—"

"What?"

"Sapphic!" she almost shouted, "and shame on you for making me say it!"

"Why not? Beatrice was beautiful and might have had many admirers. It doesn't mean she encouraged them or returned their affections in the same way, but she might have enjoyed the thrill of it, a young girl like that, teasing her mother, acting superior, pretending to be sophisticated about it all."

"My God, so you don't think I'm wrong. You think so too!"

"It's possible, but it's also possible that it was all very innocent."

"I don't know what to think! I was hoping I wasn't able to see how silly my idea was but if you think it's possible—"

"We can't exclude it, but for tonight I suggest banishing it from your mind. Otherwise you'll get no sleep."

"With my luck I'll probably drop right off to sleep and have a string of unmentionable nightmares."

After they said good night, Urbino poured some brandy and settled down in the study before trying to woo sleep himself. He took out the Contessa's description of Maria's last day.

From the time she had left the apartment building at seven-thirty with Carlo to collect Urbino's laundry and that of a wid-

ower in the Calle dell'Arcanzolo, Maria had been well observed.
The mother and son returned an hour later to the Rio della Sensa,
Carlo leaving from there to see to the rest of his duties at San
Gabriele. Maria spent most of the morning in the laundry room
of the building and went for her midday meal to the Tullio
trattoria near the Madonna dell'Orto where she was joined by
Carlo. They both then went back to the Rio della Sensa to get the
laundry and from there had gone to the widower's. The mask
maker Cavatorta said they had passed by his shop in the Calle
dell'Arcanzolo shortly before five. After that no one saw Maria
alive again except for Sister Veronica and her little group. They
hadn't seen Carlo anywhere in the church.

7   URBINO decided to take advantage of the fact that Ca-
    vatorta closed his shop on Wednesdays to stop by his
apartment in the Ghetto Nuovo early the next morning. It might
be better if there were no customers to interrupt them.

There were names on only nine of the seventeen bells at the
entrance of the tenement building in the Campo Ghetto Nuovo
but Cavatorta's wasn't one of them. A woman coming out with a
plastic shopping basket told him the mask maker lived on the
seventh floor.

As Urbino went slowly up the dark, damp stairway, he smelled
cooking and heard loud voices, mainly those of women. The stairs
got darker and mustier as he went past the fifth floor. When he
reached the seventh, he was faced with two closed doors without
any bells or name plates. He was about to knock on the one on the
right when he heard an infant crying behind it. Cavatorta was un-
married. He went across to the other door and knocked.

He had to wait only a few seconds. It was as if he had been

expected. There was neither surprise nor curiosity on the mask maker's thin face, only a slight raising of the eyebrows that Urbino found irksome.

"Couldn't you wait until tomorrow and come by the shop to ask your questions?"

Cavatorta had a reputation for knowing about something almost as soon as it happened in the Cannaregio. Perhaps one of the women in Maria's building had mentioned Urbino's visit. It couldn't have been Don Marcantonio. As far as Urbino knew, the two hadn't spoken since Cavatorta had left San Gabriele and become a mask maker, pursuing an interest that went back to a childhood fascination with the mask of Santa Teodora. His business had flourished since the revival of *carnevale*.

"You're here to ask some questions about Maria Galuppi and her long-dead daughter but I'm afraid I know nothing about the old woman except what everyone else does. I was unlucky enough to be one of the last people to see her alive. That was around five when she walked by the shop with Carlo. He was carrying some laundry, maybe yours. Don't tell me that your interest is because of some lost and soiled laundry."

"Maria didn't stop in to say hello?"

"That would have been something to see. Maria and I didn't get along. It goes a long way back. All they did was walk by about five. They didn't say a word to each other. That's all there was to it." He looked down the hall. "Would you mind stepping inside? I'd prefer that my neighbors remain convinced I have something to hide."

He led the way through the small entrance area to a room with a table in a corner next to an unmade bed. On the table was a hot plate with a dirty espresso maker.

"I'd like to say make yourself at home, but since I'm not at home here myself after twenty years, it'd be hypocritical." He sat on the edge of the bed, running a hand through his unkempt graying hair. Urbino sat in the chair by the table. "Did Bo send you?"

"Don Marcantonio? Not at all. I came on my own. I'm concerned with the way the Questura has handled the case."

"You tread dangerous ground. It isn't wise for a *forestiero* to differ with the almighty Questura. Any one of those many pieces of paper you need might be found to be out of order."

"I'm not taking an antagonistic approach. I just want to have some things settled to my own satisfaction. There can be no harm in that. Of course, you're in no way obligated to answer any questions I might ask but I was hoping you might help since you knew the Galuppis. Carlo—"

"Carlo was devoted to his mother," Cavatorta interrupted. "He loved her despite everything. Isn't that what you want to hear?"

"Despite everything?"

Cavatorta nodded with satisfaction.

"Despite the way she tyrannized him as only a mother can, was so devoted to her daughter's memory that she had little time to give him even though he was the one who was still alive. I doubt if all her bustling around was only for her beloved son in whom she might not have been all that well pleased." He made this last comment in such an arch way that Urbino pretended not to have caught his twisting of the words from Luke.

"Why didn't you get along with Maria?"

Cavatorta laughed but the dark eyes in his thin face didn't seem amused.

"I thought you would never ask. As I said, it goes back a long way. Maria never forgave me for 'giving up the cloth,' 'losing my faith,' 'turning my back on God, San Gabriele, and the blessed remains.' She had quite a few ways of expressing it, you can be sure."

"Did it go back even farther than that, to as far back as the fifties?"

It was a long shot but Cavatorta was about the right age.

"If you want to know something about Beatrice Galuppi, why don't you just ask me? Yes, it goes back to the fifties and yes, it had something—everything— to do with Beatrice."

"You were in love with her?"

The mask maker shrugged.

"I suppose I was, one of a large group," he said ruefully, "but I was about to enter the seminary. I didn't know exactly how I felt, it was a confusing time, but Maria must have known. She made it clear she wanted to save me for God and to save Beatrice for a match made in heaven—*her* idea of heaven."

"Tell me something about Beatrice."

"I've already told you everything in a nutshell. You can figure out whatever else you want to know from that."

"She was beautiful and had many admirers. Her mother was overprotective, wanting her to make the best marriage possible."

"Except that Beatrice wasn't always amenable to her mother's wishes. Sometimes she did things just to upset her. You might say she was ahead of her time. She was a lot like the girls today, she was always doing things her own way."

"Like getting involved with someone unacceptable to her mother, maybe even courting a *scandalo*?"

"A *scandalo*, no, not if she could help it. Nothing that would have made her own life more difficult. But she was temperamentally inclined to unsuitable attachments. As I said, she was always doing things her own way and was quite clever about it too."

"Did Beatrice ever mention a girl or a woman named Domenica? Did you know anyone with that name back in the fifties?"

"Domenica," Cavatorta repeated slowly. "No, I don't think so. Why?"

Instead of answering, Urbino asked him if Beatrice had ever kept a lovebird.

"What questions you ask! She might have had a whole cageful of lovebirds, parakeets, and goldfinches for all I know." He looked up with a smile on his thin lips. "All I remember is a dog, a cocker spaniel named Veronica. No, she didn't name it after Sister Veronica, she named it after the Venetian courtesan Veronica Franco. She knew a lot about the history of Venice and couldn't resist giving the dog a name like that. It drove her mother wild. She just couldn't accept the fact that her daughter wasn't the kind of girl there were so many of in those days—making the Stations of the Cross and novenas, keeping the feasts, and cherishing every word from the mouths of old phonies like Bo. But Maria was determined to think otherwise. You'd have thought Beatrice had been miraculously assumed into heaven or was another Maria Goretti instead of a suicide."

"A mother will usually think the best of her daughter. From what I've heard Beatrice was talented. Don Marcantonio told me you've seen some of her paintings."

"So that old fool did send you over! His information isn't always the most reliable. He sees things the way he would like them to be, not the way they are."

"You've never seen any of her paintings?"

"In this case he's right." Cavatorta was obviously reluctant to grant the priest even this limited claim to truth-telling. "Yes, I've seen three of Beatrice's paintings." He reached over to the table to pour himself a cup of coffee without asking Urbino if he wanted any. After taking a sip, he continued, "After I became a priest Maria treated me as if there had never been any bad feeling between us— that's how it was, anyway, until I left the priesthood. She asked me to look at some of Beatrice's work. She knew I had always been interested in art although I never saw any of Beatrice's paintings while she was alive. I ran into her once or twice at the Accademia and the Glass Museum when she was setting up her easel but I got only a brief glimpse of what she was doing. I had to wait more than ten years after she died to see some of her work—and I would never have seen anything at all if Maria had waited a few more months."

"Why is that?"

"Because I had left San Gabriele by then, had 'turned my back on God.' I left in May of sixty-seven."

"So sometime between the flood in November and May you saw Beatrice's work."

"Right. She said only one other person had ever seen what Beatrice had done—Sister Veronica. Maybe she showed them only to us because she felt that, as religious, we would keep them secret. Those paintings were something of her daughter's she wanted to have only for herself yet she wanted our opinion."

"Were they good?"

"She had some talent but not much more than all those poor fools with their easels set up along the Molo. She was young. With time she might have improved. Two were Venetian scenes, the Grand Canal at the Rialto Bridge and a view of Murano from the Cannaregio. The other was a study from Tintoretto."

"Which Tintoretto?" He remembered how upset the Contessa had been that Maria had never mentioned Beatrice's interest in the painter.

"*The Transport of the Body of Saint Mark* at the Accademia. It wasn't a particularly good copy. Beatrice didn't have the patience for that. I know what you're thinking. You're wondering if there's any significance in the fact that Beatrice chose that painting when thirty years later her mother has been murdered during the theft of the body of another saint. Coincidences aren't undreamt of in my philosophy. Are they in yours?"

As he went out into the Campo Ghetto Nuovo, Urbino asked himself if Beatrice's copying this particular Tintoretto was in fact a coincidence or if, as he had mused last night about such things, it was actually part of a design he was yet unable to see.

❧

8 NOT even the faintest traces of a design had begun to emerge an hour later when he stopped by Stefano Bellorini's studio on the Fondamenta Nuove.

"You're here about Maria Galuppi," Stefano Bellorini said as he led Urbino into his studio. Dressed in worn black corduroys and a large black turtleneck that stood out sharply against his pale skin, he looked very much the artist—and very much aware of it.

"As it turns out, I am, but first I'd like to see the frames."

He gave Stefano his coat and looked around the large open space, cluttered with the implements and materials of the man's art. Bellorini's father had bought the building as the future site of a clinic for his son when he was studying medicine at Padua. Medicine hadn't suited the artistically inclined Stefano, however, and after his father's death he had knocked down all the walls on this top floor and made it into a comfortable studio.

Stefano brought him over to a worktable at the far end of the room by two large windows looking out on the quay and the lagoon, Murano and San Michele in the distance. He moved aside what looked like a small, rusted anchor impaling a piece of wood.

"One of my found objects, but don't tell Barbara it was next to her frames."

Unwrapping the frames from pieces of worn velvet, he examined them himself for a few moments before passing them on to Urbino.

What he had seen as mere sketches at the Contessa's party three weeks ago were now close to being finished. They were made of brass and turquoise fashioned in a severe Egyptian design, blue ceramic and bronze in liquid lines, and pearls and mother-of-pearl inset in beaten copper.

"Beautiful. Barbara must be very pleased. I might have you do something similar for a photograph of my mother and father."

Bellorini beamed.

"I'd be happy to. So," he said, his eyes blinking with humor behind his round glasses as he rewrapped the frames in the velvet, "our incomparable Barbara tells me that you're playing Sherlock Holmes. She said she hoped that didn't leave her the role of Signor Watson. As she remembers him, he was a bit dull-witted and on the short and fat side."

"As usual she flatters me. All I've been doing is asking a few questions here and there to settle my own mind."

"I can understand that—what with your laundry being involved and Carlo coming to the Palazzo Uccello the way he did. Please sit down." He gestured toward several chairs and a sofa on the other side of the room away from his work area. "And let me get us a drink. I'm in the habit of having a bit of Strega about this time every morning."

"Just a swallow for me."

Urbino sat on the sofa. He could tell from the pillow and blanket that it was probably used for afternoon naps—or maybe morning naps if Stefano was in the habit of having more than just a bit of Strega at this time.

Stefano handed him his drink and sat in one of the chairs.

"How can I help you?"

"I was wondering if you might have noticed anything unusual along the quay in the week after Maria's murder."

"Like someone with your pillow slip filled with the bones—or whatever—of Santa Teodora on his back? I'm afraid not. I wish I could help you—or rather help poor Carlo. He's dead now, I know, but there's his memory to consider, his reputation even if he is gone."

"You don't believe he killed his mother either."

"I'm an artist, a craftsman, if you will, not a psychologist or criminologist. Sons do kill their mothers of course. And Maria could be demanding. I feel uncomfortable saying this since she's dead, and not just dead but—but murdered the way she was, but she had a hard side to her. Maybe you never came up against it. Neither did I," he added quickly, "but I saw it. She ordered Carlo around, chastized him for being late or dropping some of the laundry."

"Mothers do things like that from time to time, even the best of mothers."

"There was something else. The two of them were arguing one

afternoon about ten years ago in front of San Gabriele. I don't know what Carlo had done to upset her but she said something about having lost her best child. Angela was with me. She took it pretty hard since we never were able to have children of our own."

"Did you know the sister?"

"It might be more helpful to ask who didn't know her. She was familiar to just about everyone in the Cannaregio, probably in most of the other *sestieri* as well. If you knew what Beatrice Galuppi had looked like you would understand. Even Angela, the most charitable soul I've ever known, although I suppose it's not for me to say, had some resentment toward her. Women couldn't help it. She was extraordinary-looking—and to make it worse she was intelligent, talented. The women would have had to be saints to feel differently."

"And the men?"

"Just what you would expect—smitten, all of them, although I should say all of us. Without Angela back then I would have been led by the nose like everyone else. As it was, I had my share of fantasies but those were almost the days of our honeymoon, you might say."

"Yes," came his wife's voice from behind Urbino, "they were the days of our honeymoon—even if our love nest in that university apartment was more like a dungeon!"

Urbino turned to look over the back of the sofa. Angela, a flattering rosiness in her cheeks, was holding a string basket with vegetables, bread, and a newspaper.

"Don't be naughty and tell our secrets."

"Look who's talking! I had time to hear some of what you were saying, my dear! Besides, Stefano, the condition of apartments is no secret to anyone who's been in Venice as long as Urbino has."

Urbino, who had his own continuing battles with mold, rats, and water bugs at the Palazzo Uccello, gave Angela an encouraging smile. She took off her coat and knit hat and walked over to them. Noticing the bottle of Strega, she shook her head but seemed more amused than anything else. She gave Stefano a look in which there seemed a great deal of silent, wifely communication. "You artists have your weaknesses as I know only too well, Stefano, but must you be corrupting others?" She sighed indulgently and gave him a kiss on his bald spot. "So what do you think of my Stefano's work?"

"That wasn't why he came, Angela. He wanted to know if I noticed anything strange along the quay the week after the murder."

She gave a quick, high-pitched laugh.

"You bothered to ask him? He has two strikes against him. He's a man and he's an artist. They're the least reliable people to ask questions of when it comes to what they've seen. They—or should I say 'you'? I think you qualify on both counts!—you live in a different world and force us to live in it with you. No, Urbino, ask a woman. Then you might stand a chance."

Before he could ask her though, she added quickly, "But I'm afraid you're not going to have any luck with me this time. I was in bed with the flu. It always seems to hit me hard after the holidays. Thank God for Sister Veronica. If I had had to depend on Stefano, I would still be under the blankets."

"But you were at Maria's funeral."

"Just barely. I looked like a corpse." Realizing that this hadn't been the best way to express herself, she gave Urbino an embarrassed, apologetic smile. "But I might be of help nonetheless. If you want to know what's going on along the quay, ask Benedetta Razzi. She's always looking out her window. But she's a peculiar one."

She tapped her temple twice.

"Angela!"

Stefano seemed genuinely upset.

"He'll see for himself!" she said defiantly.

9 THE widow Razzi was a familiar figure in her native Cannaregio where she owned many buildings, most of them in a poor state of repair. About sixty-five with wispy white hair and faded blue eyes, she pinched her *centesimi* at the markets and yet lavished a small fortune on dolls.

When Urbino entered her parlor all he could see at first were dolls—on chairs, sofa, tables, shelves, and cabinets, even perched on an old wall clock, peeping from open drawers, and adorning the carved wooden top of a baroque mirror. Many of them were in regional costumes from Italy and other parts of Europe and the world.

"Maria Galuppi." Benedetta Razzi nodded as she lowered herself into a ripped and sagging love seat. Her long, false eyelashes only emphasized the bags and circles under her eyes. She carefully rearranged two dolls beside her. "I knew her as well as a woman could know another one much, much older. She might have been my mother."

Sister was more like it, Urbino thought, as he sat down in an overstuffed chair.

"A terrible thing to have happened to anyone," she continued. "It makes me even more content not to have any children of my own." She picked up one of the dolls—a blond girl in Tyrolean costume—and put it on her lap. "One child breaking your heart is bad enough but then to have your other one do the same years later—not to mention your head too! But what am I saying?" With an exaggerated giggle she put her hand over her mouth and looked at Urbino with wide eyes.

"There are some who don't think Carlo killed her."

"Yes, there are those. I've heard them talking."

"And what about you, Signora Razzi?"

"I don't think it makes very much difference. I always said that

Maria was dead ever since that daughter of hers died." Her head was bent over the doll as she arranged its skirt more neatly. "Of course, thirty years is a long time to be alive and also dead." There was no giggle but mirth managed to escape from her ravaged eyes.

"Did you know Beatrice Galuppi?"

She got up so quickly that the doll tumbled to the floor. Urbino rose to retrieve it but she waved him away. She snatched it up and put it down on the love seat. "My employee," she said curtly.

"I beg your pardon, Signora Razzi, but I don't—"

"My employee," she repeated impatiently. "Beatrice Galuppi was my employee, I said. No matter how uppity she was, she came to work for me like any other girl for five months. It was around the time my husband died."

"What kind of business did you have?"

"Still have! Buildings, property—more now than I did then! He left me with three buildings back in fifty-four. I was young and rich, and I made myself richer. If there had only been some way to make myself younger too or at least stay the same age, like these sweet young things." She sighed as she looked around at her dolls. "But at least I have my money and my health although I wish I could sleep better. I'm an insomniac."

She went over to the window and drew aside the drapes to look down at the Fondamenta Nuove.

"There goes Giorgio with another bottle from the wineshop. Is that his nose or a bunch of grapes? Well, he's still sober enough, I see, to be able to avoid Angela Bellorini. Probably afraid she'll use one of her meals as an excuse to poke around in his affairs the way she did when my Donato died. She's a strange one. Always wanting to give people those miserable meals of hers but give her anything yourself and she's likely to throw it in your face the way she did with the Cavatortas and a cousin of mine. Too proud, that woman."

Somehow Urbino wasn't surprised to find that the widow Razzi was just as critical of Angela Bellorini as Angela had been of her. He hardly knew the widow Razzi at all but he knew her well enough to realize that deference, not charity, was what she wanted—and preferably from a man.

She was still looking out the window.

"And there's that silly old fool Gabriela with her nasty little dog. They look more and more alike every year!"

She started to laugh at her own joke and stopped. From the direction of her gaze he could tell she was now looking out at the cemetery island.

"I might have made a mistake staying here," she said, dropping the drapes and closing off the view. "I should have moved to my building by the Madonna dell'Orto." She turned back to Urbino. "What were we talking about?"

"Beatrice Galuppi."

"My employee," she emphasized again. "Yes, Beatrice Galuppi worked for me, cleaned apartments like anyone else who needed the money, although Maria probably never saw any of it. Beatrice spent it all on clothes, paints, brushes—everything for her own sweet self. She cleaned this apartment here, too, although she liked to work where I couldn't see her."

"When?"

"I already told you—back in fifty-four! She worked until a month before she died. Didn't surprise me much when she did either."

"Did she seem depressed?"

"I know what you're getting at—depressed and then killed herself like everyone says. Well, maybe she did and maybe she didn't. What I meant was that she was sick enough the last few weeks she worked for me. I would hear her throwing up in the toilet—or trying to was more like it. She looked ready to faint once or twice and was so thirsty she took to carrying a bottle of water around with her—a fancy bottle it was, too, all cut glass. I thought it had wine in it but I sniffed it once. It was water all right," she said begrudgingly. "She looked a fright, too. She was a beauty but even a beauty can look a fright at times."

She nodded with satisfaction as she went back to the love seat.

"Did you see anything out of the ordinary in the week between Maria's death and the discovery of Santa Teodora's body down there on the quay?" When she gave him a puzzled look, he added, "From your window there. You say you suffer from insomnia."

"So did Rossini! He wrote operas from his bed, didn't even have to get up when he couldn't sleep. What I do myself is get up and see if any of my darlings are awake too. I make myself some tea and take it over to the window. Sometimes one of my sweethearts likes to keep me company."

A comfortable-looking chair was near the window and on the sill was a dirty, lace-covered pillow. He could imagine her sitting there with one of her dolls and looking down at the quay for hours.

"Did you notice anything out of the ordinary on any of those nights or maybe during the day?" he asked again.

"What I see is always ordinary, most ordinary, that's my comfort. The usual people and boats come and go—the sweepers, the deliverymen, the police, the neighbors, the tourists—always different but always the same. During the night there's hardly anyone about. It's always been that way. It's all so predictable, it's better than counting sheep. Sometimes we drop off to sleep right there, me and one of my darlings, even from time to time during the afternoon when I haven't slept at all the night before."

"Before I go, Signora Razzi, I have just a few more quick questions about Beatrice."

She picked up another doll, this one dark-haired with a mantilla, combs, and a brightly colored dress.

"May he?" she asked, bending down to confer with the little señorita. The answer must have been affirmative for she raised her head and smiled, flashing close to every one of her false teeth.

"Did you ever hear her—or her mother—mention the name Domenica?"

She fussed with the doll's dress as she shook her head.

"Did Beatrice have a pet bird, a *cocorita*?"

"I have no idea, I assure you! If she did she never brought it when she was working for me, thank God!"

"I'll be going then, Signora Razzi. Thank you for your time."

"I would rather be thanked for my good company."

"For that too. Don't get up. I can show myself out."

"I'm not an old lady, young man." She got up from the love seat and walked with him to the door. "But aren't you going to ask me anything about the American signorina? The one who jumped from the window? When I opened the door and saw you standing there, that's what I said to myself. He's here to ask me about her, I said."

"Signorina Quinton?"

"She always insisted on the 'Signorina,' made quite a point of it the first few times. She rented two floors of the Casa Silviano off the Rio della Sensa."

Urbino was familiar with the building from the outside. A few years ago a piece of its facade had broken off and damaged a tricycle that a child had left out in the *calle* during the night.

"She was a big, boring woman, God rest her soul, probably slept the whole night through, but she was no trouble at all, gave me what I asked right from the first, all in crisp new notes and in advance. I love renting to you *forestieri*. If you have any American friends looking for a place, Signor Macintyre, send them to me. We can work something out as soon as that apartment is put back in order. Now don't forget."

10 ABOUT five that afternoon Urbino was sitting in one of the pews of San Gabriele as Sister Veronica, who kept giving him uneasy glances, explained to her small group of hospice guests the story of Santa Teodora. She said nothing about the theft and the murder, perhaps at the order of the Mother

Superior or even the Vatican, but she did mention the recent reconsecration. Her guests—an elderly couple with weary looks on their faces and an obese woman in a natty fur coat—didn't seem particularly interested in any more details, however.

When she finished she told them they could stay in the church for the six o'clock Mass or return to the hospice. She would see them tomorrow at nine for the tour of Murano.

Urbino went over to her.

"It's good to have Santa Teodora back," he said.

She nodded but there was a worried look in her dark brown eyes. With her finely chiseled face and expressive eyes Sister Veronica was an attractive woman. Though over fifty she looked ten years younger, the way religious often do. She must have been beautiful as a young woman.

"It certainly is but I keep expecting someone to ask about Maria. When they do, I don't know what to say. I don't like to talk about it."

"But they're probably so filled with wrong ideas they could use a dose of the truth."

"The truth! I know less of it than anyone else, less than you do, I'm sure." It seemed almost a criticism.

"But you don't think Carlo killed his mother, do you?"

Although it was barely a second before she responded, it seemed much longer. In fact it seemed as if she didn't want to answer the question at all. But when she did it was with a fervent denial.

"Of course not. I had many opportunities to observe Carlo. Kill his mother? No, Carlo didn't kill her."

"What about the sister, Beatrice? Did you know her?"

Sister Veronica's expressive eyes had lost their worried look. In its place was something close to disapproval.

"No, I never knew her."

She turned to look at the fat woman in the fur coat who was bending over the glass case to peer into the masked face of the saint. When she looked back at Urbino, she stared at him without adding anything in clarification. It might well have been that, being from Murano and roughly the same age as Beatrice, she had heard rumors about the girl's behavior. Perhaps it had been indecorous of him to suggest they had known each other.

"But you did see some of her art work." Then, as if to give more authority to his questioning, he added, "Don Marcantonio mentioned it."

"Yes, but not until many years after her death. Since I was giving the tours here, even back then around the time of the flood, Maria trusted my opinion on art. She also knew I had an interest in Tintoretto just as her daughter had had and wanted to impress me with her talent. I don't think she doubted for a moment that there was some."

"Wasn't there?"

"Oh, there was but it needed to be developed much more. She was an amateur without any formal training, from what I know. Who's to say what she might have done if she had lived and applied herself? There was something there."

Having delivered this lukewarm praise, she cast her eye back over her little group.

"What about the Tintoretto?"

"There were two Tintorettos: *The Transport of the Body of Saint Mark* at the Accademia and *The Presentation of the Virgin* at the Madonna dell'Orto. Only details, not the whole pictures. Just the men carrying Saint Mark's body with the camel behind them and Saint Anne with her arm around the Virgin. Maria was pleased with them because of the religious themes. It made her feel better about her daughter."

She avoided his eyes.

"You saw only the two Tintorettos?"

"Oh, no," she said, looking up at him and smiling now. "She was determined to show me everything. There were some sketchbooks with nothing of much interest, also a *capriccio* derivative of

Piranesi, drawings of buildings, bridges, and piazzas. The best of the lot were copies of several scenes from the Barovier Wedding Cup at the Glass Museum. I say they were the best even though she didn't copy some of the scenes exactly as they were. She made some changes. And it might not have been such a good idea to try to capture the scenes in oils."

"All that might be why they were the best. She showed some originality."

"You might say. But don't forget that the scenes on the Wedding Cup are much simpler than the Tintorettos."

There was no disagreeing with this—and even if there were, Urbino would have avoided challenging Sister Veronica on a painter she knew and loved so well. At any rate, he had no opportunity for she had barely finished when the woman in the fur coat asked her about the murder, in an unnecessarily loud voice.

"There was a theft, you know," she said for the benefit of the elderly couple who had gone over to inspect the Cima more closely.

Sister Veronica sighed and excused herself. It didn't seem as if today was going to be one of the days she escaped without giving more details than she wanted to.

🦋

11 THIS time Cavatorta didn't ask him in. He looked as if he had just awakened, his hair more mussed than before and his thin face puffy.

"This morning you said that you saw three of Beatrice Galuppi's paintings—two scenes of Venice and a Tintoretto. Is that right?"

The mask maker crossed his arms and leaned against the doorframe.

"Your memory isn't quite as good as you'd like to think, I'm afraid. It was only a detail from a Tintoretto. But now that you've been reassured, if you'll excuse me—"

"Where did you see them?"

"At the Galuppi apartment on the Rio della Sensa. You don't think Carlo and Maria carted them all the way here, do you?"

"Were there any other paintings around?"

"Would a lithograph of the Sacred Heart of Jesus and a calendar with a picture of the Matterhorn qualify?"

"You didn't see a detail from Tintoretto's *Presentation of the Virgin* that's at the Madonna dell'Orto or—"

"Listen, Signor Macintyre. If you think you're going to pin the theft of any of Beatrice's paintings on me, don't even try. Those things were taken while I was hearing confessions at San Gabriele. I'm sorry to disappoint you. Good afternoon."

Urbino was left standing in front of the closed door, listening to Cavatorta's footsteps receding down his hallway, presumably back to a bed as rumpled as he was.

🍂

12 "I never heard of any theft, no," the Contessa said later that evening on the phone, "but I didn't know anything about her paintings to begin with either, you might recall." Obviously it still hurt that Maria hadn't confided in her. "When was the theft?"

"Around the time of the flood, sometime between then and whenever Cavatorta left the priesthood."

"For my own peace of mind I'd like to know exactly when it was. Maybe there's a good reason why I don't know anything about it. Alvise and I were up in Geneva at the clinic right after the flood—in fact, Sister Veronica came up with us for several days, which might also explain why she didn't say anything about a theft. I'll try to find out. You've been asking enough questions these last few days. For a foreigner to have asked even half as many in the days of the Council of Ten would have got him thrown straight into the *Piombi!*"

"You don't mind asking around?"

"It's not my intention to 'ask around,' as you put it. As for minding, I might even enjoy conducting a discreet little inquiry of my own—sounds so much better put that way, doesn't it? And who knows, *caro?* Maybe I'll find out why there are so many things everyone else seems to know that I don't have the vaguest notion of!"

"One thing I'm sure you do know about is Sister Veronica. Could you refresh my mind on her circumstances?"

"Her circumstances? She's a sister of the Charity of Santa Crispina."

"I mean her history."

"You mean her secular history, I assume, before *la vita nuova?* But she renounced all that when she took the veil."

In light of the changes in the Church over the last two decades and the freedom enjoyed by Sister Veronica, the Contessa's expression had more than a whiff of Victorianism.

"I know her father was a glassblower," Urbino said, "but not much else."

"There isn't much else, *caro.* When her mother died she went to live with an aunt in Naples for five or six years until she was eighteen; then she helped out in her father's shop for a while. After he died she sold the factory to his apprentice and entered the convent."

"And has been living happily ever since as a nun?"

"It would seem so."

"Why did she wait until her father died to enter the convent?"

"He disapproved."

"And she disapproved of him."

"So you do remember something else after all! Down in Naples she used to fantasize that her family was descended from the

Doges. Her aunt did everything to encourage it. She didn't have much fondness for her brother-in-law. Sister Veronica grew up disliking everything to do with glass and glassmaking but she was only an impressionable young girl then."

"An impressionable young girl who eventually found her way to the convent."

"Nothing like a Saint Augustine turnabout, if that's what you're thinking. She didn't have much of a distance to go. She's less inclined to talk about her good points than her faults, but I'm sure that however impressionable and confused she might have been, she was also devout. But why are you so interested in Sister Veronica?"

"No particular reason except that she didn't seem comfortable with the topic of Beatrice Galuppi."

"And should she have been? Despite all the changes since Vatican Two, most of which we both lament, don't forget that Sister Veronica remains a nun—something that Beatrice Galuppi never was!"

Rather than ask her any more questions, this time about Cavatorta, and risk getting her even more riled, Urbino mentioned Bellorini's frames and soothed her with his admiration for them.

❧

13 FORTIFIED the next afternoon by a substantial lunch and half a liter of wine at the Montin, Urbino went to the Europa e Regina.

He approved of Voyd's choice. The hotel, in two adjacent baroque palazzi across from the Salute, was one of those places in the city probably closest to most people's image of Venice of the Grand Canal. It was where he himself had stayed during his early visits and when he had needed a change from his bare *pensione* room near the train station while the work was being done on the Palazzo Uccello. He approached the hotel's little *campo* through the narrow alley angling off toward the Grand Canal from the main route to the Piazza. The only sounds were the muffled ones of his own footsteps and the water traffic on the Grand Canal.

He had a drink in the bar before going up to Voyd's suite. A reserved Kobke led him through the foyer to the large sitting room where reflected light from the Grand Canal played over the ceiling, walls, and antique furniture. The Salute gleamed tantalizingly beyond the terrace doors as if within touching distance.

Kobke went through a door on the far side of the room without a word. Suddenly Urbino heard a light laugh and looked in its direction.

"Down here, Mr. Macintyre."

The writer was reclining on a sofa placed to the right of the terrace doors. It was diagonal to Urbino, and Voyd's body seemed misshapen because of the angle. It was as if the man's head, impressive enough when its owner was erect, were gigantic, dwarfing the rest of his body. Beneath it were several cushions which contributed to the peculiar effect.

"I don't blame you for preferring the Salute to this sad sight." He gestured down at his reclining figure. "Before you make yourself comfortable, why don't you pour us some sherry. Everything's ready there on the sideboard. Then you can take this chair here. Just remove that notebook and all those papers."

After getting their sherries, Urbino went to the uncomfortable-looking great armchair with a high back. It was covered with a morocco notebook and loose sheets of paper with spidery handwriting. He gathered the sheets and put them on top of the notebook, then looked for a convenient place to lay everything.

"Just put them down on the floor. Christian has been reading to me from Quinton's material. A sad duty but an interesting one. Poor Quinton still had a lot ahead of her to judge by what I've been reading—or rather what I'm having read to me of late. Even holding a book is an effort, you see. It's my back, an old bicycle accident that flares up from time to time. It's made these indolent periods a regular part of my life. I sometimes think I should live like a latter-day pasha on low sofas with hundreds of little embroidered cushions around me."

A woman's laugh sounded from behind the door Kobke had gone through.

"That's Adele, Quinton's niece. She seems to keep finding scraps of her aunt's writing and insists on bringing them over herself. I'm beginning to think it's less for the sake of security than to see Christian. He's quite a charming fellow." He paused long enough to give Urbino the opportunity of saying something, then went on. "Let me be honest, Mr. Macintyre. I know why you're here. Oh, I know you're a polite young man and would have come eventually, sometime next week perhaps when you realized I was about to leave before the madness of carnival. But here you are now, still much later than I wished but earlier than you would otherwise have been."

Voyd raised the sherry to his lips, careful not to spill any on the crisp white front of his shirt. Once again woman's laughter was heard, followed by Kobke's accented voice, the words indistinguishable.

"Don't look so surprised, I'm not psychic. That's one thing I haven't been accused of although—who knows?—it might do my writing some good. It certainly had an effect on Yeats's work. But no, I owe my information to none other than Benedetta Razzi, none other than that extraordinary woman. She might find her way into one of my stories although I'm afraid I might have to tone her down to make her credible. But I believe we had a conversation—a very brief one—about such things that morning about two weeks ago in the Piazza San Marco." He gave Urbino an amused smile. "Yesterday afternoon—before I threw my back out again on the Accademia Bridge—I visited the good woman. She has a key to a locked room at the Casa Silviano. It seems that keeping a locked room, ostensibly for the use of the owner of the apartment, is some way of circumventing the rent control laws here. One of the clerks downstairs explained it to me. I thought there might be something in the room for me, more manuscripts or whatever, but Signora Razzi assured me it was impossible. One of the conditions of Quinton's rental was that she didn't have the use of the room, didn't even have access to it in an emergency. In the course of my visit with her—with her and her *bambole*, that is—she mentioned that you had been there earlier. I think she wanted to impress me with her full social life."

"And she mentioned that I asked her some questions about Maria Galuppi. You see, Mr. Voyd, after Maria Galuppi was murdered, her son came to the Palazzo Uccello on two—"

The writer waved his hand.

"Don't underestimate me, my friend. I don't know you very well but I know you well enough. There's no need to either apologize or explain. Your secure little domain, your refuge, your sanctuary—call it what you will—has been quite rudely invaded and you must have things back in order—or at least make a valiant attempt. It's a most natural desire. Like Venice we all need to protect our frail barriers."

Voyd took another careful sip before going on.

"So when you called this morning I got to thinking. There's not much else I can do in this pathetic state. I remembered our last meeting at San Gabriele after the Patriarch's service. I told you and the Contessa da Capo-Zendrini that Quinton had an interest in Maria Galuppi, that she had written me of it several times, and that I suspected that Quinton's friendship wasn't all that selfless. My poor dead friend, like all us other scribblers, was always on the lookout for material, for inspiration, for a germ that might become a story or—wonder of wonders!—even a novel. It seems I was right about that. Quinton wasn't without an ulterior motive in befriending Maria Galuppi. We writers must often plead guilty to such things, even when it comes to those closest and dearest to us. Just think of all the material that vampire Scott sucked out of poor, tortured Zelda!"

Voyd would probably have shaken his head in bemused admiration if his condition had allowed it.

After a few uncomfortable moments earlier, Urbino was beginning to appreciate the writer's volubility. It was making things easier for him.

"Why do you say you were right in assuming Margaret Quinton had a literary interest in Maria Galuppi?"

Voyd pointed to the sheets and notebook Urbino had removed from the armchair.

"I base it on the best evidence there is: Quinton's Venice notebook. Those other sheets don't pertain. She wrote them in Florence before she came here. Christian and I got through them late last night and started on the notebook. She mentions Maria Galuppi a few times along with other material more interesting to me. I assume there must be more entries about the old woman in the rest of it."

Urbino looked down at the morocco notebook. He had an urge to pick it up and start reading.

Voyd smiled.

"Nothing would make you happier than stealing away for a few hours with poor Quinton's notebook. Am I right?"

Before Urbino could answer, the door Kobke had gone through earlier opened and a pale, angular young woman came in tentatively, followed by the Dane. She looked different from the person Urbino remembered from Quinton's funeral. Then she had seemed plain with only youth to recommend her. Now she was almost pretty, with a quick smile and inner glow.

"Adele, this is Urbino Macintyre. You might remember him from your aunt's funeral."

"Of course I do. You were with the Contessa da Capo-Zendrini."

"We were just talking about your aunt, Adele. I was telling him about her Venice notebook, how fascinating it is."

"You're a much better judge of that than I am, Clifford. That's why Aunt Margaret put you in charge of her literary affairs. She knew I'd never have been able to sort out the wheat from the chaff. I just glance through the things before passing them on to you."

"But I'm sure you'll read it all eventually, my dear. At least when it's published, as it certainly will be. Her public is interested in just about everything she's done."

"What is Mr. Macintyre's interest in the Venice notebook?" Kobke asked, looking coolly at Urbino.

"Did I say he had one? I don't believe I did, Christian, but as it turns out, he happens to be most interested." He turned his head slightly so that he could see Adele Carstairs better. "As I was saying, Adele dear, your aunt's public will clamor. Oh, yes, will they ever clamor!"

"You've impressed that on me on enough occasions, Clifford, which is why I rush over whenever I discover the slightest scrap, even if it's a laundry list."

"Ah, dear Adele, is that why you've been such a bustler between the Danieli and here!"

She blushed and looked away.

"I really must be going," she said. "I'm meeting some local ladies for tea at Florian's and some others later for dinner. They're taking me under their wing, I think, because of Aunt Margaret's love for Venice."

"Would those invitations still be forthcoming if they knew what you've said about Venice?" Voyd asked with a mischievous grin.

"That was a long time ago, Clifford."

"It was hardly a month ago, as I recall." He winked at Urbino. "She'll forgive me if I repeat what she said, with the understanding that it goes no further. We wouldn't want to compromise these teas and dinners with local ladies of prominence. Adele—ages ago, as she believes—called this fair city of yours abhorrent, green, and slippery. The phrase is original with D. H. Lawrence, of course, but I assure you her delivery made it very much her own!"

"Would you get me my coat, Christian, before Clifford embarrasses me any more?" She put her hand out to Urbino. "It's a pleasure to see you again, Mr. Macintyre. Perhaps before I return to Vienna we can meet for tea or drinks away from this teaser, magnificent though he is."

After Kobke helped her into her coat, she bent down and kissed Voyd on the cheek.

As Kobke was showing her to the door, Voyd stared at Urbino with an amused expression. Urbino felt it was probably time for him to leave, too, but it was difficult with Margaret Quinton's notebook lying there on the floor within reach. He wouldn't know if there was anything of importance in it until Voyd read through the whole thing and told him, if he were so inclined. For perfectly selfish reasons he now wished that the writer would stay in Venice longer. Wouldn't it be an unlucky stroke if he didn't finish the notebook until he had returned to London? The man must have any number of things that were of greater urgency or at least more profitable to him.

"You can pick it up again, you know," the writer said. "No alarm went off before and I don't think there's any need to fear one now."

Urbino reached for the notebook, leaving the loose sheets on the floor.

"You're welcome to take it back to the comforts of your palazzo. Read it there."

Kobke had returned in time to hear Voyd's offer.

"Clifford! We just started to read it ourselves. Don't you think—"

"As you well know, Christian, we have plenty to occupy us. Besides, you have that business to tend to for me at the Palazzo Pitti. I'm sure Mr. Macintyre will be done long before you get back from Florence."

"But Clifford," Kobke said in gentler tones that Urbino found more irritating than his previous strident ones, "isn't it your responsibility to see that nothing untoward happens to any of Quinton's manuscripts?"

" 'Untoward'! As I've said many times before, my boy, I would love to meet your English tutor! Yes, I do have a responsibility, and I don't take it lightly, but I have faith in Mr. Macintyre. Take it and enjoy it, Mr. Macintyre. I hope it answers some of your questions."

Kobke seemed about to say something else but then turned and went back into the room he had entertained Adele Carstairs in. Voyd waited for him to shut the door before continuing.

"I must confess that lending you the notebook is also a way of making sure I see you again. Christian will be down in Florence and I'll be feeling very much alone, especially if I have to suffer through this indignity much longer. I would be very happy for the company and we might even get into a discussion of that Des Esseintes of yours, the recluse you admire so much. Sitting here like this today I couldn't help but wonder if he didn't have a marvelous idea after all. To have everything he needed or wanted right there around him at all times. It's a self-sufficient and reassuring existence for a person, even if one isn't bedridden—or should I say 'sofa-ridden'? I wouldn't mind having that invention of his, that row of little liqueur casks with interconnected spigots that can all be opened at the same time. Called it a mouth organ, didn't he? I'd like to have it rigged up right over my sofa here so that I could take a drop of one liqueur after another, or make unusual combinations— chartreuse verte, chartreuse jaune, Benedictine, Drambuie, Cointreau, pernod, absinthe, Grand Marnier, Amaretto! Tell me, Mr. Macintyre, do you have such a mouth organ in your little palazzo?"

"I'm more inclined to follow the spirit of Des Esseintes than the letter."

"Ah, yes, as I recall, you did tell me that you don't have any turtle carrying its jewel-encrusted carapace across your Oriental carpet."

"Tortoise," Urbino corrected. "And the tortoise died, if you remember."

"I certainly do. The poor creature was unable to bear all that beauty on its back! There's a lesson for all us aesthetes in that! And a lesson for Venice as well, I suppose! You see, Mr. Macintyre, we have a great many things we can talk about besides two dead women, no matter how interesting and endearing they were, but I realize they're what you're concerned about now. So take the Venice notebook, take it with my blessing and read it, and when you return it, we can get on to other things. Can I expect you back in a few days? Certainly before Christian returns from Florence, if you don't mind. I hope so. You'll have to show yourself out, I'm afraid. It would be best not to disturb Christian. These visits from Adele can put him in the strangest moods."

❧

14 WHAT Voyd had said about the lesson in Des Esseintes's tortoise—that all the blazing beauty set on its back had led to its death—echoed through Urbino's mind as he walked back to the Cannaregio to make his next visit. When he had been in the Protestant graveyard with the Contessa the morning of Quinton's funeral, he had pointed out to her, in his ironic way and with the help of some ill-sung lines from Wagner's *Tristan und Isolde*, that love and death embraced in this watery city. Voyd's words had reminded him, however, of yet another embrace—between beauty and death.

He took a slight detour and stood on the Rialto Bridge looking at the marble wall of Gothic and Renaissance palazzi on both sides of the Grand Canal as far as the Ca' Foscari, where there was a bend in the broad waterway. The frescoes that had once adorned the facades of the palazzi had faded and disappeared and the buildings themselves, resting on thousands of weakening, wooden stakes, were still sinking—or so many people, with little faith in all the hydraulic and architectural efforts being made, strongly believed. The weight of all the stone staircases and Murano chandeliers, all the paintings in heavy frames and the ornate period furniture, all the altarpieces and the mosaics, all the belltowers and humpbacked bridges, all the statues and fountains, all the stones of Ruskin's Venice—the weight of all this beauty could only be hastening the end if the end were to come At Quinton's service Voyd had read some lines from the dead woman's work, something about Venice having been born to die like all beauty and perhaps being destined to become even more beautiful in its passing.

As he resumed his walk to the Cannaregio, Urbino tried to shake off these thoughts which were, at best, self-indulgently romantic and, at worst, enervating, for they undermined the anger one should feel in the face of any kind of death.

When he got to the Strada Nuova his thoughts had turned to Maria, Carlo, and Beatrice. A few moments later, however, as he considered how Beatrice's beauty hadn't saved her but might in fact have been her undoing, he realized that he was still thinking of the same thing but in a different guise.

He quickened his pace. He hoped the Tullios at the trattoria near the Madonna dell'Orto would be able to give him some clear-cut facts. He had had enough of something else ever since he had left Voyd.

15   NETTA was in the kitchen next to the bar preparing one of the simple meals the Tullios offered as Bettino poured out some grappas. A group of laborers was sitting at a large table by the stove, playing cards and joking. After Bettino brought them their grappas, he came back to the bar and poured a red wine for Urbino. Although not a regular, Urbino was familiar to the Tullios. He sometimes came in midafternoon for one of Netta's meals when it was Natalia's day off.

"Yes, Maria was here," Bettino said. "She took her midday meal here maybe two, three times a week, usually about two o'clock. It was the same that day, wasn't it, Netta?"

His wife nodded as she went on chopping.

"Did she seem any different from usual?"

"Not to me, the same as she always was, but Netta, well, Netta thinks there might have been something different."

Netta came from the kitchen, wiping her hands on her apron.

"You say 'thinks,' Bettino, but I *know* there was something different. Excuse me for saying this, Signor Macintyre, but sometimes you men don't notice what you should." She nodded toward the group at the table as if they could be taken as representative of their sex. They seemed oblivious to everything but their card game and drinks. "A man's attention isn't to be relied on; sometimes he doesn't even see what's most important even if it's right under his nose."

It was almost the same thing Angela Bellorini had said yesterday.

"What was different about her, Signora Tullio?"

"In one word, excited. She said nothing strange, she talked about the usual things—the weather, her work, the food, Santa Teodora—but underneath it all, I tell you, she was excited."

Bettino shook his head, the only expression of doubt he allowed himself. His wife glared at him.

"Believe me, Signor Macintyre, she was excited about something."

"In a happy way or an anxious way?"

"She didn't seem nervous or upset—as I said, excited." She went back into the kitchen, but a few moments later put her head through the little window to look at him. "Excited, Signor Macintyre, and I don't think it was in a bad way at all. But her excitement, it made me feel a little uncomfortable. She was usually a quiet woman, calm. That day she almost seemed like a little girl squirming in church on Sunday."

Bettino said nothing until there were sounds of pans being moved around. Then, quietly: "Take what she says with a grain of salt, Signor Macintyre. I noticed nothing. Everything seemed the way it usually was. When she finished her meal, Carlo came by and they left for the Rio della Sensa to get the laundry."

As Urbino was leaving, Netta waved from the kitchen.

"Excited, Signor Macintyre, remember that, like a little girl."

She said something to her husband that set him moving briskly behind the bar.

❧

16   FIFTEEN minutes later Urbino was at the tenement on the Rio della Sensa, knocking on the door of one of the apartments on the first floor. Children were screaming behind it. A wide-eyed little girl with thick, curly black hair opened it slowly. He was about to ask for her mother when a haggard woman appeared with an infant in her arms.

"Giulietta Pagano?"

"Yes?" A look of fear came over her face. "It's about my husband, isn't it? He's had an accident."

She said it in a resigned way. When he assured her this wasn't the case, that he didn't even know her husband, she showed no sign of relief but only stood staring at him.

"Excuse me for disturbing you but this will take only a few minutes." He had to raise his voice as a child started to cry from the back of the apartment. "I would like to ask about Maria Galuppi. My name is Urbino Macintyre and I'm—I'm conducting an inquiry into her death."

Well, that was true enough. As long as she didn't ask for any credentials.

She handed the infant to the little girl and told her to wait in the kitchen.

"There's little to tell. We've been here for only a year. She was a good woman, God rest her soul. She stayed with the children once or twice but they didn't like her because of her son, they said he gave them the *malocchio*. They would tease him from the window with that song from "I due gobbi," the one the old women sing around the tree. I read that story to them all the time." Urbino nodded. He was familiar with the folktale. Two hunchbacks overhear a song of the days of the week sung by a group of old women who then remove the hump from one's back and put it on the chest of the other. "It would make Maria even angrier than him but he probably didn't even understand what it was all about. I doubt if she ever told him that particular story."

"You saw her the day she died."

"We were both doing the laundry that morning in the *lavanderia* downstairs. There was nothing unusual about her. You can't help thinking of the last time you see a person before they—they die, how they look, what they say. If anything she was more herself than usual."

There was a crash from the apartment and she called several names out sharply. There was silence but it wasn't likely to last long.

When Signora Pagano turned back to him, it was with a weary, blank look, almost as if she didn't quite remember who he was or why he was there.

"You were saying that Maria was more herself than usual."

"It was nothing much," she said hurriedly. "When I went back about three to collect my detergent, she had her arm around Carlo, she was saying they wouldn't have to be doing this forever, that after Sunday it would be different, something like that, I'm not really sure. I wasn't trying to listen. She looked embarrassed when I came in. I think sometimes she didn't want people to see how tender she was with Carlo. Maybe they would blame her for his condition, I don't know. They always seem to blame the mothers." She gave him a wry smile that only brought out her weariness more. Another crash came from somewhere behind her, as well as the cries of a child. She excused herself abruptly and closed the door.

The other tenants of the building confirmed what Signora Pagano had told him. Maria Galuppi hadn't seemed any different on the day of her death.

17   THE widower Rodolfo Tasso lived in a tiny apartment overlooking the Calle dell'Arcanzolo just a stone's throw from the Campo San Gabriele and not far from Cavatorta's mask shop. He was a retired chemist from a factory in Porto Marghera, who had managed to avoid working for the war effort under Mussolini by feigning the kind of chronic illness he had eventually contracted. In good weather he could be found at his window reading the paper, chatting with passersby, and in general conducting the diminished business of a man in his eighties. Because the amputation of several toes made it almost impossible for him to go out, he had a basket on a rope that he lowered for provisions, the morning's *Il Gazzettino*, and the mail.

Urbino could hear Tasso cursing and talking to himself as he came to answer the door.

"Who is it at this hour of the afternoon?" he complained as he opened it. He was a thin, bald man with quick, lively eyes. His pajamas and robe seemed about two sizes too big for his emaciated frame. When he saw it was Urbino, he looked embarrassed. "I'm sorry, Signor Macintyre, please come in."

When Urbino told him why he was there, the man's face seemed to crumple as if he were about to cry.

"Ah yes, poor Maria, God rest her soul. To think I remember her when she was a little girl." He lowered himself carefully into a chair near the door. "What is it that you want to know? The police have been here twice, very kind of them not to insist I go to the Questura."

"You saw Maria the day she died."

"Yes, she came by with Carlo to pick up my laundry about eight and they brought it back at four-thirty, as usual. She always came every other Monday."

"Did you notice anything different about her? Did she say anything that struck you as strange?"

"Quite the opposite. She was very happy, especially in the afternoon." His birdlike face, with its slightly irritated look, softened as he said, "And she wanted me to be happy, too. She would bring me a nice *zuppa di pesce* the next day, she said, she didn't want me to worry about my laundry, she would do it as long as she could, no matter what happened. She was filled with *gentilezza*, was Maria Galuppi. She knew how insecure and worried we old people can get, we're always afraid of being forgotten, pushed aside. But Maria assured me she would never forget me." He scratched his bald head with his thumb and looked up at Urbino with a slight frown. "But excuse me, Signor Macintyre, why are you so concerned about Maria Galuppi? The good woman is dead. All we can do now is pray for her soul."

"I might be making a fool of myself, Signor Tasso," Urbino said, deciding to be completely honest with the old man, "but I can't believe Carlo killed his mother. All this is none of my affair, surely, but I'm looking for something that will clear his name."

"And will reveal who really did it! Good for you, Signor Macintyre! Many of us would be grateful to you for that."

"There are some in the Cannaregio who think he did it because he resented the memory of his sister. Did you know her?"

"She was a vision, *la bella Beatrice*! If I had been thirty, even twenty years younger—!"

He shook his head.

"Do you know if she ever had a little bird as a pet?"

"Could have, I suppose, she had a dog, a cocker spaniel, I think it was. She was interested in many things—people, animals, why not a little bird? She was bright too, she liked making clever little jokes. She could tell you everything there was to know about the Queen of Cyprus, Tintoretto, and so many other things when she wasn't much more than a little girl. I even had a conversation with her once about Casanova! Just because she was the daughter of a washerwoman didn't mean that she didn't have a sharp mind and mightn't have gone places. She liked to point out that Tintoretto was the son of a dyer from the Cannaregio."

"Did she have many girlfriends?"

"I saw her with girls her own age on occasion but less and less as she got older. It was because of how lovely she was. The other girls couldn't help being green with envy, they told tales, ignored her, you know how it is at that age. You're wasting your energies there if you want to learn anything about Beatrice. Any woman who knew her back then would probably still be filled with envy. Couldn't trust what she said." He laughed. "And as for the men, you couldn't trust them either. She seems to have rejected every single one of them."

"Every one?"

"Ah yes, there was talk of someone special, but I don't think there was any truth in it. But who knows? It was a long time ago. I was young then myself, a mere fifty!" A wistful look came over Tasso's face and he sighed.

❧

18 THAT evening Urbino sat in the library turning over what he had learned in the past two days. He resisted the urge to start reading Quinton's Venice notebook, wanting to think things through before he did. Quinton belonged to Maria's recent past, whereas his inquiries had been taking him into her life twenty and even thirty years before.

He hoped that his interest—and, yes, let him admit it, his fascination—with Beatrice Galuppi, this beautiful girl of wit and intelligence who had died under mysterious circumstances, wasn't going to prove to be his blind spot. Surely the more he knew about Maria, the better chance he would have of discovering what had actually happened on that afternoon almost three weeks ago. To understand Maria completely he would have to understand Beatrice, and then even Carlo might fall into place. Families often had one pivotal figure, one key member around whom the others grouped and in relation to whom they even defined themselves. In the Galuppi family it had been Beatrice.

She was a problem he was determined to solve, even if it didn't bring him any closer to the ultimate answer he was seeking. Like Ruskin on his ladder at San Zanipolo, exploring behind the tomb of the Doge, he must find out the true dimensions of Beatrice. Ruskin's suspicions about the sculpted Doge had been confirmed—he had found only one hand, only one finished cheek, and one half of an ermine robe. By his own admission he had discovered a monster.

What would he, Urbino, discover about the beckoning figure of Beatrice?

Had she been having an affair with a man who had rejected her? Had she been pregnant? Had she killed herself because of it? Benedetta Razzi had described symptoms that sounded like morning sickness.

But who was this woman who had given her the gift of a lovebird and had been the source of arguments between mother and daughter? Was it possible that Beatrice had encouraged rumors of a man in order to camouflage her relationship with this Domenica? After all, no one appeared to have known of Domenica except old Marietta on the Rio della Sensa, who had overheard the heated exchange between Maria and Beatrice several weeks before the girl died.

The Contessa might shy away from the lesbian possibilities but he didn't, he couldn't. He understood them with that knowledge of things Venetian that, as Tasso had pointed out, had been one of Beatrice's characteristics. Perhaps Beatrice had been able to feel more comfortable with her love for another woman in a city that had once been a flourishing center of the so-called "unnatural vice."

Aside from all this, there was also the theft of her artwork. Had the paintings Cavatorta had not seen—if, in fact, he hadn't seen them—been stolen, or was there some other reason for his apparent ignorance? And why hadn't the rest of the paintings and sketches been taken? Had there been a discriminating thief who had selected only the more accomplished work? Sister Veronica had said that the scenes from the Wedding Cup at the Glass Museum had been the best of everything she had seen of Beatrice's work.

Having got nowhere with all this speculation, he decided to put Beatrice from his mind for a while and go over what he had learned that day about Maria. He had been struck by Netta Tullio's conviction that Maria had seemed excited the afternoon of her death. Although Giulietta Pagano and Rodolfo Tasso hadn't noticed anything unusual about her, hadn't they both perceived a greater kindness, a special consideration for her son and for Tasso himself? And hadn't she said to both Carlo and Tasso something that had indicated a coming change in her life? Could she have had a premonition of her death? But Urbino discounted this as soon as it occurred to him. What she had said to them had suggested something positive, something desirable.

In addition to all this, something else he had heard teased his mind, but exactly what it was eluded him. Despite his fluency in Italian, he feared he might have missed or overlooked something that had been said.

Deciding to wait to read Quinton's notebook until tomorrow, when he would be more alert, he took Italo Calvino's *Fiabe italiane* down from the shelf, a book he read in randomly from time to time, enjoying the Italian versions of the Brothers Grimm and Hans Christian Andersen.

He had read only a few paragraphs of "I due gobbi," the first tale he had turned to because of what Signora Pagano had told him earlier, when he closed the book with a crack.

One little piece had fallen into place. Even if it wasn't the most important, it gave him the expectation of more important ones to come.

❧

19 THE next morning he was jarred out of sleep by the phone.

"I thought I'd make it my responsibility to wake you this morning," the Contessa said. "Ever since you told Natalia she didn't have to come in until noon, I've had fears you'll sleep the whole day away."

"My God, Barbara," he said, squinting at the clock, "it's not even seven-thirty!"

"That's precisely my point, *caro*. More industrious souls are up and about at six."

Urbino, who needed at least an hour and three coffees before he could function in the morning, began to tell her listlessly about his visits of the previous day, starting with his trip to the Europa e Regina to see Voyd. By the time he had described his conversation with Rodolfo Tasso he was more alert but yearning desperately for his first cup of coffee.

"Haven't you been the sleuth! What do you make of it all?"

"Not much yet, I'm afraid, except for one thing, something I realized late last night." He sat up in bed. "Giulietta Pagano said her children used to taunt poor Carlo with the song from "I due gobbi." Maybe you know it. It's not much more than a list of the days of the week." He cleared his throat and, with the realization that this might be a small way of paying her back for her early morning call, recited in a high-pitched voice that he hoped was suggestive of an old woman's, " 'Saturday, Sunday, Monday, and Tuesday.' "

"What's come over you, Urbino, have you—?"

"But in Italian, of course," he said, savoring the Contessa's confusion, "it's 'sabato, domenica, lunedì, e martedì.' "

She took in her breath sharply.

"I see what you mean—or I think I do!"

"I made a simple enough mistake although it was really Giulietta Pagano who did. She passed it on to me. I should have picked up on it when she said that Maria told Carlo that things would be different for them after Sunday. What she must have heard was not that but something about this woman Domenica."

"But what does it mean?"

"Just what I kept asking myself last night as I tossed and turned. By the time I finally got to sleep, I convinced myself of what it must be. Maria must have meant that after she saw Domenica— after she talked with her—there would be a change of some kind. I don't believe Giulietta Pagano caught everything Maria said but Maria thought she did because she was embarrassed. It was probably nervousness at being overheard."

"Do you think that Maria was waiting for this woman at San Gabriele? That might mean . . ."

"That this Domenica killed her," Urbino finished for his friend. "If we find her we'll find the murderer."

The Contessa's response wasn't what he expected.

"Now I shall let you indulge your interest in Beatrice Galuppi to your heart's content. I thought you might be falling in love with her—posthumously of course. I don't think I would have shown you her photograph even if I had had one."

Despite her little joke, there was an unmistakable nervous edge to her voice. Obviously uncomfortable, she was probably relieved that they were speaking over the telephone instead of face-to-face.

"The fact that no one except Marietta seems to have heard of this Domenica," Urbino went on, "might be more significant than if her name were on everyone's tongue. By now she could be as old as Maria was or somewhere in her fifties—that is, if she's still alive herself."

"Mysteries within mysteries," the Contessa said without any of the enthusiasm that had been in her voice at the beginning of her reveille call. He almost expected her to hang up with a perfunctory good-bye, but instead she said, with some of her earlier animation, "But I think you've forgotten that I was going to try to find out when Beatrice's artwork was stolen. It took a trip to the Questura and as much of my charm and the da Capo-Zendrini influence as I was capable of with three absolutely obnoxious officials. And they say the carabinieri are cloddish! Anyway, it appears the Galuppi flat was broken into a week after the flood in sixty-six. Some of Beatrice's sketchbooks and paintings were taken—the copies of the Tintoretto *Presentation* and of the Wedding Cup. Maria didn't report anything else missing. And nothing, it seems, was ever recovered. Obviously Sister Veronica and I didn't know anything about the theft because we were up in Geneva at the clinic with Alvise."

There was no reason why they might not have learned later upon returning but Urbino let it pass. There had been such satisfaction in her voice at having settled at least this personally troubling detail.

"So Cavatorta must have been telling the truth when he said he never saw any of the other things. Maria asked him to look at Beatrice's work sometime between the flood in November and when he left San Gabriele in May."

"Or he could have been misleading you about the period of time."

He could feel her waiting for a response. When it didn't come, she said, "And there's something else. Maybe you'll be more impressed with what I've been able to accomplish. I also saw the report on Beatrice Galuppi's death."

His silence now was one of surprise.

"I was alone in the room for a good ten minutes. There were folders on Maria and Beatrice in the same tray as the one about the theft. There might even have been one on Carlo too but I'm not sure. I didn't have time to look through everything."

"It's strange for all the Galuppi files to have been out like that unless someone at the Questura has been reviewing Beatrice's file along with the others. Maria's murder is closed. Why would Beatrice's file be of interest to them?"

"Do you think someone wanted me to see it?"

"What did it say?"

"I read what I could as quickly as possible. As we already know, Beatrice was found in the toilet of the Galuppi flat in November of fifty-four, the fifth, I think it was. The autopsy found a massive dose of arsenic in her system, introduced"—her voice dropped as she added—"vaginally. There was a bruise on her forehead but it wasn't a death wound. It was from when she fell to the floor. According to the medical report Beatrice was a suicide and she *wasn't* pregnant."

She paused to give him a few moments to take this in but he sensed that she didn't expect or want a response quite yet.

"If she had been pregnant," she went on, "there might have been some question that her death had been caused by an abortion attempt."

"But it doesn't make sense. Even if she had been pregnant,

injecting arsenic is not one of your usual ways of bringing on an abortion, is it? You don't think she wanted her death to look like an attempted abortion, do you?"

"Why? So her mother could have been spared the shame of having a daughter who committed suicide by having instead one who died while trying to give herself an abortion? There's another possibility. She wasn't pregnant but thought she was."

"But why arsenic?"

"Maybe she didn't know it was arsenic." She gave a sigh of exasperation. "There are too many question marks and maybes involved to suit me. They didn't even find any trace of arsenic in the toilet, no pills, no vials, no syringe—just the poor girl herself."

"Who found her?"

"Maria."

Urbino tried to imagine what that moment of discovery had been like for Maria. What did she think had happened? Did she call the police right away? Had Carlo been with her? He was so lost in these thoughts that he didn't realize at first that the Contessa was saying something.

"Are you still there, Urbino? I was asking what was on your sleuthing agenda for today."

"I thought I'd go to Murano. Marietta said that Maria went there the first week of every November." He stopped and took in his breath. "My God, I just realized! There's that November date again!"

"Maybe we'll find out why it keeps popping up when we go to Murano."

"We?"

"Yes, we. Elsa is doing my hair at ten so the morning is impossible. If I ring up Angela, however, I'll be available for the afternoon. Shall we say about twelve-thirty here? We'll have Milo take us over in the boat. I haven't been using it much lately and he feels a bit neglected. I dare not tell him that if it were a gondola he couldn't get me out of it!"

❦

20 THE Contessa's motor launch left the Sacca della Misericordia and headed toward Murano. Off to their right was the cemetery island with its brick walls and cypresses. The early February sun had broken through the clouds and the lagoon shimmered ahead of them toward Burano, Torcello, and the other islands.

"If Beatrice didn't commit suicide, couldn't she have been killed by the woman she was involved with?" the Contessa asked, breaking the long but not uncomfortable silence between them.

Urbino had been staring back at the Fondamenta Nuove and trying to pick out Benedetta Razzi's building.

"So you've become reconciled to the possibility that Beatrice could have been having a relationship with another woman? You felt differently a few days ago."

"That was before I read about a Sapphic nun from seventeenth-century Tuscany. After that I'm receptive to just about anything on the topic."

She buried her hands deeper into the sleeves of her sable coat until she seemed to be hugging herself and peered through the window of the cabin. They said nothing more on the short crossing to Murano until they reached the quay in front of the superimposed arcades of the Basilica of San Donato.

"I'm still not completely convinced, though," the Contessa said with a touch of belligerence.

"I didn't think you ever could be."

Urbino helped her on to the steps of the quay.

Inside the Veneto-Byzantine church there was much to remind him of Maria. It wasn't only the relics of San Donato enshrined with the bones of the dragon that legend said he had slain but also the baroque statue of San Teodoro on the high altar. The mosaic peacocks and cockerels on the floor even had him thinking of Beatrice's lovebird.

"Yes, I knew Maria Galuppi, God rest her soul," the old sexton told them by the baptistery door in the almost empty church. "She came every November, around the Day of the Dead, even insisted I open when we were *in restauro*. She would stay five, ten minutes, say a prayer, go behind the altar there to pay her respects to our San Donato. Hardly ever said a word to me or anyone else but she always would light a candle and leave something for *i poveri*."

"What about the pastor?," Urbino asked. "Did he have any contact with her?"

"None that I ever saw. She never came to Mass or went to the rectory. She would come in, pray, then leave. Always alone."

"Do you know why she came?"

The old man looked offended.

"Our church is very beautiful. What more reason?" Looking at the Contessa, he added more softly, "But it might have been because of *il Giorno dei Morti*. As I said, she always came around then. Maybe she was remembering her dead."

Before they might ask him anything else he turned and went back into the baptistery.

21 THE iridescent lump of molten glass at the end of the long tube started to swell from the force of the *maestro's* lungs and then to take gradual, miraculous shape. Around him his workmen were fashioning what looked like vases, putting pieces of the glass paste on places the *maestro* indicated when he paused briefly from his own work.

They looked like brawny priests officiating before a glowing altar, the object of their devotion an indestructible dish filled with the burning substance only they could magically transform into all the myriad shapes of creation.

Urbino looked over at the Contessa. Surely she must have seen this dozens of times before, as he had himself, but to judge by the expression on her face you would think it was the first time.

The *maestro*, within a remarkably short period of time and with the help of only his imagination, a spatula, and a pair of pincers, formed his paste into a delicate swan.

Something out of nothing, Urbino thought as the glassmaker put the swan in the cooling gallery with numerous other little animals, vases, ashtrays, and candlesticks. Then he turned to his two visitors with an inquisitive look on his broad, flushed face.

"Signor Macintyre and I have come to Murano for information," the Contessa said in her unaccented Italian. "You are the first of the *maestri* we're speaking with."

Because the Contessa was well known on Murano through her contributions to the Glass Museum and her patronage of the glass factories, they had decided she would be the one to ask the *vetrai* most of the questions. The smile that came over Bartolomeo Pignatti's face showed how right they had been. It was as if she had paid him the highest compliment.

"I will do what I can, Contessa, but what information could I have that might be of interest to you?"

"It's about Maria Galuppi."

"*Sì, la poverina,* but I don't understand."

He took a handkerchief from his back pocket and wiped the sweat from his forehead. He was a good-looking man in his late forties with curly black hair and a trim moustache. His sleeves were rolled up to reveal well-developed arms with several scars that looked as if they were from burns.

"We would like to settle some things about her life so she can rest in peace. We've learned that she came to Murano regularly."

"*Sì,* Contessa, regularly but not often." He stuffed the handkerchief back into his pocket. "Every November like the *festa* of a saint."

"She came to see you?"

"And before me my father and most of the other *vetrai* as well. We would talk about it among ourselves. She had the same business with us all. She came to ask questions, Contessa, just like you. And always the same ones, one November after another. Did we know a girl or woman named Domenica? Never any last name and she never could tell us what this Domenica looked like. Did this Domenica ever buy from our factory a crystal dove, a *cocorita*? Did we make such things back in the fifties? She would describe it so well that I could see it in front of me every time—small, fragile, with ruffled wings, the kind of thing you learn how to do when you first begin. I have made such *uccellini* myself but never one with an elegant 'D' on the bottom."

"And she came every November, you said."

"*Sì,* for more than twenty years—and always the first week, even at the time of the big flood."

"Did you know her daughter?"

"Beatrice? More's the pity! But I heard of her although I was just a boy at the time." He didn't meet the Contessa's eyes. "My friend Alberto has an older brother, Vittorio, who was *innamorato pazzo* but it did him no good."

"Did Maria ever mention Beatrice when she came?"

"Not that I heard, only questions about this Domenica and the glass dove. She was determined to find out what glassworks the trinket came from. She was sure it was from Murano. If only I could have examined it, there might have been a chance, who knows?" He shrugged. "But it was gone, she said, she didn't have it any longer. I told her I would make her another free of charge but this didn't please her at all. Sometimes she would be angry when she left us but she would always be back again the next year."

One of the workmen asked Pignatti to come over to the furnace.

"You'll have to excuse me. I hope I've been of some help. Let me give you a suggestion. After you've talked with some of the other glassmakers you should visit Caterina Zanetti farther along the

Fondamenta dei Vetrai toward San Pietro Martire. She knows a lot about Murano—at least the Murano of many years ago. Her name isn't on the bell but look for the name of her nephew, Agostinelli."

Going from the chill wind blowing off the lagoon to the heat of the glass factories and then back again gave them no new information but the feeling that if they continued it for much longer they might find themselves confined to their beds for a week.

"Get me to the nearest restaurant," the Contessa said as they stepped out onto the quay again. "I don't care what it's like."

Buffeted by the wind, they went along the quay toward a restaurant they had passed a few minutes before. The shop windows were crowded with gaudy and cheap-looking glass objects meant to catch the eye and open the pocketbook of tourists determined to bring back something—anything—from the island of glass before the next boat left. Only occasionally was there something that might have tempted them to linger for a few moments if the weather had been better—an elegant chandelier or chain lamp hanging above all the trinkets, goblets of milk-glass filigree, fragile little cups, bowls, and salt cellars. But they hastened toward the haven of the restaurant, not even bothering to heed the warning of the soiled *menu turistico* taped to the window. They managed to satisfy themselves with simple *frittate* and a bottle of red wine and talked about everything else but glass and Maria Galuppi.

22 CATERINA Zanetti, a thin, papery-skinned woman who looked at least as old as the century itself, was propped up with pillows in an overstuffed chair by her bedroom window. The chair was positioned so that she could see what was reflected in the little mirror affixed to the outside of the window.

On a small table next to her were a Bible, an empty glass, and a half-empty bottle of grappa.

"So pleased to see you both," she said in an almost inaudible voice, pushing stray strands of white hair back under her cap. She was seeing Urbino and the Contessa for the first time but was treating them as if she had known them for years. "Can my niece get you anything?"

"*Non grazie*, Signora Zanetti," the Contessa said. "All we will trouble you for is your knowledge. We were told that you're the person to see if we want to know anything about Murano."

Signora Zanetti gave a self-satisfied smile.

"What do you want to know? I can tell you all about the Palazzo da Mula and San Pietro Martire and the dragon of San Donato. Or maybe you want to know about the Golden Book of Families or the Room of the Mirrors in the Glass Museum." Her voice was getting stronger as she went on. "Or maybe about how the daughters of the glassmakers were allowed to marry into the Venetian aristocracy?"

She looked at them expectantly.

"Not about any of those things, Signora, but about something much more recent. We would like to know about Maria Galuppi."

"*Una brutta morta.*" The old woman shook her head and sighed.

"Did you know that she came to Murano every November?"

"*Mariavergine! Certo!* I would see her in my mirror."

"Did she ever visit you?"

"Never, but Lodovico Pignatti was my good friend, God rest his soul. He would say, 'Caterina, she came again.' No need to ask who 'she' was. Always the first week of November, always the same questions about a woman and a glass bird. I would say, 'Lodovico, tell her to stay away, tell her you will call her on the telephone next year if you happen to remember this woman.' But he was a *gentiluomo*, was Lodovico. He wouldn't stop seeing her even though I told him he might end up *morto.*"

She looked at them both sharply to see the effect of her words, then reached for the grappa. Urbino poured her some. Without thanking him except for a nod, she downed it quickly.

"I was right, you see. He died three weeks after one of her visits. *I polmoni.*"

She tapped her chest with a withered hand. "He knew what I was talking about! One time didn't he get the influenza twenty-four hours after she came? And another time didn't his granddaughter have a miscarriage a week later? Then back in November of sixty-six, right after the flood, his showroom burned down, the most beautiful one on the Fondamenta dei Vetrai. He had just remodeled it. I helped him with some of the historical touches. There were new cases and mirrors, a parquet floor, an old map of Murano, a framed, handwritten quotation about the glassmakers from that ugly little man D'Annunzio, photographs of his family, friends, workers, apprentices, famous visitors to the factory—oh, so many nice things! And almost all destroyed in an hour! I saw the flames in my mirror. Poor Lodovico was never the same. I told him to redo it just the way it was before but he didn't have the heart. I think he was afraid the same thing would happen again. Although the police and insurance people said it was an accident, he argued it was arson until the day he died. But believe me—it was Maria Galuppi!"

She picked up her glass and held it out for Urbino to refill. More grappa seemed to be the only reward she wanted for having given them the benefit of her knowledge.

❧

23   "SO it was a glass bird all along," Urbino said as the boat headed back to the Cannaregio and they went over again what they had learned on Murano. The day had returned to clouds brought in by the wind, darker ones this time that threatened rain before long. "No one seems to have seen it,

which might mean that if she wore it around her neck she kept it concealed. But what do you think happened to it?"

The Contessa, who had slipped into a reflective mood since leaving Caterina Zanetti, looked back at him blankly.

"Maybe Beatrice didn't lose it as she thought," he went on. "Couldn't Maria have taken it herself to punish her daughter? Or maybe she wanted to examine it more closely or show it to someone who might now not even want to admit having seen it." He considered this latter possibility for several moments, going over in his mind the different responses to his question about Beatrice's lovebird. Deciding to think it through at another time he turned to the question of dates.

"Remember how you said yesterday that we might learn why the month of November keeps coming up—Beatrice's death, Maria's visits to Murano, the burglary of the Galuppi apartment? Well, we didn't, but we did find out that something else happened then—Lodovico Pignatti's showroom burned down. And it was in the November of the flood, the same November that Beatrice's artwork was stolen."

The Contessa was looking out the cabin window at San Michele. She drew her sable coat more closely around her and finally said something, but not anything he expected.

"Do you want to be buried on San Michele?"

"That's a morbid thought," he said, wondering if she had even been listening to him.

"I guess it's brought on by all this talk of death. And don't forget we've been there twice in less than a month."

"Don't you visit Alvise's grave?"

"Not anymore. Seeing my own name and birth date next to his disturbs me too much."

Although Urbino had never been to the da Capo-Zendrini mausoleum with the Contessa, he had sought it out one day with the help of a man from the cemetery office. It was an imposing structure with somber iron doors, two weeping angels, and statues of Catherine of Siena and Nicholas of Bari. He had found it romantic with its cracked, discolored marble and overhanging cypress but he could understand how disquieting it might be for his friend to see the empty space waiting for her own death date.

"There's the family plot back in New Orleans, of course, but I think I could see myself on San Michele, one among all the other foreigners who died at Venice."

"Don't be silly," she said as the boat slipped into the Misericordia Canal and the cemetery was lost to view. "Half of them probably had no choice and the other half had some grim notion of finally having a *pied-à-terre* in Venice. You've already got that."

This ended the brief discussion between them and they said no more for the rest of the trip. When they reached the Ca' da Capo-Zendrini, Urbino declined the Contessa's offer of a drink or the convenience of continuing on in the boat and set out for home on foot.

At the Palazzo Uccello a tearful Natalia was in the upstairs hall with an *agente di polizia*. She hurried over to Urbino and put her hand on his arm.

"Signor Macintyre, it's not my fault! I came at my usual time, maybe a few minutes later than usual, that's all. I didn't—"

But he didn't wait for her to explain. He hurried down the hall to the library. Before he went through the door, he knew what he would find or—more precisely—what he wouldn't. The room was a mess of scattered books and papers, of pulled-out drawers and gaping shelves. Someone had been in a big hurry and hadn't bothered to be neat.

He went to the shelf where he had put the Venice notebook, having slipped it in the space above two of Margaret Quinton's novels. For the first time in his life he cursed his passion for order.

❧

24 A quick call to the Contessa brought Milo within minutes to take him to the Questura but when they entered the Grand Canal from the Rio della Maddalena Urbino asked to be brought to the Europa e Regina first. The Questura could wait for as long as it would take to tell Voyd in person what had happened to the notebook the writer had entrusted to him.

A heavy rain had started but Urbino was oblivious to it.

Whoever stole the notebook had known or feared that there was incriminating evidence in its entries. As far as Urbino was concerned, its theft was yet one more argument for Carlo's innocence and even against the theory that Maria might have been killed during the snatching of Santa Teodora's body. He hoped that Commissario Gemelli would see the sense of this.

He assumed he had not misplaced his trust in the Contessa's discretion. He was less sure about Voyd, however, given his garrulity, although the writer certainly must know how important the notebook could be in relationship to Maria's murder.

That left Kobke. Maybe he was prejudiced against the Dane because of his supercilious manner but he seemed the most likely person to have said something in spite and anger before leaving for Florence. He remembered how much Kobke had disapproved of his taking the notebook.

After breaking the news to Voyd, he would broach the topic of Kobke. Perhaps without his young friend around, the writer would be more inclined to speak frankly about him.

When Milo left him off at the hotel landing, Urbino told him he could go back to the Ca' da Capo-Zendrini. After talking with Voyd, he would walk the rest of the way to the Questura despite the rain.

The door of Voyd's suite had a *Non disturbi* sign. After a few moments of wondering what he should do, he rang the bell.

When there was no response, he rang again. Perhaps Voyd was dozing or couldn't get up easily from the sofa. When there was still no answer, he turned the knob. The door opened silently. The writer must have left it unlocked to avoid getting up for room service now that Kobke was away.

Urbino stepped into the foyer.

"Mr. Voyd? Are you here? It's Urbino Macintyre."

There was no answer. He continued through the foyer to the sitting room. Once again the first thing he saw was the white baroque facade of Santa Maria della Salute, this afternoon slashed by driving lines of rain.

The second thing was Voyd lying just as before on the sofa—except that this time he had a small hole in his forehead.

The poor man's mouth was open as if he were about to say something or had just finished.

Part Four

THE BONES
OF VENICE

1 "NOT only do you refuse to come here in the police boat," Commissario Gemelli said several hours later, "but you don't even come directly. On the way you make a detour and discover a dead body. And now you're telling me that this man's death has something to do with the murder of Maria Galuppi! Need I remind you again that the case is closed?"

"I know it sounds incredible, but when you consider that Voyd was murdered and Margaret Quinton's notebook was stolen within hours of each other—"

"Even if I agree that there might be a connection between the two—other than yourself—there's no way you can convince me they're related to the Galuppi affair."

"But Voyd told me himself that Maria Galuppi and Margaret Quinton had become friendly, perhaps even to the point of exchanging confidences. I'm sure that if you looked at her letters to Voyd, you'd find—"

"I'd find, perhaps"—he stressed the word—"that this Quinton and Maria Galuppi were acquainted, that they took coffee together on occasion, that they might even have taken a picnic basket to Torcello in good weather."

"And there's another thing," Urbino went on, deciding it best to ignore Gemelli's sarcasm. "Voyd mentioned only yesterday that

Quinton had made some entries about Maria in her notebook. Voyd and his friend Kobke—"

"Now there you might have something. He's being brought back from Florence later tonight. There was more to that relationship than met the eye. They had a whole suite to themselves and Voyd paid for everything, even down to newspapers and gratuities. And there was an incident at the hotel restaurant a few nights ago, a heated exchange about a young American woman."

"Adele Carstairs?"

"We don't know her name. Why do you mention this Carstairs woman?"

"She's Margaret Quinton's niece. They've all been seeing a lot of each other."

"Yes, I remember the name now. She was very cooperative about her aunt's possessions at the Casa Silviano. Could it be that Kobke and Signorina Carstairs are on especially good terms? From what the headwaiter said Voyd was upset with his friend for always being at the Danieli when he was needed elsewhere. They had some words after the young woman left the table. I believe Signorina Carstairs is staying at the Danieli?" When Urbino didn't say anything, Gemelli smiled. "Why are you so shy of someone else's theories, Signor Macintyre? Would Signorina Carstairs wreck your own house of cards? There are many different kinds of crimes of passion, you know."

2   THREE days later at four-thirty in the afternoon, Adele Carstairs, in a black dress with a beige lace collar, sat on the sofa in the small parlor of the Palazzo Uccello. Above her was a Bronzino the Contessa had given Urbino several years ago. The tautness and look of restrained inner agitation of the Florentine

lady, in her pearls and brocade, mirrored those of the young American woman to an extent that was almost comical—even down to the way their long, thin fingers were splayed in their laps. Kobke, more casual than usual in a Missoni pullover in brown, beige, and blue, was pacing back and forth in front of the closed doors to the balcony. When he saw Urbino, he strode across the room to him.

"At last, Mr. Macintyre," he said as if he had been kept waiting for hours. "We have very little time."

Urbino took the young woman's hand.

"It's good to see you again, Miss Carstairs."

"I wish the circumstances were different. The last time we saw each other it was with dear Clifford—" She reached in her pocketbook for a handkerchief and dabbed at her eyes.

When Kobke looked at her sharply, she slipped the handkerchief back into her purse.

"It was Adele's idea to come here this afternoon. I'm not sure that fool of a commissioner would approve."

"He had to be that way with you, Christian."

"That way with me! He had me there for three hours asking the same questions over and over again! I wouldn't even repeat some of the things he asked about Clifford."

To Urbino's surprise Kobke colored.

"Don't forget he had me there for an hour myself. We shouldn't criticize him for doing his job so thoroughly."

"I'm not talking about thoroughness. I'm talking about indiscretion."

"But how is he going to find out who killed poor Clifford unless he asks all kinds of questions? Besides, Christian, what's indiscreet for you might not be for a Latin."

Kobke turned away and went over to the balcony doors, pulling aside the drape to look down into the garden.

"Christian has been through a great deal, Mr. Macintyre. They told him he couldn't stay at the Europa e Regina any longer. The suite was closed off for a day, then there was a problem about the bill, so we thought he would move to the Danieli. He'll leave for Vienna as soon as he can. I'm sure something can be worked out with the Hotel Sacher." She glanced nervously over at Kobke.

Vienna in winter, Urbino thought, not the best time for love under the lindens but yet it might indicate some finer discrimination. He was about to ask what had brought her to Vienna when she went on.

"Clifford owned the flat in Knightsbridge, you see, and poor Christian doesn't know if he'll be able to get his things—there's lots of clothes and artwork—let alone stay there. Of course, we'll both go to London for the memorial service whenever that will be, but—"

"How you do run on, Adele dear," Kobke said, dropping the drape and turning back to them. "I am sure Mr. Macintyre has little interest in our plans. Don't you think you should tell him why you came?"

Urbino asked if they would like something to drink but Kobke declined for them both and gave his companion a pointed stare. She opened her purse and took out some folded sheets of paper.

"Here, take these," she said to Urbino.

There were six or seven sheets, some lined, others blocked in the Continental manner, covered with a small, crabbed handwriting, with a lot of deletions and insertions. A three-by-five file card almost slipped to the floor.

"That's the very last of Aunt Margaret's writings, Mr. Macintyre."

"But why are you giving them to me?"

"My thoughts exactly, Mr. Macintyre," put in Kobke.

Adele Carstairs looked embarrassed.

"I thought you might keep them for a while. Look them over, do what you want with them. The truth is that I'm almost afraid to have them myself after what happened to you and Clifford. Don't get the wrong impression. I certainly don't want to put you in a delicate or—God forbid—dangerous situation, but I thought you might be able to do some good with them. As I mentioned the other day, I didn't read most of the things I came across and now I have an aversion to them. You showed such an interest in Aunt Margaret's writing and Clifford did give you the notebook"—she stirred uneasily on the sofa, pointedly not looking at Kobke, who was standing with his arms folded across his chest and a long-suffering expression on his face—"so I thought that giving them to you was the sensible thing to do. I haven't told anyone about all this."

"Except me, of course," Kobke said, breaking his pose to walk across the room and sit on the sofa. He took the young woman's hands in his. "And I advised a safe-deposit box or—even better— just ripping them up and throwing them into a canal. You see, Mr. Macintyre, there's something you don't know. It explains why Adele is so worried about those papers. Most of Quinton's writings were taken from the suite at the Europa e Regina, also some of Clifford's letters to her, the ones he collected from the Casa Silviano last month. Nothing else was missing—no money, nothing. We can't delude ourselves any longer that Clifford's murder didn't have something to do with Quinton's writing."

He looked at Urbino levelly.

"And Quinton's letters to him? Did he have any of them here in Venice?"

"Those letters couldn't have been stolen even if Clifford's flat in Knightsbridge had been broken into. He burned them in December, every single one! I was there when he did it. But don't get the wrong idea, Mr. Macintyre, he wasn't singling out Quinton's letters for the fire. He threw all the ones he had into it. It was a big roaring blaze."

"But I don't understand."

"It was part of an agreement he made with his correspondents. He wanted them to destroy all his letters and he would do the same with theirs. Clifford had a horror of the biographer." He allowed himself a slight smile as he said this. "He wanted to make things as difficult as possible."

"Did your aunt destroy Voyd's letters?"

"Obviously not, Mr. Macintyre," Kobke answered for her. "As I recall, the topic came up at your friend the Contessa's party. Clifford had just taken dozens of his letters from the Casa Silviano. I'm sure that none of his correspondents was so foolish as to have destroyed any of his letters. I certainly didn't. Clifford wrote the most magnificent ones."

"I know nothing of all this," Adele Carstairs said. "I do know that Aunt Margaret and Clifford wrote a great many letters to each other since they first met here in Venice—more than thirty years of correspondence." She sighed, perhaps at the thought of a relationship of such length ending so sadly for them both in the place where it had begun. "So, then, Mr. Macintyre, you will take those things? Even though you realize that—that there's perhaps some connection between my aunt's writing and Clifford's death? Who knows? There might be something there that could be of help. I suppose I could have offered them to the police but that commissioner would probably have thought I was ridiculous. Besides, somehow it didn't seem quite right." She stood up. "We must be going. We've imposed on you long enough. I'll be at the Danieli until the end of the week. After that you can contact me at the Hotel Sacher in Vienna."

"Before you go, Miss Carstairs, I'd like to ask you something about your aunt. I hope you don't consider it impertinent or disrespectful but I'm sure you will realize how important it is. Do you believe your aunt killed herself?"

Where he had expected a moment, however brief, indicating reflection, perhaps regret or reluctance, she answered him immediately with an unblinking look.

"It pains me to say it, Mr. Macintyre, but yes. She made two other attempts. One before I was born, about fifty-one or fifty-two. She had come back to Schenectady to settle her father's affairs after he died. The second time was fifteen years later in Tangier where she was staying with friends and working on a travel book. So when I got the call in Vienna, my first thought was that she had succeeded at last, God rest her soul. You see, Mr. Macintyre, my aunt might have been a very talented woman, someone whose work will live long after her, but it wasn't enough to keep her going. She gave up a long time ago. She needed something more and never found it."

When she finished, she smiled bravely, not for Urbino but for her Danish companion who was already putting an arm around her shoulders.

3 URBINO was determined not to make the same mistake twice. He would sit down and read what Adele Carstairs had just given him. And when he finished, he would lock it in the safe, something he should have done with the Venice notebook.

After telling Natalia she could leave for the day, he went to the library, put the third act of *Tristan und Isolde* on the turntable, and settled into the Brustolon armchair with some Corvo within arm's reach on the large convent table, cluttered with books and papers he hadn't yet restored to their proper places. As the shepherd's horn sounded—inspired by the lugubrious cry of the gondolier— he started to read, slowly at first.

He gradually became accustomed to the scribbled corrections and the intricacies of Quinton's script and was able to read more quickly. The first few sheets were filled with various observations, all of them rather brief and most about Venice.

In Venice, actually Murano, they invented the mirror, not to mention quite a few other things, but I keep thinking about mirrors, always mirrors. The reason isn't far to find, not with all this water, all these surfaces reflecting and distorting. The

Italian for "a stretch of water" is *uno specchio d'acqua*—"a mirror of water"—and "to be as clean as a new pin" (something I devoutly wish for!) is "to be as clean as a mirror"—a much better image.

There must be dozens of mirrors here in this apartment. Did Signora Razzi take all the mirrors from her other buildings and put them here? Does she have any in her own apartment? What frightens me isn't that they reflect all my lines, my graying hair, my haggardness, my fading blue eyes, showing all the years I've lived and making me apprehensive of the ones still to come. No, it isn't that although sometimes I think it is. But last night I realized it was something much different. When I went to fix my hair in the ormolu mirror in the hall, I was afraid that when I looked it wouldn't be me, that my features would have changed and I wouldn't even recognize the person I saw. There looking back at me would be a stranger.

Cannaregio (also Canareggio, Cannareggio): bamboo district, region of cane, region of bamboo. Sounds more like a quarter in an Oriental city, but of course Venice does have an Oriental aspect, doesn't it?

Why not say to him: Just look at a map of Venice or look down on the city from a plane. Does it look like a lute? two fish swallowing each other? a whale? two hands interlocked? or does it really look like a distorted, broken heart?

Yesterday at the Accademia I assured myself that I was safe. Not only might I observe without becoming any more involved than I wanted to be but there was a point beyond which—no matter what my intentions—it was impossible for me to go. There was certainly little chance I might find myself within the frame, surrounded by all that old polished wood. Wasn't that the stuff of Oriental tales and of imaginations much more vivid than my own?

Can there be one single solitary day untinged with melancholy in this city? I doubt it and I don't think I would wish it. I've been melancholy (lovely word!) elsewhere but never with such pleasure.

My conversation last night makes me think that there might be a story in it somewhere. Or maybe not in what Maria told me but in this: Somewhere there exists a lost Tintoretto on the theme of the theft of the body of Santa Teodora from Sicily, and a man (but why not a woman?) is obsessed with finding it. She can't and commissions a fake.

She looked up at the ceiling. From below upwards the figures seemed to be floating in space above her head, swimming against a blue that receded from her eyes the more she looked at it. *Sotto in su,* from below upwards, she remembered from the guide. If only one's own life could be seen from this kind of distance so that all the cumbersome and embarrassing shapes and memories floated freely as if they were filled with a hydrogen that didn't just make them light but gave them a luminosity, too. And then she remembered— hydrogen exploded, didn't it?

How about this for my historical novel? The story of the sailors from the Lido who went to Alexandria to steal the body of St. Mark and hid it beneath a pile of pork. Would this be more interesting than something on the glassblowers of old Murano?

When the weather gets better, I want to make a circuit of some of the islands in the lagoon, those I've already seen and others. Not just San Michele crowded almost obscenely with its graves or Murano that always seems to smoke and smolder in my imagination but Burano, home of lace, also green and silent Torcello, San Francesco del Deserto with its friars, and all those *isole del dolore* dedicated to the care of the insane, the leprous, the tubercular. One of them used to be set aside for the sick pilgrims who wandered and searched for cures at whatever shrines they chose to believe in.

Murano. You hear the name and think of glass: *avventurine, reticelli, millefiori, lattisuol, retortoli,* beautiful, romantic names. But thinking of glass I think of death. Death and glass are sisters. The fragility of the glass, the frozen deathlike stare of all those little animals and ballerinas and clowns, the inescapable feeling of death and dying you get when you see all the cheap work. Death and glass at the court of Louis Quatorze where the glassmakers were poisoned after they had rendered up what had kept them alive—their secret of how to make the magical substance. And didn't the Muranesi bring their own form of death into the world when they invented the mirror into which we peer for signs of decay and the inevitable failure of not being the person we used to see there?

These entries covered three sheets, front and back. Even if the entries themselves hadn't made it clear that Quinton had recorded them at different times, the various inks and the marked variation in the handwriting would have. Urbino assumed that the entries were the kind he might have found in the Venice notebook. In fact, she very well might have copied them into the notebook afterward. The other four sheets appeared to have been written all at once or copied from another source.

She was always wandering in some Venice of the heart where she didn't so much lose her way as seem to lose it, to take a turn she thought would lead her away from it all, only to find it confronting her again without any warning when she thought she was far, far away from it. The Campo of Pain, the Piazza of Grief, the House of Loss.

And so it was appropriate that she not only came to Venice after Paris but that she decided to stay awhile. It was easier having arrived in November. There were more rooms, fewer people, and the sense that everything was being protected by fog from something which, though as inevitable as the coming of true winter, would itself pass if one only had patience.

Lillian had patience. Hadn't she shown how much those last weeks in London, especially during that last meeting in Regent's Park? If John hadn't appreciated it, it wasn't for any inability on her part to mark time, to hold herself back from saying and doing what she wanted.

In the end, however, it might have been better if she had had less patience and more of something else she was still trying to name months later.

Even the vaguely Oriental aspect of the city seemed appropriate. She remembered reading in a book when she was hardly more than a schoolgirl that "l'Orient commence à Venise." John was an Arabist and insisted on referring to the Middle East as the Near East, the Orient of old. Their first disagreement had been in a Lebanese restaurant when she had told him she hated the song they were playing, that in fact she hated that kind of music. It never seemed to resolve anything, always seemed to leave things up in the air or to end them on a dying fall. It had only made it worse when John had told her the song was called "From Here Begins an Old Story."

Even then, so close to the beginning, those words had chilled her, had seemed to be a prophecy. And now she felt that they showed their truest meaning here in the serenest city on earth, the city where strange things were supposed to happen to you.

Yes, Lillian said to herself as she wandered the city, yes, at least I know how it's supposed to be. Knowing this prepares me for anything, even for nothing.

She found a room not far from the Zattere. Two or three times a week she went to the Ca' Pesaro to look at Klimt's *Salome*. She knew it was perhaps perverse, this fascination with the Klimt when she had the Tintorettos and Veroneses and Carpaccios all around her. Vienna was certainly a more appropriate place for Klimt. Yet, almost against her will, she was drawn to the painting, associating it with the Salome mosaic in the San Marco Baptistery. It made no difference when she read that Klimt's painting was actually of Judith, for hadn't Judith been responsible for the death of a man, too?

One evening after having been to see the Klimt she was sitting in her room and felt a sudden chill, followed a few minutes later by a burning sensation in her face and a buzzing in her ears. She opened the window for some air despite the chill outside. As she stood at the open window, she looked down into the *calle* and saw a man, perhaps forty, perhaps older. He was leaning against the closed shutters of the pharmacy. Wasn't he the man she had noticed several days before at San Rocco? Wasn't he the one who had lingered for a long time today in front of the Klimt?

When she went out for dinner several hours later, he was still in the *calle*.

What would be the greater mistake? To acknowledge his presence or pretend she didn't notice? She hurried past him, her eyes averted. She was relieved that he didn't follow her but then she saw him again in the Campo Santa Margherita, looking through a café window with a cigarette in his hand and a smile on his face. He must have come from a different direction.

She turned around and hurried back to her room.

The next day, and for days afterward, the papers seemed to be filled with news of death and destruction. Floods and earthquakes, fires and famines, murders and suicides. She read all the articles and then, not satisfied, all the obituary notices. She sought out the death announcements posted in the parishes, scrutinizing the photographs and wondering about the lives of the dead.

She started to go to funeral Masses in the early morning, sometimes hiring a boat to take her in the cortege to the cemetery island.

After a week of not seeing the man anywhere she found herself standing next to him in the back of the Church of the Carmini during a Requiem Mass. He touched her sleeve.

"Ah, you too are interested in the city's dead," he said in English with only the faint trace of an accent.

Lillian rushed from the church. She found a working-class bar by the maritime station where she drank several glasses of wine, trying to understand why she felt not just frightened and threatened but also strangely exhilarated.

The next day she went to the cemetery island again, not as part of a cortege but on her own late in the afternoon.

She didn't see the man at the grave of Pound or the Baron Corvo or Stravinsky but there he was at the tomb of Diaghilev. She noticed him from the far end of the Orthodox section and realized she had known he would be there.

As she approached him, he smiled and picked something up from the top of Diaghilev's tomb. She looked at it, squinting in exaggerated fashion—not in order to see better but because she wanted him to realize she was making an effort to understand, even if it was only this one small detail. She wanted him to see the effort and strain on her face.

"A slipper," he whispered.

Not a glass slipper, but a ballet shoe, moldy and faded, with withered flowers nestling in it as if it were their coffin.

Like the Middle Eastern music mentioned at the beginning, there was no resolution to the story. It just ended.

All that remained was the index card. On it were two numbers and not even a dozen words:

The Death of Domenica—title??
Secondo Fabriani, La Storia di Murano, 137, 192

A few minutes later he phoned the Contessa.
"'The Death of Domenica'? What does it mean?" she asked.
"Your copy of Fabriani might tell us."
"I'm afraid it will have to wait until tomorrow. I'm having an early dinner with Stefano and Angela, then we're joining Sister Veronica for the chamber music concert at La Fenice. We would have asked you to come except that I know how much you dislike Haydn."
"Cancel, Barbara."

"Cancel? At the last minute? I couldn't possibly."

He didn't say anything, knowing that silence, not insistence, was usually the best tactic with her. It shouldn't take her more than a few minutes to realize how important it was that they resolve this new development as soon as possible.

After a few moments she sighed.

"Well, all right, if you really think it can't wait until tomorrow."

"It could, but if it did, I doubt if I'd get any sleep. I'd keep wondering about those pages. Are you familiar with the book?"

"It's one of the ones she borrowed. I read it years ago. I'm afraid I skimmed a lot of it. It's quite a tome."

"Fortunately, Quinton left behind specific page references. I'll be there in half an hour. That should give you time to make your apologies and have the book ready and waiting. Let's hope we can learn something."

4   THE Contessa put the ceramic elephant down on the table with the other animals and asked Urbino to read the passage out loud again.

"There's an engraving by Visentini on the bottom of the page." He held the book up so she could see it. "The only passage she could have been referring to is the one I already read." He started to read it again, this time translating it into English as if this might reveal a facet that hadn't been apparent a few moments before:

The art of glassmaking was most jealously guarded in the Venetian state for the glassblowers knew secrets coveted by other cities and nations. So valued was the art of the glass-makers that they were sometimes given amnesty for serious crimes so that they could continue their precious, secret art. On the other hand, if any of them left the Venetian state, he

was put under immediate sentence of death and was often
sought out and made to suffer this ultimate penalty.

When he finished, the Contessa shook her head.

"Not much there. What about the other reference?"

Urbino turned to the other page Quinton had listed on the card
and skimmed several detailed paragraphs on the glass *maestri*. He
was beginning to think that this reference was also without interest
when he reached the last paragraph. He drew in his breath.

"What is it?"

Without answering, he went over the whole page again, this
time more slowly in case he had missed something, but this
second reading only confirmed the first. The last paragraph was
the only one of importance for them—and had been, he would
think, for Maria Galuppi as well.

"Well, what is it, Urbino?"

Instead of saying anything he read to her in a quiet, unhurried
voice: " 'One of the earliest glassmakers whose name is known to
us is Domenica, an otherwise obscure man alluded to in a
fourteenth-century manuscript.' "

In the moments afterward they could hear the siren of a fire-
boat farther down the Grand Canal. As it faded, the Contessa
stood up quickly, her lap rug falling to the floor.

"Domenica," she said in almost a whisper. "But Beatrice's Domenica was a woman! We're looking for a woman!"

"Are we?" Urbino closed the book and got up. "What we know
is that Maria was looking for a woman, a woman named Domenica. The last time we know she was asking about a woman was
on her annual visit to Murano during the first week of November.
Maybe Maria and Margaret Quinton became friendly sometime
after the first week of November—friendly enough, that is, to
learn something about each other."

He walked back and forth in front of the sofa, his hands thrust
into his trouser pockets.

"Their friendship grew," he went on, "they had many conversations—this we know from Voyd—and somehow during one of those conversations the name Domenica came up. Once it did, especially in reference to Murano, wasn't it only natural for Quinton to tell Maria what she knew about a glassblower from old Murano named Domenica—a Domenica who was a man? The result was that Maria ended up learning a valuable piece of information—after having been misled just as we've been." He looked at the Contessa, his eyes shining. "It's all so neat and logical."

"Perhaps too much so," she said as she settled herself on the sofa again. "This Domenica lived hundreds of years ago. Why does there have to be a link to Beatrice?"

"Remember, the dove was made of glass. If it had been made of anything else, we could consider all this just an oddity, a coincidence."

"In either case, made of glass or not, everyone would assume Domenica was a woman when they heard the name."

A puzzled look came over the Contessa's face, as if she had forgotten exactly what position it was she was arguing.

"Everyone except someone like Beatrice herself. Remember what Rodolfo Tasso said about how much she seemed to know about things Venetian." He thought for a moment. "Of course, she might have picked up this obscure little detail from her Domenica, whoever he was." Before she might correct him he added, "Or whoever he is if he's still alive."

"I don't know. It could still be a woman." She seemed to be finding it hard to relinquish what had been almost impossible for her to accept before. "Quinton's notebook might easily prove you wrong."

"More likely than not it would confirm all this. Or Voyd might have remembered. He said Quinton mentioned Maria in her letters but even those are lost to us."

He quickly explained what Kobke had told him earlier about

Voyd's burning all his correspondence in December back in London.

"But what about letters that might have come afterward?"

"I'll ask Kobke. Some letters might still be around—maybe in London or in Gemelli's hands. Those letters—if they exist—could establish some crucial dates. On her last November visit Maria was asking about a woman. Sometime between then and when she was murdered she might have learned she had been going in the wrong direction, asking the wrong questions. It may have been enough to put her right after all those years. And in finally discovering who Domenica was—a man who might have been someone close to her own age, even a trusted friend, who knows?—she might very well have brought about her own death. This person could have every reason to want to remain unknown. Arsenic is more usually a means of murder, not suicide."

The Contessa stared at him in surprise, then looked down at her lap rug.

"Was there anything in the rest of what you read of her writing that might be of help?"

"It doesn't seem so, although everything was about Venice in one way or another. There was an unfinished story and some random observations and comments—most of it rather melancholy and self-absorbed. It's not hard to see she was suicidal." He paused in his pacing. "There was one thing, though, that might be of importance. She mentioned a conversation she had with Maria. She didn't say what it was about—maybe she put that in the notebook—but she did say there might be a story in it."

The Contessa raised her head and looked up at him.

"Do you think it was about Beatrice? Or this—this Domenica?"

"Perhaps, but in the next sentence she said that a better idea for a story might be a lost Tintoretto on the theft of the body of Santa Teodora from Sicily. Of course, no such Tintoretto exists as far as we know."

She nodded woodenly.

"Could whatever it was that Maria told her and this idea of an unknown Tintoretto have been related in some way?"

"It's possible. And then there's the coincidence of Santa Teodora." He shook his head slowly. "You know, reading only those scraps has made me realize even more why someone might have been willing to kill for the notebook."

❧

5   LATER that night, back at the Palazzo Uccello, Urbino devoted himself to the two books he had brought back from the Contessa's: Fabriani's history of Murano and Martino de Martini's massive study of the art of glassmaking.

After rereading the passage on Domenica he skimmed through the rest of the Fabriani. He indulged himself for a while by first seeking out the chapters that highlighted the intrigue, jealousy, and violence that had glass at their heart, then the sections—this a much gentler tale—of aristocratic dalliance and grand passion played out in the gardens of Murano far from the watchful eyes of Venice. He ended by searching for a familiar name or association among the old Murano glass *maestri*—Barovier, Toso, Ferro, Salviati, Fuga, Seguso.

It was almost midnight before he opened the Martino de Martini book on glassmaking. Several initial chapters about the Saracens, Egyptians, and Romans almost put him to sleep. The chapter on the chemistry of glassmaking was even worse and he started to close the book when a word in a paragraph ahead hooked his eye.

He knew there was now no possibility of his falling asleep soon as he read:

In order to create that much prized emerald green glass in all of its purity and to avoid any undesirable yellowish tone, it is necessary to add tin oxide or arsenic.

6 URBINO left the Palazzo Uccello early the next morning for the Biblioteca Marciana. The sun was breaking through the clouds and it promised to be a nice day. The *calli* were crowded with housewives carrying string shopping bags and plastic baskets filled with groceries. Schoolchildren shouted at each other, deliverymen maneuvered wheelbarrows up and down the bridges, old women stepped carefully alongside their muzzled dogs, and groups of tourists made their way toward San Marco. Although *carnevale* was still more than two weeks away, he encountered several people in masks and was startled when a respectable-looking woman with a Gucci purse pelted him with confetti that fell soddenly to the pavement outside a pastry shop in the Campo Santa Maria Formosa.

While having a coffee in the busy, smoke-filled café under the clock tower, he called Kobke at the Danieli. The Dane, who was about to go to Verona for the day with Adele Carstairs, was less supercilious than usual, his characteristic ironic tone replaced by something like reserve.

"We'll be leaving for the station in half an hour. We could arrange to meet you for a drink here this evening."

"Some other time, thank you. This will take only a few minutes. Yesterday you said that Voyd burned his correspondence in December. Did that include all of Quinton's letters?"

"As far as I know. Why?"

Urbino didn't think it was necessary to go into detail with Kobke. It might not even be prudent. "I wanted to see if she mentioned anything about a project about Murano. There was an entry about it in those sheets."

"Oh." Kobke sounded relieved. "I don't know anything about that. He said he burned everything but he might have held back a letter or two. He didn't get any letters from Quinton after the burning, though. I picked up the mail every day."

"Do you know if Quinton wrote Adele Carstairs from Venice?"

"Adele hardly got any letters from her at all. In fact, they didn't see much of each other in the last five years. She was surprised to get everything—everything, that is, except the royalties on the books. Those went to Clifford. I don't know who they go to now."

As Urbino walked across to the library, he wondered whether Kobke was in Voyd's will. Either way, Urbino was sure he wouldn't languish. Adele Carstairs was going to find it difficult to get rid of him—that is, assuming she wanted to.

As he went up the stairs to the main reading room, he reminded himself that he should find out exactly when the two of them were going up to Vienna. He didn't want them to leave before he had a chance to ask them more questions. At this point he didn't know what those questions might be.

The reading room was overheated and he had some difficulty focusing on the entries made in the card catalogue in ornate handwriting. He eventually found what he was looking for, however— an encyclopedia of poisons. He copied the necessary information on a slip of paper and gave it to the woman at the request counter. When the book finally arrived, after what seemed like an hour, he brought it back to his table and looked in the index under "arsenic."

There was more than he expected.

He learned about the Austrian miners who ate arsenic for strength and about the use of the chemical in papermaking, taxidermy, and—he was relieved to find it confirmed here— glassmaking. He read about the Arab chemist who discovered arsenic in the eighth century and about the large quantities found in Napoleon's body in 1840 when it proved possible to make a second death mask as distinct as the first. He spent many minutes studying a chart of the most famous cases of arsenic poisoning since the seventeenth century and reading detailed accounts of some. His favorite was the nineteenth-century Maybrick case in which the young wife was found guilty of poisoning her husband even though he had been known to consume arsenic in the mistaken belief that it was an aphrodisiac. He familiarized himself with the symptoms of arsenic poisoning—nausea, vomiting, diarrhea, intense thirst, weight and hair loss. He was surprised to learn that arsenic had not only found its way into many cosmetics—women in southern Austria used to swear that it improved their complexions—but that it had also been an ingredient in medicinal tonics recommended by doctors and pharmacists.

Misused, it brought almost certain death, but in the proper hands and with no malevolent intent it was beneficial. If it did not exist people would have had to go without many things until a substitute was found. How many fewer preserved animals and how much less peeling, faded wallpaper in shades and patterns of green would have graced the rooms and offices of his New Orleans youth? Well, perhaps in these instances, he thought to himself with a little smile, it might not have been such a loss after all.

As he closed the book, he considered the implications of several things he had just learned. He needed a drink.

He went to Florian's and on this occasion was happy not to have the company of the Contessa although, as it was, his thoughts frequently carried him in her direction. As he gazed out at the Piazza, flooded by gentle sunlight, his mind played over various pieces of information. It didn't take him long to realize that he had to go back to Murano. But first he had to talk to several people again.

He decided against another Campari soda and struck out for the Cannaregio, savoring the mild weather that they would be lucky to have for even a few more hours. Two gondolas, filled with laughing tourists, glided past each other beneath the Ponte Guerra as he was walking over it. He felt both euphoric and also peculiarly grim. It was a combination of expectation and fear.

He stopped beneath the church campanile in the Campo Santa Maria Formosa. Although he wanted to do what had to be done as quickly as possible, he nonetheless lingered for a few minutes to look at the monstrous leering head at the base of the bell tower, one of many that could be found throughout the city. As he gazed at its flat nose, grossly misshapen mouth, and protruding teeth, he didn't see it so much as Ruskin had—as an emblem of the evil spirit to which Venice was abandoned in the late Renaissance—but as a horribly exaggerated version of Carlo Galuppi.

This must be the way the poor man had looked to the children who had followed him down the alleys and across the squares, taunting and laughing and at times throwing things. Unless the man could be cleared of his mother's murder, this image of him as an ugly soulless monster would be remembered as yet one more grotesque in the already teeming Venetian menagerie of strange beasts.

Urbino vowed to do all he could to prevent this from happening. There was someone who, although not physically deformed, was a monster of a different kind, someone who had murdered Beatrice Galuppi, her mother, and Voyd, and had contributed to Carlo's suicide. Of this he no longer had any doubt. This person might even have played a role in the suicide of Margaret Quinton and might not yet be finished if threatened again with the possibility of exposure after many years of careful concealment.

As he walked across the Campo Santa Maria Formosa, Urbino hoped he would be able to rip the benign mask from this person's face and reveal the monster beneath.

❧

7   "IN my opinion it's a dying art," Don Marcantonio said, "just like the priesthood."
He looked at Urbino over the tops of his round, thick glasses to see if his little joke had been appreciated. They were in his austere parlor, where they had discussed Beatrice Galuppi a week

ago. Perhaps not finding the appreciation he had hoped for in his visitor, Don Marcantonio looked behind Urbino at the lithograph of Saint Lawrence being grilled over the coals. It was a copy of the painting at the Gesuiti. Urbino's own gaze wavered between the old priest's face and the mallard hen and drake next to the candelabra on the darkwood sideboard.

"Young people aren't attracted to either calling anymore," Don Marcantonio added.

"I'm not speaking of the young people today but of thirty years ago," Urbino explained.

The priest shrugged his shoulders.

"When you are as old as I am, you make little distinction between the youth of today and three decades ago. The same applied then. I don't remember anyone from San Gabriele who studied glassmaking. I would have made it a point to know. We might have replaced a few glass items here and there. Sister Veronica hasn't been much use to us in that respect."

"I've seen Luigi Cavatorta about Beatrice Galuppi's paintings."

"Now there you have the opposite side of the coin to no vocations at all. Cavatorta should never have become a priest to begin with. His mother, God rest her soul, is to blame for that. She would get a privileged place in heaven having a son who was a priest. That's what she thought; don't think many of these mothers don't! Now look what's happened to him. *Una vergogna!* That's one mother who should have been more like some of the parents around here who can't decide if it's worse to have a son who's a priest, a glassblower, or a common laborer."

He shook his head and sighed, getting up slowly. It was obvious he considered their conversation over. There wasn't going to be any brandy or tea offered on this occasion.

"I've meant to ask you about your lovely ducks before," Urbino said as they were leaving the parlor. "Where did you have them done?"

"I did them myself a long, long time ago when I had the strength for such things and for traipsing around the lagoon at daybreak."

He stared at Urbino but said nothing more although his eyes flicked in the direction of the sideboard. Perhaps he was aware of just how disquieting it might be for others that a man of the cloth could not only kill animals but also go to not a little trouble to preserve them as trophies. In fact, Urbino wasn't quite sure which of the two acts was more disturbing and—he had to admit—more intriguing.

When Urbino mentioned Sister Veronica as he was about to go through the outer door that Sister Giuseppina held open, Don Marcantonio frowned but there was an element of satisfaction in his voice when he said,

"She's certainly not at Santa Crispina. Our sisters seem to be everywhere but where they should be these days." He looked down at the diminutive Sister Giuseppina. "Murano, isn't it, Sister? The Glass Museum with her little group?"

Sister Giuseppina said nothing but she gave Don Marcantonio a look of disapproval that had the priest backing away from the door and almost forgetting to say good-bye to Urbino.

❧

8 BENEDETTA Razzi's building was conveniently near the boat station for Murano. The woman, dressed in a faded, floral-print robe frayed along the hem, was holding her Tyrolean doll when she answered his ring.

"I wondered when you would be back, young man," she said as she looked up at him flirtatiously through the bristles of her false eyelashes. "Come in, come in."

She shuffled ahead in her worn slippers and eased herself into the love seat crowded with dolls.

"Does death or suicide bring you here this time?"

"Signorina Quinton."

"You lost interest in Beatrice and the Galuppi family?"

"Not at all. What I have to ask might have some bearing on the deaths of *all* the Galuppis."

"My! It must be a very difficult question then—or a difficult answer." She looked down at the doll cradled in her arm and said into its face, "Can we manage it, *amore mio*? You see," she said, turning back to Urbino, "last night was as bad as the others. My sweethearts and I spent most of the night with open eyes. So if it's a complicated question you have, we might not be up to it." She set the doll down on her lap.

"I don't mean to be inquisitive, Signora Razzi, and I certainly don't want you to think I'm meddling in your business affairs, but I've learned that there was a locked room at the Casa Silviano."

"Still is one, and always will be," she said a bit defiantly. "That American writer told you."

"Yes, Signor Voyd."

She gave no indication that she had heard of Voyd's murder. If she knew and was pretending not to, he would let her continue with her little game. And if she didn't know, it might be best not to explain that yet another death was associated with the Galuppis and Margaret Quinton.

"What business is it of yours, this room? That was an agreement between the American signorina and me."

Urbino hoped he looked properly chastened.

"Of course it's none of my affair, Signora Razzi, but it's important to know if Signorina Quinton left anything behind in the room." He paused before adding: "Papers, letters, things of that nature."

"She never went in the room! It was locked and it's locked now. Whatever she left behind her niece already has. Why are so many people interested in that dead woman's writing anyway? Was she Dante? D'Annunzio?" A blank look came over her face as she failed to think of a third writer or perhaps one whose name began with the same letter. She stood up, catching the doll before it tumbled to the floor. "It's not right of you to ask me all these questions when you didn't even bring a little something for my darlings this time. The first time I excused you but I was sure you would know better when you came back. I would have put it with their other things." She nodded in the direction of a small tiered table covered with all kinds of tiny trinkets, most of them miniature versions of real objects—little cups and saucers, a menagerie of glass animals, tiny porcelain masks that would fit over a doll's face, miniature books, and even a delicate candelabra with candles no bigger than pencil leads.

"It's quite a collection. I hope you'll forgive me."

He started to make movements to leave but not without feeling that there was still something of importance she might tell him.

"Next time I'll bring you something special."

"Not for me, remember, but for my sweethearts," she said as she led him to the door, the Tyrolean doll clutched in one hand.

9   THE weather had changed again and the lagoon was wreathed with fog that drifted over the water. Where everything had been golden and sunny only an hour ago, now the dominant color was pearly gray and the wake of the boat opalescent. It wasn't so foggy, however, that they needed someone to watch from the bow and once or twice Urbino was able to glimpse the dim outlines of another craft not far away. Never did the other craft turn out to be a black and gold funeral gondola making its way back from San Michele, but somehow this was what he kept expecting to see, even down to the drooping red chrysanthemums that would be on its bow.

The fog lifted suddenly, but briefly, and the island of glass came into view beyond the stretch of water that now showed as flat and silvery as a mirror. Murano neither smoked nor smoldered as Quinton had said it did in her imagination but for a few moments seemed to beckon him onward. It was soon lost again in a swirl of fog, however, and he was left feeling teased and even mocked.

It took him some time to find Sister Veronica and her group at the Glass Museum. He went up the main staircase to the suite of exhibition rooms, where he passed the showcases displaying the best and the worst of Venetian glass, most of it looking dusty. His own preference was for the crystal-clear items that Murano had prided itself on until seventeenth-century excess took over—cups, dishes, vases, goblets, chalices, ampules, all in simple, delicate designs. As for many of the other things—glass horses and mice, a menagerie of vases, drinking glasses with snake-entwined stems, liqueur bottles fashioned to look like pistols, ceremonial glass trumpets, pagoda-shaped, dolphin-encrusted chandeliers—at least they were better than the even more vulgar objects outside in the shops.

Sister Veronica was in the room with the masterpieces from the fifteenth and sixteenth centuries. She stood with several elderly women and a middle-aged man in front of the glass bell that covered the Barovier Wedding Cup that Beatrice Galuppi had copied scenes from. It was a delicate goblet about nine inches tall with a smooth blue surface decorated with several enameled scenes and portraits: of the bride and groom, a bridal procession on horseback, and a fountain in which several naked young women bathed.

Once again, as he had last week in the Church of San Gabriele, Urbino listened to what Sister Veronica was saying.

"Without question this is the most exquisite piece in the Glass Museum. It was blown and decorated in the second half of the fifteenth century by Angelo Barovier of the distinguished glass-making family. Although it is said to be patterned after a Chinese original brought back to Venice in a caravan, I prefer to think it was the original creation of the Barovier *maestro* himself. Notice its lovely violet-blue color and how perfect, how dramatic its form is. As you can see, depicted around its rim are the aristocratic nuptial couple, the wedding procession, and an allegory of youth. Although the couple for whom it was made are now only dust, it is still here to remind us of their marriage and to show us what heights earthly beauty can reach even in something as lowly and humble as a cup.

"If you would like to make a similar gift yourself, you will find copies in many of the shops here on Murano." She gave an embarrassed smile. "But I assure you I get absolutely no commission if you decide to buy anything later. Before we leave you might want to look at the fragment of a glazed drinking glass from the fifteenth century found in the ruins of the Campanile of San Marco after it fell down in 1902 'like a gentleman,' as it was said, without hurting anyone at all."

When she finished, she smiled at Urbino and came over to him.

"Good morning, Signor Macintyre. Are you here to reacquaint yourself with Venetian glass? Tintoretto is my specialty but you are welcome to join us for the rest of our tour here. You might even give us the benefit of your own knowledge. I'm afraid there are terrible gaps in what I know about glass and glassmaking despite my family background."

"Actually I came to ask you another question or two. As it turns out, it's about the Wedding Cup."

"But I'm afraid you've just heard almost everything I know about it. If it's more detailed information you want, I have a book back at Santa Crispina that you're welcome to look at."

"The information I want is about Beatrice Galuppi's copy of the Wedding Cup. You said it was well done but that she had made changes, had tried to show her originality."

"*You're* the one who mentioned originality, Signor Macintyre." She turned her head to look at her little group, who were gathered in front of the case against the far wall. "It wasn't a complete copy but only of some of the details: the bride and groom and the scene of the fountain of youth." She looked down at the cup beneath its glass bell. "It's been a long time but yes, I remember that it was well done."

"And the changes?"

"She gave in to some youthful self-indulgence. It was a matter of vanity, *not* originality. Beatrice Galuppi was blessed with beauty but that didn't mean she had to paint her own face instead of the bride's plain one. Always staring into a mirror, she probably was."

"And the groom?"

She laughed but it was a nervous laugh.

"Your guess is right. You would think a vain girl like that would have kept him just as he was. He's very handsome, very aristocratic." They looked down at the Wedding Cup. The imposing profile of the young nobleman with his long brown hair and cap indisputably supported her point. "But she would have her fun."

"What do you mean?"

"The groom's features were somewhat more coarse, the nose less aquiline, maybe even the colors were less true, with redder tones, I'm not really sure. I don't think she took as much care with him. There was something vaguely familiar about his face but I can't say that I recognized it. Maybe I felt that way because it reminded me of those Renaissance profiles of Pico della Mirandola, Lorenzo dei Medici, and Savonarola. But the portrait on the original itself reminds me of them, too. It's in the same style; he even has a cap like the ones you see in those portraits."

"What did Maria say when you told her about the changes?"

Sister Veronica averted her eyes.

"I didn't tell her. I told her the painting was as lovely as the original here. It wasn't really a lie, you see. She only wanted to have her daughter praised. She said that Beatrice was very protective about this particular painting, that she never even wanted her to look at it. Beatrice had once given it or lent it to someone who hadn't taken good care of it. She was in tears when she got it back and she just hid it away. How could I not praise the work? I gave Maria what she wanted, what she needed."

Urbino was tempted to tell her that she had been wrong, that Maria had wanted nothing more nor less than the truth. She had been searching for it for twenty years.

As if she wanted to make up for what she hadn't told Maria twenty years ago, Sister Veronica now said quickly, "But of course nothing could come close to the original, even if Beatrice hadn't indulged herself. It's not just the scenes themselves that make the cup what it is but the shape, the texture, the workmanship. She could never have captured that, no matter how good she was. Have you seen any of her work yourself?"

Urbino shook his head. It might be helpful to try to locate what hadn't been stolen. Had the pieces been in Maria's apartment when she was murdered? And where might they be now?

"Then you have no idea what a talented copyist she was. I know Signor Cavatorta doesn't agree with me, but she had a skilled hand, a fine eye—and she would have been even better, much better, if the Lord hadn't had other plans for her." She seemed eager to repair whatever poor impression she might have given of Beatrice but then she added, "The talented as well as the good can die young."

"What about her copy of the Tintoretto at the Madonna del' Orto?"

"I didn't care very much for it, although I suppose it was good in its way, but I'm inclined to be more demanding when it comes to the divine Tintoretto."

"And the *capriccio*?"

"She approached it too much as a game—juxtaposing scenes from the Cannaregio, the Rialto, and Murano the way she did. There was very little Piranesi in it."

Urbino thanked her and apologized for having taken her away

from her group. Before he left, he walked slowly around the glass bell. As Sister Veronica had said, the Wedding Cup was exquisite. The enameled love scenes and portraits of the bride and groom brought to mind Keats's words—"unravished bride of quietness."

Keats of course had been referring to the Grecian urn itself as a bride but here on the Wedding Cup was an actual bride—and she did, in fact, look properly unravished.

The quietness was something else, however.

There were things about the Wedding Cup that came close to screaming but as he turned to leave, he realized that however loud the scream sounded to him, it meant nothing unless it also rang true. And to be sure of that he needed to know still more.

10 "ARSENIC?" Bartolomeo Pignatti whispered the word even though no one else was in the showroom but the two of them. He had his lunch—a simple one of bread, cheese, roasted peppers, and red wine—spread out on one of the display cases. All around them were glass shelves and mirrors reflecting the vases, ashtrays, animals, figurines, glass pencils, lamps, and other wares of the Pignatti glassworks. There was still perspiration on the glassmaker's forehead from his hours in front of the furnace. He took out his handkerchief from his back pocket. "Why do you ask about arsenic, Signor Macintyre?"

"There's no need to be concerned."

"I want nothing to do with the police if I can help it. One of the things our father taught us was never to trust them, never depend on them. We've never had much cause to. The Pignatti family has always tried to lead its life with honor."

"I'm sure of that, Signor Pignatti, but not even the Pignatti family, no matter now it conducts its life, has control over people who choose to live differently."

"What is it you want to know?"

There was a note of resignation in his voice. He cut a piece of cheese and put it into his mouth with the edge of the knife.

"Do you use arsenic here?"

Pignatti swallowed and picked up his glass of wine before answering.

"Tin oxide, we use tin oxide. I can show you our records. Nothing but tin oxide."

Urbino took a sip of the wine which was the only thing he had accepted when Pignatti had offered to share his meal with him.

"So you don't use arsenic to make your emerald-green glass?"

Pignatti raised his eyebrows.

"You know something of our art, I see. Centuries ago that knowledge might have brought you death—and certainly the death of the glassmaker who gave you the information."

"It wasn't a person but a book."

"A book," he said scornfully, "everything is in books today. Not long ago the only way to learn our art was from a glass *maestro*. But to answer your question, Signor Macintyre, we do not use arsenic at the Pignatti Glass Factory, not anymore, none of the glass factories do."

"When did you stop?"

"It must be a good thirty years ago, just after I started learning from my father. Even back then, as I remember, it was difficult to get, as you can imagine, although it was well known that we glassmakers needed it. There were papers to sign, care to be taken. It should have been as difficult to come by in the days of the Borgias!"

"Did your father keep the arsenic locked up?"

"Most of the time, certainly at night when we were closed. During the working hours it depended."

"On what?"

"On whether we had need of it. It was used not only for the emerald-green color but to reduce silver ions to elementary silver—for that we use iron today and, as I said, tin oxide for the emerald-green. My father always said the colors were better with the arsenic but I never noticed much difference. He was a *perfezionista;* he preferred the old ways, God rest his soul."

"Did he ever notice if any of his arsenic was unaccounted for?"

"If he did he never said anything to me about it. He might have noticed if large amounts were missing from one time to another, but other than that . . ."

"So someone could have taken a little at a time over a period of days or weeks without his necessarily noticing?"

"Who is this 'someone' you're talking about?"

"You said you were an apprentice here over thirty years ago. That was about the time Beatrice Galuppi died, wasn't it?"

A cloud passed over Pignatti's handsome face.

"I've already told you and the Contessa that I never knew her."

"Yes, I remember what you said. Tell me, were there other apprentices here then?"

"Several."

"Do you remember them?"

"Fairly well. There were twin brothers from the Castello. One of them had the skill, I think the other came just to be with his brother. They left after a month or so, went to Argentina. Still there now, someone told me, married to twin sisters."

"What about the others?"

"One other—a man from Padua, about five years older than me"

"What did he look like?"

"As handsome as the others were ugly. And his name was Giovanni Fabbri, can you imagine! How many Giovanni Fabbris do we have here in Italy? They're like your John Smiths in America and England. Isn't that what the name is there? We would joke about it, ask him if it was his real name, try to get a look at his *carta d'identità*, but I stopped after my father told me not to tease him. 'Maybe he has his reasons' is what he said, 'and who are you to say it isn't his real name?' He was very protective of him, made me feel a little jealous, I admit, all the more so because his work was better than ours. When we had our picture taken together, one of the twins put his fingers behind Fabbri's head for horns. My father got very angry. We had to take the picture over again."

"Do you know where this Fabbri is today?"

Pignatti shook his head.

"He left about three months after the *gemelli*, said he had to go back to Padua. He always seemed nervous. I think he was having problems at home, but he never talked about them. He hardly told us anything about himself. He might still be in Padua, but you know how it is these days, people don't stay where they were born anymore."

The glassmaker gave a deep sigh.

"Did he ever come back here again?"

"Not as far as I know, but I left for the army not too long after that, then traveled around for a year, settled down in Canada, got married. My wife and I came back after the flood in sixty-six. My father was getting old by then and needed someone to help out, all he had was a nephew and my two sisters. I had to learn everything all over again."

Now Urbino thought he understood Pignatti's sigh a few moments before. He had probably been thinking about his own attempt at escape years ago only to find himself now in the place where he had begun. But he had little to complain about from a professional point of view. The Pignatti glassworks were thriving and, according to the Contessa, were one of the best on Murano.

"So you never saw this Giovanni Fabbri again?"

"And why should I? I doubt if he would have wanted to pay any friendly calls, at least not once my father died. I wasn't very nice to him. You know how young people are. No, I never saw him again. Of course, that was thirty years ago when I knew him. I might pass him by every week on the quay and not even know it was him."

He couldn't resist looking at himself briefly in one of the mirrors across from him and admiring his own dark good looks which were probably only a mature version of what they had been in the fifties.

"And the photograph?"

"The photograph?" Pignatti looked away from the mirror with a puzzled frown. "What photograph?"

"The one of you apprentices."

"Oh that! It used to hang right there." He indicated an area behind the counter now occupied by shelves and backed by a mirror that displayed an array of glass pencils of different shapes, sizes, and colors. "That was twenty years ago—more than that now—before the fire."

"Is there a negative?"

"My father couldn't bear to have any reminders of what the showroom used to look like. It was very elegant in an old-fashioned way. He made no attempt to replace anything. He kept it simple, the way you see it now—just the shelves and the mirrors. He even threw away some of the things saved from the flames. He was convinced it was arson, that someone envied him his showroom. He didn't want to take the chance again. He might even have thought it would be bad luck."

As Urbino walked slowly back to the boat landing, stopping only to have a sandwich and another glass of wine in a crowded bar, he remembered what Caterina Zanetti had said about Maria Galuppi's annual visit bringing Lodovico Pignatti bad luck.

11 WHEN the water-bus from Murano slipped through the fog to San Michele, Urbino got off in front of the bone-white chapel. He could catch one of the next boats back to Venice.

He went through the gateway with its Gothic carving of Saint Michael and the dragon to the cloister, empty except for himself and an old woman walking in the opposite direction and carrying a bunch of white chrysanthemums. She had probably put fresh flowers in their place but these old ones would last a few more days, perhaps next to a votive light and a picture of her deceased.

At the information office across from the cemetery entrance he asked the old friar, muffled in a scarf and wearing gloves with the tips of the fingers cut off, for the location of the Galuppi graves. Although Urbino had a general idea of where they were, he didn't want to waste time wandering around. On another occasion it might be enjoyable but not this afternoon. The friar wrote the information on a small map of the cemetery and pushed it through the opening.

"And where is Beatrice Galuppi buried?"

"It's right in front of you, young man."

The friar nodded toward the sheet of paper.

"Would you please check your records, Frate? Beatrice Galuppi."

Urbino thought he knew what the friar would find but he had to be sure. The friar seemed surprised by the information he eventually located after several minutes of incoherent mumbling. He shouldn't have been surprised at all, however, for better than Urbino he must have known that the deceased from poor families seldom enjoyed perpetual rest but one of only twelve years' duration, the realization that had so troubled Urbino during Maria's funeral.

"Beatrice Galuppi was disinterred and taken to the common grave site."

"Where is that?"

"Let me check the dates again. Here it is. The remains of Beatrice Galuppi would have been consigned to the area of mass graves." He showed Urbino where it was on the map. "This was several years after we stopped sending the remains to Sant'Ariano farther out in the lagoon."

Urbino knew the island although only by reputation as he did the island for the insane. Sant'Ariano was the old Ossario, the Island of the Bones, the final resting place for the deceased poor after their twelve years on San Michele. Today it was no longer used for this purpose—or for any other. It was just a remote island on the edge of the lagoon, littered with bones, shunned and ignored and not even listed on most of the detailed maps of the area.

"Exactly when was Beatrice Galuppi disinterred, Frate?"

"Her *campo* was scheduled for November sixth, 1966. That would make it only a few days after the flood."

"What is the procedure for disinterment?"

"If the survivors have not contacted us about their intentions, we send them a notice, asking them what they wish to do with the remains of the deceased. We also post signs in the *campo* and here at the office with the dates of disinterment, but so many of the survivors never visit the graves. Twelve years is more than enough time to forget."

"What alternatives do the survivors have?"

"The remains can be removed to another part of the cemetery and given perpetual care or put into one of our own ossuaries and deposited in a wall. What usually happens is consignment to a common grave on the island. As I said, up to twenty-five or thirty years ago the remains were sent to Sant'Ariano. Rarely—usually only in the case of *forestieri*—is the body taken to a cemetery in another city or country. If you have any more questions, you might ask Lapo Grossi. He's working in the *campo* of the Galuppi mother and son this afternoon. He has been here a very long time. He knows everything there is to know about San Michele."

As Urbino went to the field where Grossi was working, walking down one of the many paths that cut geometrically through the island of the dead, he didn't feel the same self-indulgent melancholy as he had in the Protestant graveyard the morning of Quinton's burial. This afternoon, whose fog and gray sky were themselves funereal, the rows of graves with their names, dates, inscriptions, and photographs seemed so many futile attempts not so much to deny death its sting or give reverence to the dead as to assure the living that they couldn't—wouldn't—ever forget their beloved dead. The saddest words someone had said to him after his parents had been killed were by a well-meaning neighbor: "You'll get over it, Urbino. My mother died eight years ago and I can't remember what she looked like, what she sounded like."

Was there a second death after the first? The death of memory?

But then the image of the old woman with the white chrysanthemums came to him. She was remembering, and after she was gone, perhaps there would be someone for her—someone to light a candle, bring fresh flowers, and most important of all, speak with love and affection of a familiar face, a familiar voice. Yes, there was the old woman, and others like her, others like Maria who had never forgotten her daughter. The more he learned about Maria, the clearer it was that she had always been remembering her daughter, even, he was sure now, until the very second of her death.

No matter what Lapo Grossi knew or didn't know, it couldn't shake Urbino's conviction.

"I remember very well," old Grossi said as he eased down his wheelbarrow. He was a man whose appearance was well suited to his job—tall, cadaverously thin, with eyes and mouth that were mere slits. He might have been used as an emblem of the Isle of the Dead. "What interest is it of yours?"

Urbino immediately understood what kind of person he was dealing with. Grossi's sense of proprietorship about his domain was matched by a suspicious nature developed over many years of service. As he reached into his pocket and took out a ten-thousand *lira* note, he hoped that there was a third component in the man's nature—not necessarily greed but an understanding that everything should have a price.

Grossi stuffed the money into his filthy pants pocket.

"I still don't know what interest it is of yours, but—"

He waved a dirt-encrusted gloved hand in the air.

"Beatrice Galuppi was disinterred on November sixth, 1966," Urbino said to encourage him.

"I don't remember the exact date, but it was after the flood. We had a lot of work to do here, you couldn't imagine, *tutto in disordine*, folks that came to see their plots almost dropped dead on the spot themselves. With all that work for me I wasn't looking for more on account of Maria Galuppi's daughter."

"More work? But isn't it part of your job to disinter and deal with the remains?"

"That it is—and I used to do it almost all by myself until not very long ago. Would you believe I'll be seventy-six on the Feast of the Redeemer?"

"Unbelievable, Signor Grossi! It might be your hard work that keeps you so fit."

The old man smiled. He was certainly vigorous for his years but most likely the two younger men who were standing near a row of disinterred graves, surrounded by dirt, broken pieces of concrete, and dried flowers, did all the strenuous work.

"But what did you mean when you said it was more work on account of Maria Galuppi's daughter?"

"It was, I tell you!"

He looked down at the ground and seemed reluctant to go on. Whether it was a true or feigned reluctance, Urbino couldn't tell. Whatever it was, he decided to pull out another ten-thousand *lira* note, then added another. Grossi snatched them away more quickly than the first with a nervous glance in the direction of the two young men.

"And not just more work, understand," he said, lowering his voice, "but not exactly regular either. And I pride myself after these more than fifty years with keeping to the regular way of doing things."

"In what way was it irregular?"

The old man glared at him.

"When I say it wasn't regular I don't mean it was illegal. From the way you said 'irregular'—"

Urbino quickly assured him he had meant no offense.

"What I meant by not regular," the man went on, "is that what she wanted me to do wasn't the usual way of doing things—not anymore, it wasn't."

"By 'she' you mean Maria Galuppi?"

"Who else? Although why something should be done for years and years and then no more is a mystery to me. For years we would take the poor old bones on a scow out to Sant'Ariano, and then back in sixty, sixty-one there was an end to it all. Now we just take them to the other side of the island and put them all together, a sad sight, believe me. I wonder what they'll do when there's no room, but I won't be around to see that."

"So Maria Galuppi didn't want you to throw her daughter with the other bodies."

Grossi gave him an offended look.

"We don't throw the bodies. There's a way of doing things that's proper and respectful. But yes, no matter how delicate and respectful we should have treated her daughter, she didn't want her put in a common grave. Of course, not having hardly enough money for herself and Carlo she had little choice. That's where she got me to help."

"How?"

Urbino was afraid Grossi was going to hold out for yet more

money but his hesitation seemed more emotional then merce-
nary. He sighed.

"I had to take her daughter's body and put it in one of those
over there." He nodded toward several low stone buildings that
Urbino, on his walk to see Grossi, had assumed were small mau-
soleums. "Just overnight, you understand. The next night Carlo
and I brought the remains over to Sant'Ariano. You should have
seen the man, blubbering and shaking all over the place. It came
to my mind when I heard he killed his mother. How could such
a fellow bring himself to do it, I ask you?"

"But I don't understand," Urbino said, thinking it best to avoid
any discussion of Carlo's role in his mother's death. "What difference could it have been to Maria Galuppi to have her daughter
on Sant'Ariano instead of here on San Michele?"

"I asked her the same question, hoping with all my work that
she would see the sense of it. All she said at first was 'Because of
a picture I saw once, a picture of a lot of bones.' I asked what she
meant and she said she had seen a photo of a strange place, a
cellar in Rome somewhere, in a church, I think, where all the
bones of hundreds and hundreds of monks were piled up for
everybody to see. She had never seen it herself, she said, only the
picture, but it had been enough. 'A sign from the monks it was,'
she said, 'telling me what to do with my own sweet little saint. I
have no money to give her anything better.' That's what made the
difference for her, I guess—that monks were buried the same way.
It comforted her. But maybe if she had seen how all those bones
are scrambled together on the ground she would have changed
her mind. You should have seen poor Carlo! Doing the tarantella
he was, so he wouldn't be stepping on any of the bones!"

"Would you remember where you left the girl's body? From
what you say the bodies don't seem to have been buried."

"Most of them weren't. Carlo and I left his sister's body near a
thick clump of bushes. That whole island is just about nothing but
bushes and weeds, weeds and bushes—and all those bones ev-

erywhere. I think I could remember, but I've never gone back. I was never asked to do anything like that again, you can be sure!"

"But you could take me to the spot, then."

"I suppose so, but—"

A fleeting look of fear came into his eyes.

"If I ever ask you to do that, Signor Grossi, you can be sure that you would be in no trouble. And I would pay you a great deal more than Maria Galuppi was able to."

The gravedigger scowled.

"I never took any money from that poor woman! It was an act of charity. I did it for Maria and for the memory of Beatrice Galuppi. To think she had been reduced to that sad bundle we brought over to Sant'Ariano!"

With this the gravedigger turned back to his work, leaving Urbino with not only the information about Beatrice Galuppi's body but also the comforting feeling that he had found in Lapo Grossi yet another one of those who remembered.

12 WHEN Urbino got off the vaporetto at the Fondamenta Nuove and turned away from the lagoon toward the Grand Canal, something in his conversation with Don Marcantonio earlier in the day kept tugging at his mind—something about Cavatorta perhaps? Or was it the old priest's comments about glassmaking? With a rather grim appropriateness he had called it a dying art.

Urbino still hadn't sorted it out by the time he joined the current of people in the Strada Nuova. When he reached the Cannaregio, he went to the bar at the Ponte del Giglio across from the Palazzo Labia and chatted a few minutes with Marcello over glasses of Cynar, a drink made from artichokes that the genial *padrone* had introduced him to his first month in Venice. Marcello didn't refer to the recent violence in the Cannaregio but instead talked about the various celebrations that had already begun for *carnevale*.

When Marcello went off to tend to other customers, Urbino was visited with doubts and confusions as he sipped his Cynar. He reluctantly considered the possibility that he might have made a basic error in his thinking. He had gone ahead on the assumption that there was a direct and important link between Maria Galuppi's murder, the death of Beatrice over thirty years ago, and the burning down of the Pignatti showroom in November of 1966. He reminded himself for reassurance, however, that Maria Galuppi had made those visits to the glassblowers on the anniversary of her daughter's death. And hadn't he just learned from Bartolomeo Pignatti that arsenic had been used at their glass factory back in the fifties?

On his way back to the Palazzo Uccello he went down the Calle dell'Arcanzolo that angled off from the Campo San Gabriele. Cavatorta's shop was near the mouth of the *calle* not far from the entrance to the Convent of the Charity of Santa Crispina. The tall, thin mask maker was pushing up the shutters.

"Aren't you the eager one," Cavatorta said. "Don't tell me you don't have your mask for *carnevale* yet? And here I always thought you and the Contessa were the type to have yours months ahead of time."

Urbino followed him in as he switched on the lights. The shop was dark even at the brightest time of the day. Cavatorta had wisely taken advantage of this drawback by positioning a battery of lamps to illuminate the masks on the walls and shelves. It was an eerie effect, with masks of various colors, shapes, sizes, materials, and designs glowing and staring out with hollow eyes and casting bizarre shadows. There were silvery crescent moons and glowing suns with rays streaming from around their edges; court jesters; large lion faces with thick golden manes; masks of the plague doctor with his cone-shaped nose and of Arlecchino, Pulcinella, Pantalone, Brighella, and other commedia dell'arte figures, three-quarter *volti* designed to allow their wearers to eat and drink without removing them, and delicate oval *morette* worn by women or by men disguised as women during the bacchanal of *carnevale*. There was a shelf of dainty porcelain masks that brought a touch of the Orient to the shop and a whole wall of primitive masks in the African style interspersed with ones on ancient Roman models. Many masks were adorned with feathers, lace, sequins, false jewels, and artificial hair, some of them expressing a whimsy that Urbino was surprised to find playful and pleasantly childlike.

"May I suggest *il medico?*"

Cavatorta started to reach for the plague doctor but Urbino ignored the insinuation of nosiness and went to a display on the other side of the room. Unintentionally, Cavatorta was giving him a welcome opening. There were two things he wanted to know, and it seemed easier to begin with the masks since to talk about them was the obvious thing to do.

"I am interested in a mask as a matter of fact."

He took down a large white harlequin with black lips, eyes rimmed in black and gold, and a drooping three-pointed hat with black and white lozenges and tiny brass bells. It was striking but he preferred something more stark. He put back the harlequin and took down a crimson *volto*. The half-mask was simple in design. He might even end up wearing it for *carnevale*.

"I'll take this one."

Cavatorta said nothing as he wrapped it but eyed him a few times with a raised eyebrow.

"Most of your masks are papier-mâché, aren't they?"

"As you can see."

"And you make them yourself. I mean the mask shells."

"I know what you mean. I'm a mask maker, Signor Macintyre. If you want to see my molds, they're in the back. 'No charge for looking,' as they say on Murano but in my case I mean it. No need to worry about being pressured into buying another mask. After you."

Cavatorta had an ironic smile on his face as he showed Urbino his cluttered workroom behind the shop with its molds, pails, paints and brushes, cardboard, shallow pans, and scissors used in the making and designing of masks. Urbino pointed to a pile of unpainted porcelain masks in a corner.

"Do you make those as well?"

"Those, my dear Signor Macintyre, are from a factory outside of Florence. Would you like their address? Are you thinking of dabbling in mask making? As long as you promise to be only a dilettante about it and nothing more, I might be induced to give you the benefit of my knowledge—unless, that is, you prefer knowledge of a more arcane nature, like the old Tridentine Mass?"

He laughed at his own joke as he shut the light in the workroom and followed Urbino out. He went behind the counter and took out a pair of scissors, using the smaller blade to pick at his nails. His fingers were short and fat, as if they belonged to a different person. Putting one of his fingers up to his mouth, he looked at Urbino with amusement.

Now, when the time had come for him to ask his second question, Urbino found himself saying good-bye to Cavatorta instead and walking out into the Calle dell'Arcanzolo. His reluctance wasn't because of the mask maker's ironical manner. He was almost immune to that by now and knew it too was a mask as surely as any of those displayed in the man's shop. What held him back was fear. To ask the question would be, perhaps, to get the answer he wanted, but at what cost? The answer he already had didn't settle things one way or the other.

Cavatorta wasn't stupid. He didn't even pretend to be. It wasn't one of the poses he so readily assumed. Hadn't he looked at Urbino as if to say that he knew not only that there was an unasked question but also exactly what that question was? Or was Urbino seeing things that weren't there?

He knew of another place he might get the information he needed, but with the Contessa as well there was fear, fear that she too would understand what the answer could mean and he wasn't quite ready for that.

He would have to take the chance with her. He didn't have much choice.

But he had walked halfway down the Calle dell'Arcanzolo when he turned around. It might be better to ask Cavatorta after all. The Contessa hadn't brought up the topic of the Cavatortas in reference to Beatrice's artwork, which suggested either ignorance, a lapse of memory, or—this was hard for him to understand—intentional concealment. It was better to try to settle things at once.

Cavatorta was still behind the counter, thumbing through one of the pamphlets that described the history and art of mask making. Urbino felt that the best approach now was a direct one, and he asked the mask maker about his father, the man who had been a good friend to Alvise da Capo-Zendrini. Urbino suspected the man had had a convenient, uncomplicated method of paying his way at wedding feasts.

Urbino's first surprise was that the usually evasive Cavatorta, the pamphlet still in his hand, answered so readily. The second was that the answer to his question about the late Cavatorta's form of liberality was just what he had expected.

13 LATER that evening, after Urbino and the Contessa had avoided any serious discussion while Lucia served them the veal and truffles dish she claimed any restaurant in town would pay a fortune for, they retired to the Contessa's cluttered *salotto*. There, with tea set down for her and brandy for him, she played a Scarlatti sonata on the Cristofori that was said to have belonged to the composer himself. Usually an accomplished player, tonight she was having a bit of difficulty with all the crossing of hands, broad skips, and rapidly repeated notes. She had seemed under a strain during dinner that was now going into her playing. She began another sonata, this one by Bach, then turned away from the harpsichord.

"I've been as patient as I can, *caro*. What have you learned since leaving here last night?"

He told her slowly, methodically, enjoying the opportunity to review things himself. Predictably, she was most interested in what he had to tell her about Beatrice's disinterment and Maria's arrangement with Lapo Grossi. She sat in silence as he filled her in on it all, including what he had learned about arsenic from his various sources and about his visit with Sister Veronica at the Glass Museum. When he had told her about everything except his decision to go back to Cavatorta's shop only moments after leaving it, he could see she had questions, but before she could say anything he asked her to refresh his memory about the police report on Beatrice's death.

"As I told you," she began, sounding suddenly tired, "she was found dead by Maria in the toilet of their flat on the Rio della Sensa. Officially she killed herself with a massive dose of arsenic on the fifth of November 1954."

"Exactly how would a woman go about inducing an abortion?"

"But Beatrice Galuppi wasn't pregnant, remember."

"Nonetheless . . ."

In a weary, even voice as if she were being forced to indulge him she said, "Falling down a flight of stairs might do it, a blow to the abdomen, I suppose, maybe excessive exercise. This is a bit out of my usual range of knowledge, never having had a child or, more to the point," she added quickly, "never even having been pregnant. Instruments of various types are what you hear of in the desperate cases. Then there's medication, drugs, but exactly what kinds I wouldn't know. Anything more technical than that you would have to get from a physician but I suggest you be discreet if you do. Venice is a very small town."

"Precisely. Do you think Maria would have helped her daughter abort—I mean *if* she had been pregnant?"

"Certainly not!"

"But would she have helped cover up an abortion?"

"Possibly, but you keep forgetting that Beatrice wasn't pregnant. The medical report—"

"Then Maria might have removed any possible traces in the toilet—*if* her daughter had been pregnant and tried to abort the fetus," he persisted.

"It's certainly possible. I would probably do the same in the same circumstances—who knows? A mother's love for her child is very strong, sometimes I think it must be the strongest love there is."

There was a note of regret in her voice as she said this last.

"Not to mention a mother's concern for her daughter's reputation."

He waited for the Contessa to ask one of her own questions but she seemed to be waiting for him to go on. He thought for a few moments before he did, taking a sip of his brandy.

"This Giovanni Fabbri, the apprentice that Pignatti told me about—he's our Domenica. I have no proof, not yet, but my instincts tell me he has to be."

"But who was Giovanni Fabbri?" The Contessa looked at him searchingly, clearly hoping he had the answer and—if he had it—that he would tell her. Her face clouded when he gave no answer but instead asked her a question himself.

"Did Sister Veronica know Cavatorta's father?"

"Yes, through San Gabriele. He was a devout man."

"What about before she became a nun? When she was helping her father in the glass shop on Murano? Didn't you say that Cavatorta's father sold some property to a glassblower on Murano?"

"Right, but that was after she became a nun and after Cavatorta left the priesthood. I didn't know her in the fifties when she returned to Murano from Naples. I've always assumed she didn't get to know Cavatorta's father until she came to Santa Crispina.

From what I understand, she was more or less immured during her years on Murano."

To remind himself more than anything else, Urbino mentioned how Sister Veronica had told him she hadn't known Beatrice.

"There you are! And most likely neither did she know Franco Cavatorta during the fifties. Her father didn't let her traipse all over Venice. But if it's so important, why don't you just ask her when she got to know him?" She gave him a judicious look as she put down her cup and saucer. "Urbino, you disappoint me. I have the strangest feeling you're not telling me everything."

"To be honest, Barbara, I'm not sure about certain things yet."

"You're giving me the facts—or most of them—but you're not giving me the rest. You've got ideas"—she said it as if it were a disease or a heresy—"you've got theories."

"Cara," he said soothingly, "if I have any ideas or theories they're all mixed up and confused at this point. Give me some time, just a little time—and promise me one thing."

"What's that, caro?"

"That you won't mention any of what we've discussed tonight to anyone, to anyone at all."

"I promise."

❧

14 WHAT he had told the Contessa was true. He was confused, he was mixed up, yet it was the confusion that he knew often came before clarity.

When he returned to the Palazzo Uccello, he felt restless and almost went out again for a long walk. He was happy he had eaten at the Contessa's for he knew he would hardly have taken a bite on his own. He usually got in a state like this—nervous, excited, restless, barely eating or sleeping—when he was trying to puzzle out a problem or make an important decision. He remembered an October night ten years ago before he had moved to Venice. He had left every light on in the house on St. Charles and gone out several times, walking to Tulane and through Audubon Park and the French Quarter as he tried to decide whether to maintain a small apartment in New Orleans after selling the family house. His decision, made at four in the morning over beignets and chicory coffee at the Café du Monde, had been to burn all his bridges in order to live in the city with hundreds of them.

Tonight he felt the same way. He walked from one floor to another, from the top story with its unoccupied servants' quarters down to the ground floor, not unlike a warehouse built around an enclosed, unused docking area for boats, filled with odds and ends of furniture raised on platforms to protect them from the high water.

He reexamined everything that had happened in November of 1966, now having the disinterment of Beatrice and her removal to the Ossario of Sant'Ariano to add to the list. He thought a great deal about Beatrice's copy of the Barovier Wedding Cup and the uses and effects of arsenic. He tried to penetrate the mask of Giovanni Fabbri of Padua—also known as Domenica, he was convinced—and to understand what course of events might have brought him to murder three times and what role the glass lovebird had played. There was a great deal more for him to consider, among other items Margaret Quinton's writings, Clifford Voyd, Santa Teodora, all the things he had learned from those who had known the Galuppis and especially what Cavatorta had told him about his father.

He went over it all until he became as muddled as before. Then for a few brief, even more disturbing moments everything seemed probable—every connection, every hypothesis, every "theory," to use the Contessa's word. His mind began to reel. Where meaning had been eluding him before, it now mocked him by seeming to be everywhere, one thing canceling out another. He even began to question that Domenica was a man. Almost everything pointed in this direction and yet, inexplicably, a vestige of his former assumption about Beatrice's friend trailed itself across his weary mind. It had nothing to do with plausibility and yet he couldn't shake it.

Then, in the deadest time of the night, he remembered what had been teasing him earlier in Don Marcantonio's comments, and from this he passed so quickly to what seemed the answer that he was afraid to go over it again more methodically. When he did, however, the answer still seemed as clear and irrefutable as when it had first come to him.

When he finally got to sleep, he had troubled dreams. Floating before him were the faces of Carlo, Maria, and Beatrice, and an indistinct one that seemed sometimes a man, sometimes a woman. Santa Teodora's face with its prominent nose and receding chin kept dissolving into these others.

He awoke exhausted but excited. When he called the Contessa at nine, she had already gone out and Lucia said she wouldn't be back until about midafternoon. She had gone for a dress fitting and then was meeting a group of friends at Florian's about ten.

After he hung up, he took a quick shower, wrote a note to Natalia, and left the Palazzo Uccello. If he stopped by Florian's on the way to the Questura, he might be able to see the Contessa alone before the others arrived.

※

15 HE had no such luck.
"It's just us scheming women," the Contessa said when he went to her usual table in front of the window in the Chinese salon. "We'll allow you to stay for a little while, won't we, my dears?"—she shared a quick smile with Angela Bellorini and Adele Carstairs—"but then I'm afraid we'll ask you to catch up Stefano

and Mr. Kobke over at the Correr if you want some company. I'm sure you'll find them staring at Carpaccio's courtesans."

"So you haven't left for Vienna yet," he said to Quinton's niece after declining their invitation to sit down.

"We go tomorrow afternoon. I've just been trying to convince the Contessa and Angela to join us in our compartment before the train leaves."

"How many times have I told you to call me Barbara?"

The girl looked flustered as she went on, "It's not the Orient Express, of course, but Christian and I are having champagne and some food sent in from Do Forni's. Do join us, Mr. Macintyre."

"Come now, Adele, just look at the poor man. His hair needs combing and it doesn't look as if he's shaved this morning. Doesn't that tell you he doesn't have a moment to spare?"

"I'm here now, aren't I?"

The Contessa laughed.

"You're here, yes, but why are you here? Tell him why we think he's here Angela dear."

Angela seemed embarrassed and colored slightly beneath her sallow cheeks.

"Go on, *cara*, tell him. Oh, never mind, I'll do it myself. You want to know if Adele here has anything stuffed up her elegant sleeves, something from her dear *zia* whom we all miss so much, don't you?"

Angela spoke now, lightly, quietly, "It was Benedetta Razzi. Didn't I tell you last week that she knows everyone's business? She also tells everyone's business, I'm afraid."

"Yes, she called Adele and said you were looking for wills or love letters or deeds—oh, she seems to have been wild in her imaginings. But tell him, Adele."

Quinton's niece was less reluctant than Angela had been to respond to the Contessa's prompting.

"There's nothing left, Mr. Macintyre, absolutely, positively nothing."

"How sad you look, Urbino dear." He was sure he looked nothing of the sort but he allowed the Contessa her playfulness if this was what it was. "Adele told us over lunch last week how elated you were to get the Venetian notebook."

She said this as if she had had no contact with him since then. All he could assume was that his friend, as she so often did, was playing a role with Angela and Adele and was pursuing it as far as it would take her, hoping he would understand that she was just having a bit of harmless entertainment.

"The truth of the matter, Barbara—and you other ladies—is that I came here merely to have a coffee which I haven't even had a chance to order yet." He quickly remedied the situation and brought another chair over to the table. "So Mr. Kobke and Stefano are off together?"

"Yes, they are off together. And to answer the implied question, they are also enjoying each other's company, I'm sure. They have a great deal in common—the artistic temperament, you know. But of course one needn't be an artist to have the temperament."

"They do like each other," Angela offered as the waiter put down Urbino's espresso, "now that they've got to know each other, thanks to Barbara. They just didn't get off to a good start."

Urbino remembered the afternoon several weeks before when they had seemed to be having words right here at Florian's.

"They've worked through whatever silly little problems they might have had," the Contessa said.

"Misunderstandings," Angela clarified. "Stefano says it was his fault. He collided with Mr. Kobke in the foyer here and they had a few words. Everything is fine now."

"Christian is very understanding," Adele said as if the Dane had had to excuse the grossest of behaviors.

Angela raised her chin slightly but had nothing more to add.

"Harmony, that's what I like," the Contessa said.

"I couldn't agree with you more." Urbino finished his espresso in one swallow. He stood up and had them all staring at him when he added, "I'm in search of it myself. You'll have to excuse me, ladies."

❧

16 AS Urbino spoke Gemelli fiddled with a paperweight, loosened his collar with a finger, and near the end got up and leaned on the file cabinet to gaze out the window at the canal below. When Urbino finished, Gemelli looked over at him with a smile.

"And so you want me to go over there and make an arrest for the murders of Beatrice Galuppi, Maria Galuppi, and the *Americano*. What about the Signorina Quinton? We have orderly procedure even here in Italy, Signor Macintyre. Have you ever heard of *prova indiziaria*? Circumstantial evidence it's called in English. Everything you've told me, including all this business with a love-bird and a wedding bell—"

"A wedding cup, Commissario."

"It's all very interesting and a credit to your ingenuity but exactly what can I do with it?"

"Isn't it enough to reopen the case?"

"Reopen the case! You can't imagine what we'd have to go through! Your puzzle fits together nicely but it doesn't constitute proof."

Urbino decided to take a different tack. He sensed that Gemelli, despite his protestations, was not completely rejecting his theory. Could he have learned something on his own? Had he begun to doubt Carlo's guilt? The Contessa had said that the files of Beatrice and Maria had been in the tray together as if someone had been reviewing them. Whatever it was, Gemelli seemed to want to be convinced but he was a man with a lot of personal and professional pride who would have to account to those above him.

"How difficult would it be, Commissario, to examine the body of Santa Teodora?"

"Examine it? What do you mean?"

"Have tests done by scientists and doctors, something like an autopsy."

"An autopsy on a thousand-year-old body! Don't be ridiculous!"

"But how difficult would it be?" Urbino persisted.

"It wouldn't be difficult, it would be impossible! Surely you realize it wouldn't be only a police matter. The Vatican would be involved, and you know what that means."

"I understand how difficult it would be but suppose we had something incontrovertible, something substantial, something the Vatican or any other authority couldn't ignore?"

"What would that be?"

"The *real* body of Santa Teodora."

17 IT seemed to take them forever to get from San Michele to Sant'Ariano. The police boat made it quickly enough to Torcello but although the Isle of Bones wasn't far away—and in fact was in sight for the remainder of the trip—they had had to zigzag through the narrow channels among the mud flats for more than half an hour. The Venetian lagoon was very shallow in most areas, especially this one, and boats had to be careful not to stray outside the markers.

This long approach to Sant'Ariano, Urbino thought, was not unlike a dream or more exactly a nightmare: the self immobilized, making only paralyzed progress toward a goal or away from a danger.

They passed islets that either showed no signs of human life or had only small, ramshackle wooden structures used by duck hunters for shelter, the kind that Don Marcantonio must have huddled in during the early morning hours when he was a young man. With the tide going out, there was a great deal of mud visible and the reeds and the wooden poles marking the channels stood high. Urbino kept glancing at the pilot, a mere boy who couldn't have had much experience in these waters, for fear he might run the boat aground. The best craft for these shallows were the light flat-bottomed *sandoli* they encountered occasionally, their passengers looking curiously at the police launch.

They were in one of the remotest sections of the lagoon. An analogy might be drawn between this northernmost area of the lagoon and the parish of San Gabriele in the Cannaregio, so seldom traversed by anyone except those who lived and worked there.

Gemelli, Grossi, and Urbino had been silent for most of the trip, long before they had even come in sight of the Isle of Bones. The old gravedigger still didn't seem to have recovered from his shock at seeing Urbino walk across the *campo santo* with the Commissario an hour before. He had looked as if he expected to be taken into immediate custody and thrown into one of the old dank cells in the Ducal Palace.

Gemelli's silence was like a professional decorum or pose although Urbino suspected he was using these moments in late morning as the boat made its tortuous way to consider the advisability of having gone off on what might turn out to be a wild-goose chase.

At first Urbino had tried to engage them in conversation but soon left them to their own thoughts, filled as he was with his own anxious reflections.

And so, in silence, the police launch continued its slow approach to the Isle of Bones two weeks before Ash Wednesday.

❧

18 THE boat emerged from between the wooden poles and docked at a low wooden wharf.

"Well, here we are at last," Gemelli said. "Let's get this over with."

They got out of the boat and walked from the wharf through mud and reeds until they reached a white gate with a grille that gave a view of a porch beyond it. When Urbino looked through the grille after Gemelli had stepped aside, he was startled to see an austere wooden Christ that looked like something done by a Flemish artist.

Gemelli pointed to the padlock and chain on the gate.

"Do you have a key?" he asked Grossi.

The old gravedigger shook his head and started to say something but couldn't find the words. Despite the chill wind blowing from the lagoon his forehead was slick with sweat.

"Not a good idea to break the lock," Gemelli said, "although it looks like it would be easy enough. Let's go this way." He pointed to a section of the white wall to the left of the gate. "You stay with the boat," he called to the young man on the wharf.

Urbino wondered if Gemelli could be afraid someone might appear and take the boat. From the look of neglect it didn't seem as if anyone had been near Sant'Ariano in years. Urbino and Grossi followed Gemelli to the wall. It was about five feet high.

"I'll go first," Gemelli said. He climbed to the top and turned to help Grossi. After several heavy-breathing moments, with Urbino giving support from below, the old man was up beside Gemelli. Urbino then negotiated the wall more easily than he expected and dropped down to the other side.

There was very little on the low island but scrubby bushes and weeds and what at first looked like the whitest of sand. But only a few steps showed Urbino that he wasn't walking on soft yielding sand but on bones. Skulls, vertebrae, clavicles, thighbones, ribs, and finger bones—these and all the other parts of the human skeleton were to be found in a mad jumble that only the trumpet at the Last Judgment might make any order of. Urbino was appalled, and the Commissario looked no less affected although he must have seen quite a few disturbing things in his job. Only Grossi seemed unruffled by the grim sight. He looked not at the vast expanse of bones beneath the weeds and bushes but fearfully at Gemelli, almost as if he expected to be held responsible for the scene.

Urbino didn't see how he would be able to bring himself to walk another step, not if it meant treading on bones the oldest of which must have dated back to at least the seventeenth century.

Gemelli broke the silence.

"Where did you bring the body?" He turned to Urbino and added under his breath, "It's been more than twenty years. He'll probably just take us to any old pile of bones. How would we know the difference?"

Grossi was already several feet ahead, stepping unfastidiously but nimbly through the field of bones. There seemed no hesitation in his movements. Gemelli started to follow and, with a sigh, Urbino did the same.

Any number of times he felt as if he were going to lose his balance. Sometimes it was because he was trying to avoid stepping on a skull or rib or God knew what else. At other times it was the treacherously uneven ground beneath him. At first he didn't know if it would be best to keep his eyes averted or not. After a few minutes he decided there was little sense in looking at what he was treading on. He could do nothing but follow behind Grossi and Gemelli. What good would it do to examine every time whatever had been reduced to powder and shards beneath his feet?

Grossi came to a stop by a cluster of spiky bushes against a slight rise in the ground. He stood there waiting for Gemelli and Urbino to catch up with him. Gemelli got there first and stood looking down at the ground. When Urbino got to the spot a few moments later he saw what Gemelli was looking at.

Initially his eyes registered only the same scramble of bones that were Sant'Ariano's distinctive blanket, the only difference being that these bones were piled a little higher than the others.

But gradually he perceived there was something beneath the bones that they didn't quite conceal. It wasn't the true earth of Sant'Ariano but a mass of what looked like tattered clothing.

Grossi, without any direction from Gemelli, bent over and started to handle the bones, picking them up and tossing them aside as if they were so many rocks and stones at a construction site. Urbino wondered at the years—probably several decades of service on Sant'Ariano before it stopped being the bone depository—that could be read in the dispassion with which Grossi did his work.

Urbino watched the mass beneath the bones being exposed as small lizards darted away for cover. Finally Grossi's labors subsided.

On the ground against the hummock was a form about five feet long wrapped in a piece of cloth that was faded, threadbare, and rotted at many spots. It was obviously a body in an unconventional shroud.

Gemelli looked from the form to Urbino.

"What are we supposed to do now?"

It was a question that came more from annoyance than confusion.

"We take it back. It should be examined for arsenic poisoning."

"After thirty years?"

Urbino quickly explained how large quantities of arsenic had been discovered in Napoleon's body twenty years after it was buried on St. Helena and brought to Les Invalides.

"But what's the point of looking for arsenic? It's on record that Beatrice Galuppi died of arsenic poisoning, self-administered."

"But what if this body shows no traces of arsenic?"

"Then we'll have to assume that Signor Grossi made a mistake. It's quite likely after all these years."

"He could have but I don't think so. But there's no point in arguing something we can't prove now one way or the other. Why don't we take a closer look?"

"And what will that prove?"

"Possibly nothing but I think we should, don't you?" He turned to Grossi. "Would you remove some of the material from around that end?" He gestured to what he assumed must be the head.

The gravedigger looked at Gemelli, who nodded, then Grossi bent down and unwrapped the cloth as best he could. Some of it came apart in his hands. He stood up.

They stared down at what looked like a heavily tanned face with a lot of black hair but no teeth. Beneath the head was once-white material, torn, soiled, rotting, but bearing a striking similarity to the yellowed gown covering the body in the Church of San Gabriele. Although they didn't remove the shroud from the bottom of the figure, Urbino was sure the feet were shod in little scarlet slippers. But the telling details as far as he was concerned were the prominent nose and receding chin that had so recently haunted his dreams.

Before Gemelli said anything, Urbino started talking. He had to convince the Commissario to take the body back to Venice.

He pointed out that technically speaking the body had been illegally removed to Sant'Ariano, since the boat of bones that used to plow between San Michele and the island had not been in operation at the time. And there was no point in worrying about next of kin since both Maria and Carlo were dead and had left no relatives. Besides, by the nature of Sant'Ariano, the bones and remains of the dead were anonymous and actually belonged to no one unless it was the city of Venice itself. And since there was a possibility that an examination—

"But papers, Macintyre," Gemelli interrupted him impatiently. "Papers, papers, papers. You know how our system works. You know how *your* system works. Things must be done in the proper way—special forms, signatures, stamps, seals, and then more signatures."

"You'll just have to make the decision yourself and take the responsibility."

It might have been this appeal to his position and authority, or the prospect of taking a gamble that might pay off handsomely in a professional way, or the realization that it was somewhat ridiculous to consider either decorum or due process in the middle of a field of bones. Whatever it was, Urbino could tell from the way Gemelli sighed and put his hands on his hips that he had decided to take back the body.

After covering the exposed face as best he could, the Commissario helped Grossi lift the shrouded figure and carry it back to the wall. Once again Urbino walked behind them.

It was no easier going back. He only hoped that Grossi, who was in front, had the good sense to take the same route. That way Urbino could console himself with having disturbed and crushed the smallest number of bones possible.

Once again they had little to say on the trip back to San Michele where they left Grossi off, Gemelli assuring him there was nothing to worry about.

As the boat headed for the Fondamenta Nuove, Urbino pointed out that Gemelli would have to trouble the old gravedigger again after tests on the body showed no trace of arsenic.

"There you go again, Macintyre. I've gone this far with you but I don't intend to go much beyond that. I can't. It will give me a great deal of satisfaction when that poor body is found to be riddled with arsenic. Maybe then you'll be finished once and for all." Urbino thought he had no more to say, but then he cleared his throat and added, "As I said back at the Questura, your theory proves nothing. Even if there's no arsenic in this body, it wouldn't prove anything." He looked at Urbino with something close to an appeal in his eyes. "I would need proof, you see." Then in a more official manner he said, "You've been snooping around a bit too much as it is. I'd suggest staying in your palazzo for a change."

When the boat pulled up to the Fondamenta Nuove, he offered one final piece of advice: "Don't do anything rash."

❦

19 BENEDETTA Razzi lived only a short distance from where the police launch had left him but first he went to a café and had several *tramezzini* and a glass of wine. From the phone in the corner he called the Ca' da Capo-Zendrini.

"She came back with her friends an hour ago, Signor Macintyre, but then they went out again right away. Milo took them to the Giudecca to Signora Borelli's. The Signora called after the Contessa left this morning. She sounded very upset. The Contessa said that you might go there too if you could."

Urbino could imagine what the problem was at the Ca' Borelli. Oriana and Filippo had a tempestuous relationship filled with extramarital affairs, separations, and passionate reconciliations, all conducted with operatic excess and, if possible, with a large audience. It therefore wasn't unusual to have the Bellorinis, Adele Carstairs, and Christian Kobke accompanying the Contessa to the Giudecca for the latest crisis in their lives.

He left no message for her except to say he would call again.

He went to a small gift shop near San Zanipolo with a good selection of contemporary glass. The shutters were partway down. Although it was almost an hour before the shop usually reopened, he knocked insistently on the shutter. He frequented the shop, having bought numerous Christmas gifts for his aunts back in New Orleans. The owner and his wife, well into their seventies, usually took their midday meal and siesta in the back room. The shutter was raised slowly and the husband looked out with a frown, blinking rapidly at the brighter light.

"*Chiuso.*" Then, seeing who it was, the frown was replaced with puzzlement. "It's you, Signor Macintyre. But we're still closed as you see."

"I'm sorry to disturb you, Signor Falco"—he smiled apologetically at the portly man and his wife, who was now peeking through the curtain that shut off the back room from the shop—"but it's something of an emergency."

He went inside to the window display and took a small glass swan from the shelf.

"I'll take this. There's no need to wrap it," he said, putting it in his pocket. He took out a twenty-thousand *lira* note and handed it to Falco. He apologized again for having disturbed them and started to leave.

"But a whole *famiglia* is only ten thousand, Signor Macintyre." His wife nudged her husband aside as she went up to the window.

"How very nice two or three *famiglie* would be for your Palazzo Uccello, Signor Macintyre. Would you like to look at our other *uccellini?* We have ducks, flamingos, chickens, peacocks, and owls. They're all made over on Murano. We have nothing from those Chinese countries here in the shop."

"No, thank you, Signora Falco, this is all I need."

❧

20 BENEDETTA Razzi didn't seem surprised to see him when she opened the door of her apartment fifteen minutes later.

"You see I didn't come empty-handed this time," he said when she led him into the parlor. A small white porcelain face with slanted eyes, black hair, and an elaborate headdress peered at him from the pocket of her robe.

"How lovely! I adore swans. Such graceful feminine creatures, don't you agree?" He followed her as she brought it over to the oval table. "I'll put it right next to their other little animals. It's their first swan."

Urbino looked down at the collection, wondering how many of the objects were from recent visitors.

"But you didn't come by just to make my sweethearts a little gift, did you?"

It was more a statement than a question.

"I hoped it could be something nicer," he said evasively. "Unfortunately I couldn't find exactly what I wanted."

"What was that?"

"A lovebird."

"A lovebird?" A flush began to show beneath her heavy makeup before she turned away to rearrange some dolls on a nearby shelf. "But swans are romantic too. I saw a ballet many years ago in Milan. It was about swans and was very romantic."

As she continued to handle the dolls on the shelf, Urbino picked up and examined a glass elephant, one of the porcelain masks, and a chess-piece knight. Benedetta Razzi was looking at him out of the corner of her eye.

"Your dolls have many admirers. So many interesting things here. Who was kind enough to give them this?"

He held up the miniature candelabra.

She finished with the dolls before answering with an uncharacteristic coolness.

"You should understand that I make no distinctions. Everything is part of their collection. People give what they can. It makes no difference who gives what. You wouldn't want me to go telling everyone who comes here that it was you who gave them the swan, would you?"

"Why not?"

"Someone might not think it was as fine a gift as you could give—who knows? But as I say I make no distinctions. The important thing is that my visitors bring my sweethearts something—anything." She stared at him for a few moments and then surprised him by saying, "You still want to know about that room, I think. But as I told you yesterday, it was locked when she was there. I hardly ever open it."

"I'm not concerned about the locked room anymore. I believe you."

"We're so glad to hear you do. I wish I could say the same for others."

"What do you mean?"

"So you are still concerned about it! I had an argument about keeping the room locked and it's no one's business but my own. When I suggested sending someone over about the apartment, Signor Macintyre, I didn't mean a *veneziano*, I meant a *forestiero*."

"I didn't send anyone over."

"Well, that mask maker from San Gabriele came by yesterday evening—the one who used to be a priest."

"Did he say I sent him?"

"No, but when I told him you had been to see me earlier and also another time he didn't seem surprised."

"What did he want?"

"An apartment, a better one than the one he has in the Ghetto Nuovo. He asked specifically about the Casa Silviano. I'm surprised it took him so long to come by if you weren't the one to tell him. Most people hear about a death and come before the funeral arrangements are even made."

"Is he going to take the apartment?"

"Over my dead body! Even if he could afford it—which I doubt from the way he was dressed—I would never rent any part of the Casa Silviano to anyone but *forestieri*. Once you get the Italians in they never leave. You might as well just give them the building outright! And even if this Cavatorta wasn't Italian I'd still not rent it to him. He's not a very nice man, completely ignored my little ones and started to insinuate that the police might like to know that I keep a locked room at the Casa Silviano. It's not really illegal, you know. He obviously thought I'd get frightened and agree to let him rent the apartment cheaply, but we sent him right on his way, almost pushed him out the door. I was sure you had sent him."

"He came here on his own, I assure you, Signora Razzi."

She was looking at him so suspiciously that he felt uncomfortable asking her what he had originally gone there to find out.

"When I was here yesterday, you said something about other people being interested in Signorina Quinton's writing. What others did you mean?"

A guarded look came into her small eyes with their long artificial lashes.

"Did I say anything about so many others? Other than yourself there was Signor Voyd." She still showed no sign that she knew of his death. "Also the young niece."

When she mentioned Adele Carstairs, she shifted her eyes away from him and surveyed the gifts crowded on the table.

"She didn't always come alone, though, not the last time. She had that good-looking young man with her. My sweethearts fell in love with him as soon as they saw him."

The face she turned up to him now was shining. Urbino found it difficult to understand but it seemed that Christian Kobke was quite the charmer.

❦

21   HIS next move was decided for him when he called the Ca' da Capo-Zendrini again from the café next door to Benedetta Razzi's building.

"She's not back yet, Signor Macintyre," Lucia said, "but she called a few minutes ago from Signor Bellorini's studio. Milo took them from the Giudecca. She said you could join her there until six or come here later. Sister Veronica will be stopping by about eight."

As he hung up, Urbino marveled at the busy schedule the Contessa seemed to have arranged for herself today. Now she was at Bellorini's studio only a few minutes' walk along the quay. Were Adele Carstairs and Kobke still with her? If he knew for sure, he would be able to plan things better.

One thing he should do was let Gemelli know where he was going to be, but when he called the Questura the Commissario wasn't in. As he put the phone back on its hook, he hoped he had been able to convince Gemelli's assistant of what should be done and how it might be best to do it. Yet he knew he couldn't count on getting any help at all. Hadn't Gemelli warned him not to do anything rash?

The shops were opening now and he found a stationery store not far from the quay. He didn't have time to go all the way to Valese's for something elegant. A simple student's notebook would have to do. He wrote "Venezia" on the cover with his fountain pen in a thin spidery hand. He wished he could do something with all the blank pages but he'd have to leave them the way they were. Unfortunately the Contessa had sharp eyes.

To deceive the Contessa was not something he was looking forward to. He would have avoided it, he would have run in the other direction if only he could have. But he had started something and it was now, he hoped, near its end. Hadn't he decided almost from the beginning that he couldn't allow himself to be influenced by anything but the need to uncover the truth?

He put the notebook under his arm as he returned to the quay. When he passed by Benedetta Razzi's building, he restrained himself from looking up at her window. There seemed no need to. He could feel her looking down at him. A few minutes later, however, as he walked along the quay, he had reason to doubt this as well as whatever else came into his mind. After all, it was improbable, wasn't it, that one of the two nuns in modified habits stepping into

a crowded vaporetto could be Sister Veronica? Or that the thin
man he had just glimpsed turning down a *calle* up ahead was
Cavatorta? His nerves must be collaborating with one of the
city's peculiarities: So often it seemed as if you had just missed
someone you knew, as you saw a person leaving the far side of
a *campo* or being swallowed by the shadows of a *sottoportego*. He
thought he had become accustomed to the city's trickery but
maybe this was one of the many differences between him and
a true Venetian.

The Contessa and Bellorini were sipping Strega when he arrived at the studio. No one was there but the two of them.
Perhaps Milo had taken Adele Carstairs and Kobke back to the
Danieli and Angela had gone with them. Despite the conviction
that had been with him since the early morning hours, he had a
momentary doubt as to whether he should proceed as he had
planned, whether it might not be better to wait until every possible thing was in place. The dream that had disturbed his sleep
last night flashed its images across his mind.

After giving Stefano his coat and putting the notebook down on
the little table by the door, he walked to the far side of the room
to the small area set aside for socializing. Stefano, apologizing for
having nothing else to offer him, poured a glass of Strega.

The Contessa sat on the sofa across from the windows that
looked down on the *calle* below. The work area was set up near
the larger windows that gave on to the lagoon and the north
light. Urbino was glad the Contessa was sitting where she was,
with Stefano in an old armchair to one side, for if he went to the
windows across from them and turned around to face them . . .

"You came, Urbino! You're a darling. What do you think?"

She pointed to the worktable on the other side of the room. He
went over and saw the three frames with her family photographs
mounted in them.

He picked them up one by one. The frames enhanced the old
photographs, and the photographs contributed a patina to the

newly fashioned frames. It was a harmonious marriage between
Bellorini's art and the Contessa's history.

"You're both to be congratulated."

He had been sincere in his praise but a slight frown furrowed
the Contessa's forehead.

"You got here so quickly," she said. "I called Lucia only a short
time ago." She gave him a quizzical little smile. "Where were
you?"

"Benedetta Razzi's."

"Benedetta Razzi's? Again? Whatever for? You were just there
yesterday, weren't you?"

Was this how she had kept her promise of not mentioning
anything they had discussed yesterday?

"Yes, I was."

He looked toward the little table by the door.

"A mission of charity, most likely," Stefano said. "Benedetta
Razzi is always eager for visitors. It sometimes makes me feel
guilty not to be more attentive."

"You two have made your own visit of charity, I hear."

"Yes, with Angela, Adele, and Christian," the Contessa said.
The use of Kobke's first name wasn't lost on Urbino. "You'll never
guess what's happened. Filippo left Oriana. You wouldn't believe
what a scene there was. Filippo came back for some of his things.
He's staying at the Cipriani. I kept thinking of the opening of
Anna Karenina. How does it go? Something about happy and un-
happy families and the poor wife discovering an intrigue."

She looked at him for help but before he could say anything
Stefano jumped in.

"Of course in Oriana's case the intrigue was the other way
around. Maybe now her young friend from Dorsoduro will finally
move in."

"Stefano, please! He's just a friend—almost a son to her—"

She looked at Urbino with entreaty in her eyes. It was as if to
say: There's trouble all around us. Be gentle. I can't take too much.

"I'm sure they'll work things out," he said, making another glance in the direction of the door. He saw they both noticed. They've gone through this so many times before, haven't they? I'm sorry if I don't sound concerned. It's just that I'm a bit distracted. The most extraordinary thing has happened."

The Contessa suddenly showed an interest in the way her brooch was pinned to her dress, so it was Stefano who asked the obvious question.

"And what is that?"

Before answering, Urbino walked over to the entrance hallway and took the notebook from the little table.

"Nothing more extraordinary looking than this."

He held it up and walked toward them.

"And whatever is *that?*" the Contessa asked, abandoning her brooch.

"A notebook."

"Well, we can see that well enough."

"It's a notebook that Benedetta Razzi found in the locked room in the Casa Silviano. It's one of Margaret Quinton's notebooks."

"But that's impossible!" She looked at Stefano, then back at Urbino. "That room has been locked for as long as I've known her."

"She can't figure it out herself. But there it was, she said, lying on the floor not far from the door."

Urbino went over to one of the windows and leaned against the sill with his back angled toward the door.

"It's fortunate that Adele Carstairs and Kobke haven't gone up to Vienna yet. That gives me more than a day to look this over. I doubt if she'll mind." He riffled the pages. "Although it shouldn't take long to read through what's here. There isn't much." He squinted at a page and turned it to catch the late afternoon light that was coming over his left shoulder.

"But why did Benedetta Razzi give it to you?" the Contessa asked. "And how did it get into that room to begin with?"

Urbino responded to her first question only.

"She's sick and tired of all this poking around, all these questions. I think she's also afraid of being found doing something illegal with that room. I told her I'd take the notebook off her hands and give it to the niece with an explanation. She doesn't seem to know that Voyd was murdered because of Quinton's writing and I thought it best not to tell her. If she knew, she would have been even more eager to get this notebook off her hands."

He bent down over the notebook again. Stefano poured another Strega for himself and the Contessa but Urbino had hardly touched his. He needed a clear mind.

"There seems to be something about you, Barbara."

"About me? Are you sure?"

"I'm fairly sure. Give me a minute to make it out. Her writing isn't easy to read. It's an old-fashioned kind of hand."

He was silent for a few moments while he composed his thoughts. Then—calling up all his inventive and histrionic skills and remembering how he used to entertain his ailing mother in her bedroom by reading out loud from the *Times-Picayune* imaginary articles about her friends—he began.

" 'Stopped by the Ca' da C-Z.' " He stopped and looked up at them. "She uses quite a few abbreviations. Let me see. 'Stopped by the Ca' da C-Z to pay a visit and borrow some books. I could tell the Contessa wasn't keen on lending them but I managed to convince the dear woman it was *pour l'art*. To think that someone wouldn't trust *me* with books!' "

The Contessa stiffened.

"No, I was not 'keen' about it, as she expresses it! You know how I feel about letting any of my books out of the library. I worried about it for days."

He nodded and continued to look at the page, then turned it and began at the top of the next. Hoping his face was reflecting increasing interest and amazement, he said, "She *was* very friendly with Maria. Not exactly a meeting of equal minds but she seems to have found something interesting in the old woman. I suppose she was always on the lookout for material, as Voyd said."

"What is it?" the Contessa asked impatiently. "It's not polite to be reading and not telling us anything, is it, Stefano?"

Even if she had expected an answer, it didn't seem as if she would get one from Bellorini. He sat looking down into his Strega.

"Wait then. Let me go back a bit." Urbino ran his eye back up the page and began to read again haltingly, having the ostensible excuse of Quinton's handwriting. " 'I—I don't see why I can't treat the—the whole topic of the glassblower from old Murano in a brief form, maybe a short story or novella. It could end with the—with the death of Domenica.' "

After pausing to clear his throat he continued: " 'It's a worthwhile idea but it might be difficult to bring off because of all the period detail. I wonder if the dear Contessa would be kind enough to lend me more of her collection. It would be so much better than being—than being alternately fried and frozen at the B.M.' That must be the Biblioteca Marciana, don't you think?"

He gave them a quick glance.

"Right after that she mentions Maria for the first time: 'It might be less trouble to turn my attention to old Maria's story. But there are two problems with that.' " He made a point of turning the page to the light before going on. " 'There's—there's what she told me that I can't perhaps use, and then there are all those huge—huge hells.' "

" 'Hells'?" The Contessa frowned. "Are you sure?"

"Yes, 'hells'—no, wait a minute, 'holes,' yes, 'holes.' She seemed particularly fascinated with what Maria had to tell her. She goes into more detail." He stared at the page, then moved his eyes down to the bottom. "Oh my God, I—"

Looking up quickly to see what reaction he was getting, he saw barely a flicker on either face. He hoped Gemelli had got his

message or the Questura had acted on it. He even wished now
that Adele Carstairs and Kobke were there with them. Angela,
however, was a different matter entirely. He remembered enough
about his study of mathematics many years ago with the Jesuits to
know that every equation had at least one unknown.

He felt he had no choice but to go on. He bent down over the
notebook again for the coup de grâce, this time forgetting to
pretend to puzzle out Quinton's handwriting.

" 'Maria was very excited this afternoon and at first I couldn't
understand what she was saying. I asked her to speak more slowly.
I still don't understand exactly what she meant by some man
named Giovanni Fabbri but she said that this Fabbri and the
mysterious Domenica she's always talking about were actually—' "

He turned the page and was about to continue when a voice
sounded from the door.

"That will be enough!"

Urbino turned around, and the Contessa twisted her body to
look over the back of the sofa. Angela Bellorini was standing in
front of the closed door. She must have come in while he was
reading, noticed by no one but her husband, who now got up
from his chair and walked toward her. On the woman's face was
a sneer, which did nothing for her already unattractive features.
But it was the pistol in her hand that looked most unattractive.

"It would have been so much better if you didn't have such a
long nose, Urbino—better for you and for poor, dear Barbara."

Angela Bellorini made the mistake of gesturing abruptly with
the pistol at the Contessa.

What happened next happened quickly. There was a loud
scream—it was the Contessa's. There was a cry—it was Angela's
as she rushed toward the Contessa. There was a crash—it was the
door being pushed open, revealing three grim faces behind it, one
of them Commissario Gemelli's.

Epilogue

MURDER
AT FLORIAN'S

❧

"SO I was right," the Contessa said to Urbino at their customary table in the Chinese salon at Florian's. "A woman was involved—but did it have to be Angela?"

It was late afternoon of the kind of pearly gray day that Sargent captured so well in *Venise par temps gris*, their first meeting since the Contessa had decided to forgive him for what she called his "cool deception" of her at Bellorini's studio.

The shock of learning that her friends were the source of the villainy—and learning it in the way she had—had kept her indisposed at the Ca' da Capo-Zendrini for almost a week while Urbino had met with Gemelli, the Substitute Prosecutor, and other officials at the Questura. The Commissario, though harshly critical of how he had gone about things, was nonetheless grudgingly appreciative and had shown it by passing on much of what had been learned from the Bellorinis. Urbino had been doing the same with his friend for the past half hour.

The Contessa was looking at him and nodding her head slowly.

"A woman *was* involved," she emphasized, as if his silence indicated that he had somehow forgotten or disagreed.

He sipped his Campari soda. Why point out to her that at the beginning, when they had thought there was a particular friendship between Beatrice Galuppi and a mysterious woman named

Domenica, she had shied away from the possibility of a woman
being involved? This afternoon, however, the Contessa was seeing things the way she wanted to. She thought she was entitled
to because of all she had lost a week ago at Bellorini's studio. He
hadn't told her of his own eleventh hour suspicions that a woman
might somehow be implicated, the most logical woman being the
wife of the man to whom the evidence pointed. The Contessa
might have accused him of taking undue advantage of hindsight—
something that she was now showing was hers alone to do.

"And then there was the poison," she added after a few more
moments with a touch of exasperation in her voice. "It's a woman's
way."

"Isn't that rather sexist and narrow-minded, my dear?"

"I suppose I am rather sexist and narrow-minded but I don't
think it's done me—or others—much harm, has it? I've been
looking into poisoning, you see. Most of the cases I've come
across—especially arsenic for some reason—involved women. Let
me see: There's the black widow Florence Maybrick, Madeleine
Smith, Marie Besnard, Marie Lafarge." She counted them off on
her well-manicured fingers, then waved her hand. "Oh, and many,
many others."

"It reminds me of something Kobke said before they left for
Vienna. By the way, you were very much missed at Adele's little
get-together."

"I can't believe you went."

"I felt I had some explaining to do. I didn't want Adele to think
there had actually been another notebook if she heard what happened at Stefano's. When I was about to leave, Kobke said that
neither he nor Adele could imagine Angela as a criminal, as someone in the same league, so to speak, as the women you've mentioned. Neither would Voyd have been able to, he said. Voyd
seems to have found her quite ordinary."

"That's how much they know about it." It was as if Angela had
been insulted and needed someone to defend her reputation. He

almost expected the Contessa to point out that the woman had a good heart. She had brought all those meals to the needy over the years and she had been a good friend, hadn't she? But instead she said, a bit wearily, "Most of those women I mentioned were ordinary, quite ordinary. At any rate, Christian has forgotten something. Angela didn't do it all by herself."

"But she did start things going thirty years ago. I think Kobke holds her just as responsible as Stefano for killing Voyd for the Venice notebook—which, from what Stefano says, had nothing incriminating in it."

"The point is that we were all so deceived by them both. Of course Angela was only a girl when it started. She had just married and learned not only that Stefano had had an affair before they were married but that it was still continuing—and with the worst girl imaginable, the bright and beautiful Beatrice Galuppi. To complicate matters, Beatrice believed she was pregnant and threatened to go to Stefano's father. Angela had learned she could never have children. I always thought that was what brought them closer together, the way it did Alvise and me. I felt a bond with them because of it."

"You might say that Stefano's flaw was his weakness. If he had been stronger, then maybe all the Galuppis would still be alive—and Voyd too of course."

"How do you figure that?"

"It's obvious, isn't it?" He took another sip of his Campari soda. "Stefano would have had the courage to tell his father he wanted to be a glassblower instead of a doctor or whatever dream his father had for him. He wouldn't have had to go to Murano in secret when his father thought he was in Padua. Although his father was one of those parents Don Marcantonio mentioned—the ones who don't know if it's worse for their sons to be priests or glassblowers—he might have come around eventually. Who knows? If Stefano had been stronger, he might even have divorced Angela and married Beatrice if they were still so much in love."

The Contessa gave him an exaggeratedly disdainful look.

"Divorce didn't exist in Italy back then. And Stefano would have risked losing his father's fortune if he didn't come around. A lot of money was involved, more than enough for Stefano to go to art school after his father died several years after Beatrice—enough for that and for him to pursue a less than lucrative career. That's what he and Angela have been living on."

"That's one of the things I meant by his weakness. Part of it was to be so influenced by his father, to feel he had a need for the money to make his way. Why not try for an annulment since they couldn't have children? Or go off with Beatrice and live outside of Italy?"

" 'Ages ago these lovers fled away into the storm,' " she recited with a little smile. "How do you square such romantic notions with your interest in that decadent Des Esseintes? I'm sure, though, that Beatrice would probably have jumped at the chance of leaving everything behind her, but why assume she would have had Stefano without the money? From what he says Beatrice had no idea his father was so set on his marrying into Angela's family—until she found him actually giving in. For almost a whole year afterward she seems to have hoped things would be resolved somehow in her favor. When you're young and beautiful you think you're going to have an easy time of life. She was her mother's darling and the fantasy sweetheart of just about every man and boy in the Cannaregio, so why shouldn't she win out in the end? Why couldn't she have both Stefano *and* the old man's money? She was in love and she was ambitious—a rather dangerous combination, wouldn't you say? Who knows what plans she might have been making to get Angela out of the way? I don't mean murder, of course, but perhaps persuading Stefano to get an annulment and settle things with his father. I'm afraid Stefano was caught between two scheming women. You know how I feel about Stefano's talent—despite all these horrors, those frames are absolutely beautiful—but I never thought that he was particularly intelligent. You say things might have been different if he had been stronger. I say what the poor man needed was more intelligence."

"More intelligence—and a little less innocence."

"Less innocence! Don't forget that although Angela began everything, Stefano was the one to go to San Gabriele to meet Maria and hit her with the candelabra. *He* went to the Europa e Regina."

"True, but what I meant was that a less innocent person—or call it a person with a more highly developed sense of suspicion at that time in his life—would have found it more than a little peculiar that his own injured wife would not only help him solve the problem of a pregnant girlfriend but give him the very things—the arsenic solution and the syringe—to do it with."

"You're running away from me, *caro*. Remember that I've been almost on my *letto di morte* this past week. I'm in the dark, I'm groping even now."

It was an opportunity to remind her that she had refused to talk to him even on the phone, but instead he asked her what it was that she didn't know.

"What *do* I know would be a better question. I'm groping, I tell you. Just because I've done my research on arsenic doesn't mean I know what you're talking about. Do you mean that Angela just made a little package with arsenic and a syringe and sent Stefano on his merry way to Beatrice? Who would have thought he was such a fool? Who would have thought she was such a cool one?"

"Not quite that cool, not at first. It wasn't as if she had planned to kill Beatrice from the beginning, from when she knew that they had had an affair and were continuing it. And at first her reasons for asking him to take some arsenic from the Pignatti glass factory were innocent enough—to deal with the rats in their Padua flat. Even when she learned right after they were married about his relationship with Beatrice, she only wanted to get her revenge in a malicious but not homicidal way—just enough arsenic, she decided, to destroy Beatrice's good looks, to ruin her skin and have her lose her glorious mane. She had the perfect opportunity since she was bringing those meals over to Benedetta Razzi when Beatrice was working for her. It was easy enough to arrange, I suppose. As you pointed out, a little more intelligence might have saved everyone. Angela was intelligent enough to know some of the symptoms of chronic arsenic poisoning but not the ones that led Beatrice to think she was pregnant—the nausea, the thirst, the change in her monthly cycle."

The Contessa nodded.

"I see. Otherwise she would have realized Beatrice wasn't pregnant. But I wonder what would have happened then? Would she have continued to give Beatrice the poison in small doses?"

Urbino shrugged.

"What we do know is that, believing her to be pregnant and having her threaten to reveal everything, Angela snapped. She loved Stefano despite his continued infidelity and there was also the prospect of the Bellorini money once Stefano's father died. Love and money, both threatened by someone she had no fondness for to begin with. An overdose of arsenic would solve her problems—would solve *their* problems—but she couldn't take Stefano into her confidence. He had to believe he was merely giving Beatrice the means to abort the baby. One wonders how much he had learned from his own brief medical studies to let Angela take the initiative like that and not even question it. As for Beatrice, she would have trusted anything he told her to do since he had, after all, been studying medicine, in his fashion, for a while. Despite her threats to go to his father, she had no desire to remain pregnant. I wonder how much of an effort was made at the time to find the syringe or whatever they thought had been used to administer the arsenic? And I keep coming back to why Stefano didn't question Angela's motives in giving him the solution and the syringe. The fact that he didn't know arsenic was involved at that point makes little difference."

"Marriage is a mystery, believe me."

"I suppose you would say that what also falls into the category of a mystery is the way Stefano stuck by Angela when he realized what she had done."

"What would you call it?"

"Fear."

"Fear of Angela? But what she did was mainly for love of him. I don't believe the money was all that important to her."

"If that was the case, then it was a love to be feared. But I wasn't thinking of that. I was thinking of his fear of being caught. After all, he was the one who gave Beatrice the means of her death—handed them over, albeit unwittingly. He was lucky to have Maria remove the evidence when she found her daughter in the toilet but I doubt if he would have been able to convince the police that he didn't know what he was doing."

"And that's why he set fire to Pignatti's showroom and stole the paintings and sketchbooks back in the November of the flood—this same fear?"

"Exactly. That's when Maria stepped up her inquiries about Beatrice's death and started to ask all those questions about Domenica and the glass dove Stefano made for Beatrice. He was afraid of anything that might associate him with Beatrice or glassmaking."

"Beatrice and Stefano were typical lovers, weren't they? Using the name Domenica the way they did—it was a way to conceal their relationship, I know, but it's the kind of thing lovers enjoy doing. A whole secret world of assignations, furtive looks, private words and associations. Yet lovers can also be so indiscreet. They make incriminating gifts, they write letters, they have pictures taken that will later come back to haunt them, they take unnecessary chances. I think they enjoy the risk."

If she was speaking from experience, she gave no indication other than the validity of what she said.

"Didn't one of those women in Maria's building say that Beatrice used to tease her mother with the name Domenica?"

"Yes. As you were just suggesting, it was their lovers' secrecy and ingenuity that led to the uncovering of the crime against her."

"I can't understand why Maria didn't suspect Stefano to begin with."

"For one thing she didn't know him as well back then as she came to know him later—and it was mainly through you that she did. Also, Beatrice and Stefano managed to keep their secret well. They had the luck of lovers in that respect. There was little enough to link them together. And don't forget that they succeeded in convincing Maria for a long time—for many years after Beatrice's death, in fact—that she was looking for a woman friend who had exerted a bad influence over her. It threw Maria off."

"But as it turns out, she *was* looking for a woman and so were we—a man *and* a woman, that is. We were misled ourselves but in a different way. But I can see that we would never have been led to Angela's part in it unless we—excuse me, unless *you*—figured out that Stefano was Domenica. In this case, *cherchez la femme*—even if we had definitely known a woman was involved—wouldn't have done much good."

Was this a mild reparation for her insistence earlier that she had known a woman had been involved? The beginning of a smile tipped the corners of her mouth.

"It didn't do Maria much good," Urbino said. "It was only when she learned from Quinton that Domenica had been a male glass-blower from old Murano that she started to think along different lines. Maybe she remembered seeing Bellorini on the boat to Murano when he was supposed to be in Padua at the university. She always got off at San Michele to visit her husband's grave, but Stefano would have continued on in the same boat to Murano—or she might have seen him on the return trip. She went back and forth a lot between Venice and San Michele even before her daughter died."

"Until the flood of sixty-six."

"No reason to go after that. Beatrice was scheduled to be disinterred early that month, and Maria was determined her daughter wouldn't end up in a mass grave the way her husband had. There was all the confusion after the flood to help Carlo with the exchange of the two bodies. It was a neat, if daring arrangement, with Lapo Grossi unknowingly carting off the body of Santa Teodora to Sant'Ariano where I guess Maria felt it would be more proper for it to lie than a mass grave. There was that photograph she had seen of the Cappuchin catacombs in Rome—or at least I assume that's what it was. It comforted her that there was some kind of acceptable religious tradition in what she was doing. Her devotion to her daughter, though, was obviously stronger than her devotion to Santa Teodora. She had her daughter right there at San Gabriele and had secreted the glass dove with her for safekeeping. Maria had taken the trinket from Beatrice after all. It was never lost as Beatrice thought. Everything must have made perfect sense to Maria. Remember that the twelve years were up and she had no money for perpetual care."

"I didn't know anything about it. If she had only mentioned it to me, or someone else had, Alvise and I would have been more than glad to help her. What she must have thought of the da Capo-Zendrini mausoleum!"

"Things like that probably never even occurred to her. She was determined to solve her problem the way she could. It was the form her devotion to her daughter took. It seems a bit gruesome the way she always had her daughter's body there to look at. I wonder if there were times when she thought she was really looking at the body of Santa Teodora, but most likely not. How could she ever have forgotten? And for more than twenty years no one else even noticed the difference. It shows what faith can do—not to mention a mask, slippers, gloves, and a long gown! I'm sure that what Carlo had to go through had a great deal to do with his peculiarities over the past twenty years, including his suicide on San Michele."

The Contessa nodded.

"It's comforting, isn't it," she said, "that not only is the Patriarch reconsecrating Santa Teodora's body but that they're also setting up a fund for the perpetual care of the Galuppi graves?"

"I happen to know you're playing a big role in that," Urbino said.

"And I happen to know that you made a large contribution yourself by buying two thirty-year-old paintings that had been left in a lumber room of the building on the Rio della Sensa. I'm looking forward to seeing them."

They were silent for a few minutes as they looked out at the darkening Piazza. Although *carnevale* was celebrated throughout the city, it was here in the Piazza, roofed now with low dark clouds threatening rain, that the festivities were focused. A stage, its curtain closed now, faced the Basilica at the west end. A row of grinning white masks, soon to be illuminated with the coming of night, adorned the perimeter of the Piazza above the arcades. For what seemed the third time since Urbino and the Contessa had sat down a Viennese waltz was blaring over the loudspeakers. Revelers strolled across the open space and under the arcades and congregated in front of the souvenir and refreshment stands. Others occupied the canopied deck outside Quadri's or sought a better view on the long ramp in the middle of the square where they had to compete for space with costumed figures who were there only to be seen and photographed. However many people there were in the Piazza now, there was no comparison to the throngs who would descend during the next week as *carnevale* reached its final frenzy. Urbino longed for Ash Wednesday when the Piazza as well as the whole city would return to its serene winter self.

"About Beatrice's Wedding Cup painting," the Contessa began, turning away from the Piazza. "I just don't understand why Stefano waited so long to steal it."

"For one thing, he learned that Maria had just shown all the artwork to Sister Veronica. He could only assume that the Wed-

ding Cup painting was part of it although there was always the
possibility that Beatrice had thrown it away out of anger when he
returned it after he got married. But from what Sister Veronica
said Maria told her—that Beatrice was in tears when she got the
painting back and that she hid it away—it seems the poor girl was
more hurt than angry."

"But Sister Veronica didn't meet him until about fifteen years
ago. I introduced them. Being over on Murano, and under her
father's eye, she was isolated. Then when she entered Santa Crispina she was just as isolated—that is, until Vatican Two came
along."

"She did say that the face of the groom was vaguely familiar.
Because Stefano has changed so much since the fifties he really
didn't have much to fear from her on that account. And Maria
didn't have the best vision. As for Carlo, the poor man wasn't the
type to notice things like that. But what if Beatrice's work were
shown to someone who had known Stefano back then? Admit-
tedly the face of the groom wasn't as identifiable as Beatrice's was
but Sister Veronica said Beatrice had used reddish tones. Someone might have associated her portrait of the groom with Stefano
because of the coloring. And how did he know that there might
not be other pictures of him of some kind—in the sketchbooks,
for example? At any rate, he would have got his hands on that
painting even if the face had been less obviously his or not even
his at all."

"But without his profile on it, what would there have been to
link him with it?"

"Several things. Stefano would visit Beatrice at the Glass Museum when she was copying the scenes from the Wedding Cup.
He would slip over from Pignatti's or stop by on the way there.
Although they tried to keep things secret, they sometimes didn't
care, all of the hiding was too much for them. Once Beatrice was
dead—murdered—and he heard Maria was showing the painting
around, he was afraid that sooner or later someone might link the

two. Actually he was afraid it could happen even if no one saw the painting or—if someone did—even if he wasn't recognized."

"But didn't he risk drawing attention by stealing the Wedding Cup painting even though he tried to camouflage it by taking the Tintoretto, too? He would have been better off to have done nothing."

"Not necessarily. You're forgetting Cavatorta."

Urbino was now approaching more delicate ground as far as the Contessa was concerned. She was looking at him without any apparent awareness of what he meant, of what he was about to say.

"When Stefano and Angela were married," he went on, "Cavatorta's father, on behalf of the whole family, gave them a gift, a copy of the Barovier Wedding Cup. He gave it to all the married couples he knew. A rather convenient and appropriate gift."

"And how did you find this out?"

"Cavatorta told me the last time I visited him."

"You never told me that!"

Her voice was sharp and there was a mottled look to her face. She seemed upset, embarrassed, maybe even a little afraid.

"No, I didn't. I thought it would be better to think things through. Angela and Stefano are such good friends of yours and—"

"You didn't trust me, did you? It's as simple as that. What did you think I'd do? Warn them? Or did you think that somehow I—"

"Don't be ridiculous, Barbara. I never thought anything of the kind."

"Just go on with what you were saying."

Her voice was low, but intense. Something more than his decision not to tell her about what he had learned from Cavatorta was bothering her.

"The Bellorinis rejected the gift. I know you must have heard how they sent a gift back to the Cavatortas even if you didn't know what the gift was."

"But why?"

"Cavatorta told me he saw Beatrice at the Glass Museum once or twice. Stefano might have thought he and Beatrice had been seen together and that Cavatorta had influenced his father to send the Wedding Cup as a gift, as some kind of taunt, a sign that he knew the two of them were involved. Even back then, it seems, Cavatorta wasn't the nicest person around. Stefano saw no reason to trust him."

"But that gift was given to everyone, you said."

"To everyone up until the death of Cavatorta's father twenty years ago. But Stefano didn't know that at the time and neither did Angela. It would seem that you yourself weren't aware of it until I mentioned it." She nodded perfunctorily and glanced out at the Piazza. "When he got married, he had nothing to fear, and he was angry with Cavatorta. Maybe he had a need to confess. They say unfaithful spouses want to be found out. And maybe he couldn't hide his anger at Cavatorta. Angela would have wanted an explanation and so he told her the truth, gambling that she would throw her lot in with him against Cavatorta. He told her about Beatrice and returned the Wedding Cup painting. There was no way Angela was going to have that around!"

"But the affair wasn't over, was it?"

"It continued for months after the marriage, not the way it had before but they were seeing each other whenever they could. A clean break is always the best but people think that tapering off, withdrawing gradually, will be less traumatic, that somehow they'll get off easier that way."

"So Stefano managed to enlist Angela's aid."

"Exactly. He told her that the gift was an affront to them both. Only after Beatrice died did he worry that their behavior might have given something away, that the Wedding Cup painting was probably still among Beatrice's things. Stefano was all the more upset when he found out that Cavatorta's father gave the same gift to everyone, that Cavatorta hadn't necessarily meant it as a taunt. That's why the story got around that Angela had been offended at getting a so-called common gift. They probably encouraged the story themselves at that point, taking advantage of the Cavatorta tradition even if it didn't make them look good."

"I see. So if Cavatorta saw the painting Beatrice had done even without recognizing Stefano—or even if he knew about its existence—he might have remembered the way the Bellorinis responded to the gift and started thinking."

"It was certainly a possibility. And it was the risk I took myself when I asked Cavatorta if he remembered the gift his father had given the Bellorinis. I'm not sure if he knows that a painting of the Wedding Cup ever existed. When I asked him about the theft, he was abrupt with me and didn't give me a chance to mention that particular painting of Beatrice's. Unless either Maria or Sister Veronica said something, how would he know? I was taking a chance asking him about the gift. He might have come to conclusions on his own, might have tried to take some action himself, maybe even blackmail. Cavatorta didn't care for Stefano and Stefano must have remained suspicious about Cavatorta to the end, even paranoid. Don't forget how Stefano reacted the night of your party to Cavatorta's comment that 'those who wear green must be sure of themselves.' Stefano might have thought that somehow Cavatorta knew that arsenic was used to get a desirable shade of green in glassmaking. When you're guilty, everything seems to point a finger at you."

This seemed to give the Contessa something to think about for a few minutes as she stared at the portrait of two scantily-clad women over the opposite banquette.

"So when Maria told him there was something that could still connect him with her daughter and that it was in the glass coffin, he had to get it back," she said dully, as if she were reciting a lesson.

"There was absolutely no way for him to know it wasn't something much more incriminating. But I don't think he had any intention of paying her the money she wanted for Carlo's security—or any intention of killing her either, as he says. He hit out at her when she tried to prevent him from opening the glass coffin, then he had to do some quick thinking and put the body in my pillow slip. If only Carlo had come out of the confessional then—or even looked out—but unfortunately, his mother had him well trained. And no one noticed Stefano returning to his studio. Of course he was sometimes seen bringing back things he had found along the quay or in a *calle*. He showed me an *art trouvé* piece when I was at the studio last month"—at this the Contessa shook her head slowly, her taste not encompassing even a tenth of the modern art at Peggy Guggenheim's or the Biennale—"so if anyone saw him that day it might not have been thought out of the ordinary. Once back at the studio he and Angela retrieved the glass dove and destroyed it, then disposed of the body in the dustbin, not realizing they were handling the partially preserved body of Beatrice. Voyd's murder and the theft of the Venice notebook—not to mention what might have happened to both of us at the studio last week if Gemelli hadn't decided to monitor my movements—were their final, desperate efforts to prevent their exposure, to keep their secret."

"My God, but their relationship must have been strange! Thirty years—more than thirty years!—with that secret between them. What a terrible way to live. There must be times when you don't even know you're letting your guard down, at other times you probably don't even know you're living a lie. Maybe the strain over all those years explains why they've been so cooperative with the police. They must have been souls in pain, especially toward the end."

Was the strained look on her own face because she was thinking of all the hours—all the innocent, enjoyable hours for her—spent in the company of the Bellorinis and their secret?

"Probably their secret is what kept them together all those years," he said by way of pulling her from these troubling thoughts. "Their secret *was* their marriage. You might even say it was the child they never had."

She gave him a skeptical look.

"Try to curb your imagination just a little, *caro*." She picked up a cake. "Exactly what was old Lodovico Pignatti's role in all this?" she asked, the cake poised at her lips.

"Innocent enough. He probably saw no danger or difficulty in keeping Stefano's apprenticeship a secret and was sure that sooner or later the old tyrant was bound to realize his son wasn't studying in Padua as he thought. It was only a family disagreement he didn't care to get more involved in. Then, with the old man more than ten years dead, Pignatti could see no reason for not putting up that photograph when he renovated his showroom. When Stefano and Angela found out, they decided it would be a good idea to set fire to the showroom."

"That seems a drastic measure. Why not try to convince Pignatti not to use the photo?"

"He might have become suspicious. About this time Maria was starting to come around with her questions, don't forget, and Pignatti probably knew that Beatrice had died of arsenic poisoning. In a way arson was a clean way of doing it."

"Except what was to prevent Pignatti from putting up another copy?"

"Stefano took a chance that paid off. Pignatti was too disheartened to redo the showroom the way it had been before. He died not long after that."

Dusting off her fingers, the Contessa stood up abruptly.

"Do you have a *gettone*?"

He reached into his pocket and gave her a phone token.

"I won't be long."

As she was going through the foyer, she stopped the waiter and said something to him. He smiled and nodded.

She was gone for more than ten minutes. When she came back, she was followed by the waiter carrying a bottle of Veuve Clicquot and two glasses on a tray. She didn't speak until after the waiter had opened the champagne and poured out two glasses.

"I have something to confess, *caro*, and I needed something stronger than tea to do it on. And we do have cause for celebration." She took a sip of the champagne. "The call I just made was to the house. Before I tell you what this is all about, you must promise not to be angry. You see, Urbino, Franco Cavatorta gave Alvise and me a copy of the Barovier Wedding Cup when we were married, too."

"But, Barbara, why didn't you mention it? If I had known sooner, I might—"

"But that's just it, Urbino," she interrupted. "I didn't know myself until a few minutes ago."

"What do you mean?"

She took another sip—this a much deeper one—before going on.

"Do you remember all the gifts you've ever received, especially when you get so many at one time? This was more than thirty years ago. Maybe I never even knew what Franco Cavatorta gave us. Remember, Alvise was a count. We had a huge wedding. Gifts were coming in for weeks before and after the wedding."

There was a touch of haughtiness in her delivery which he was sure had more to do with embarrassment than pride.

"So how can you be sure now?"

"Lucia looked it up for me. Alvise and I hired a girl from the university to make a list of the gifts and the people who gave them. She wrote them down in a book Alvise's mother had used for the same purpose. She made out most of the thank-you notes, too, even signed our names." She met his eyes almost defiantly as if she were ready to counter any accusation of social impropriety. "It's the way these things are usually done, Urbino."

"Especially among you counts and countesses," he couldn't resist saying. "But it doesn't make any difference now, does it?"

"I just hope that you didn't think at any point that I knew and didn't want to mention it."

"I thought that if you did know you hadn't realized its possible significance." She took this slight—and somewhat evasive—criticism without even a flicker. "It might not have seemed that important to you. I didn't start thinking along the right lines myself until my talk with Sister Veronica at the Glass Museum the day before the scene at Stefano's studio. No, it never occurred to me that you might have known and made a conscious decision not to say anything."

"Thank you for that."

"I preferred to ask Cavatorta despite the risk involved. I didn't want to upset you. I knew that if I raised the subject I would have to tell you more than was good for you."

The smile she gave him now was part appreciation and part, he assumed, the Veuve Clicquot she had drunk so quickly. He was glad she didn't point out to him that he had been somewhat neglectful of her good when he had gone to Bellorini's studio with his plan.

"Thank you, *caro*, and forgive me for being so stupid. When I was a schoolgirl at St. Brigid's, I always got the top grades in memorization: Tennyson, Hopkins, even half an essay by Cardinal Newman. But lately—" She sighed and reached for her glass only to find it almost empty. Urbino refilled it. "But you have to understand that I'm not sure I even knew to begin with so how could I have forgotten?"

It was one final apology and excuse.

"Where is the Wedding Cup now?"

"Probably crammed into that room on the top floor with a thousand other bits and pieces. Alvise used to say that that room was like the section of the Vatican Museum with all the gifts to the Popes. I haven't been in it for years and years. We'll have to poke around in there one of these days. I've been afraid of stirring up memories but maybe it's time. It might even be fun."

They both looked out into the Piazza. Two figures dressed as traditional nuns, in black robes and veils and white coifs and wimples, passed under the arcade in front of their window, arm in arm and kissing. Whether they were two men, two women, or a man and a woman was impossible to know, but any of these combinations was unacceptable to the Contessa as long as they were dressed the way they were. She shook her head slowly.

"Thank God the reconsecration ceremony at San Gabriele is scheduled after all this insanity. I assume you'll be given a place of honor."

"I'll be right next to you, Barbara, if that's what you mean although I'd prefer not to be there at all. You can be sure it'll be mobbed because of all the publicity."

"There's that, yes, but there should be a lot of people there for better reasons than curiosity. After all, there's a great deal to celebrate. Santa Teodora's body is in remarkable condition after twenty years on Sant'Ariano."

"Not all that good really. It's more a matter of only the head. As in the case of Beatrice, there isn't much left to the rest of the body. That old gown seems to have covered a lot of secrets over the years."

"*As* I was saying," the Contessa continued with a slight frown, "there's talk that what we have is yet one more miracle of our little saint from Syracuse."

"Either that or we don't know the real circumstances of her death. Who knows? She could have died from arsenic poisoning," he said, barely suppressing a smile. "Maybe that's why her body was so well-preserved to begin with." Before she could reprimand him, he added, "I know—not in the best taste."

"Not in any taste at all." She looked at him severely, then her face softened. "You did an amazing job, you know. You've got your harmony back. You've restored it to us all."

"Not for long, I'm afraid."

He nodded toward the *carnevale* crowd getting thicker out in the Piazza.

"We'll just have to suffer through it all for the next week, my dear Urbino. This is the last time I'll be anywhere near the Piazza until the madness is over."

She looked toward the door where the waiter was standing and caught his eye.

"Tell me, *caro*, do you intend to turn this into an avocation? It might not be incompatible with your *Venetian Lives*, you know."

"Turn what into an avocation?"

"Your sleuthing, of course. You've had such success with your first case."

"Venice, I'm afraid, is too quiet a town to make that a real possibility."

"A quiet kind of town!" She almost shouted it as the waiter stopped at the table. "How can you say such a thing after what we've all been through?"

"*Cosa desidera*, Contessa?" the waiter asked.

"First you can tell my young friend here that it's perfectly conceivable that a murder might take place right here at Florian's!"

"*Come*, Contessa?"

Urbino laughed. The Contessa, as usual when it came to things Venetian, was probably right.

ELLIOTT ROOSEVELT'S
DELIGHTFUL MYSTERY SERIES

MURDER IN THE ROSE GARDEN
70529-X/$4.95US/$5.95Can

MURDER IN THE OVAL OFFICE
70528-1/$4.99US/$5.99Can

MURDER AND THE FIRST LADY
69937-0/$4.50US/$5.50Can

THE HYDE PARK MURDER
70058-1/$4.50US/$5.50Can

MURDER AT HOBCAW BARONY
70021-2/$4.50US/$5.50Can

THE WHITE HOUSE PANTRY MURDER
70404-8/$3.95US/$4.95Can

MURDER AT THE PALACE
70405-6/$4.99US/$5.99Can

Coming Soon

MURDER IN THE BLUE ROOM
71237-7/$4.99US/$5.99Can

America's Reigning
Whodunit Queen

Charlotte MacLeod
WRITING AS
Alisa Craig

Join the club in Lobelia Falls—

THE GRUB-AND-STAKERS MOVE A MOUNTAIN
70331-9/$3.50 US/$4.25 Can
THE GRUB-AND-STAKERS QUILT A BEE
70337-8/$3.50 US/$4.25 Can
THE GRUB-AND-STAKERS PINCH A POKE
75538-6/$3.50 US/$4.25 Can
THE GRUB-AND-STAKERS SPIN A YARN
75540-8/$3.50 US/$4.25 Can

And for more disarmingly charming mysteries—

THE TERRIBLE TIDE	70336-X/$3.50 US/$4.50 Can
A DISMAL THING TO DO	70338-6/$3.99 US/$4.99 Can
A PINT OF MURDER	70334-3/$3.50 US/$4.25 Can
TROUBLE IN THE BRASSES	75539-4/$3.50 US/$4.25 Can
MURDER GOES MUMMING	70335-1/$3.99 US/$4.99 Can